Strike Force

TAKE NO QUARTER

DESIREE HOLT

TAKE NO QUARTER

Dedication

So many people help me produce a book, beginning with Joseph Trainor, cop and former Air Force non-com, who answers my myriad questions; Margie Hager, my beta reader extraordinaire and incredible friend; my fabulous virtual assistant, Maria Connor; and last but far from least, the very talented and eagle-eyed editor Rebecca Fairfax, who makes my books sing. I love you all and dedicate this book to you.

Chapter One

"Fifteen minutes to the drop zone." Lt. Slade Donovan, code name Shadow, spoke into his throat mic, giving the members of his Delta Force team, code name Sierra, a head's-up.

They were flying through the night in a Boeing MH/AH-6M Little Bird helicopter flown by a Special Operations Aviation Regiment pilot. SOAR provided aviation support for Special Forces and had been dialed up to fly this mission. Coincidentally, the pilot, Lt. John Wannamaker, had flown this team on other assignments before, which gave everyone a secure feeling. *'Nothing like knowing your team,'* Slade always told them.

Trey McIntyre, code name Storm, leaned back against the inner hull of the chopper, closed his eyes and began the process of centering himself. Next to him and across from him, other members of Team Sierra were doing the same thing. This included the newest additions, Brock Sullivan and Axel Weber. The whole team had just completed six grueling weeks of training to make sure the newbies fit into the team. Being able to trust that each person knew what he was doing was just as important as the tasks themselves.

Under normal circumstances, they would not be deploying so soon after finishing their last op, but just as they'd wrapped up the training session, word had come down from the brass that Dana Roberts, a journalist, had been kidnapped by the Lopez Garcia cartel she was investigating, and Sierra Team was tasked with retrieving her. This was not their first adventure with *narcotrafficantes*. Sierra Team had been deployed before as part of larger missions to work in concert with the Mexican military when an especially vicious cartel situation had arisen.

Trey had wondered why the cartel hadn't killed the woman, since journalists who wrote unfavorably about cartels were not too popular. This year alone three had been beheaded and placed in a public square for people to see, although not by this cartel. Then he'd learned that the cartel had contacted the media conglomerate she worked for and asked for twenty million in United States dollars or they'd send her home in pieces. Cartels were never about to pass up an opportunity for a big payday.

Of course, the briefing made them aware that Lopez Garcia's style was a little different from the other cartel leaders'. They called him *El Lobo. The wolf.* Wolves, Trey knew, were among the world's smartest, most perceptive animals — and also one of the most vicious and bloodthirsty. The word was Lopez Garcia ran his cartel like an alpha wolf ran his pack, with prescribed, ritualistic behavior and a defined pecking order. Everyone acknowledged that this kidnapping was abnormal behavior for him and his cartel... If someone had gone off the reservation and done this on their own, there could be a lot of bloodshed over it.

This team was due some leave time after three back-to-back missions and had been on the verge of getting to it, but when the call had come to gear up, they'd killed that idea. Each of them was aware that the primary focus of all units of 1st Special Forces Operational Detachment — Delta — was counterterrorism and hostage rescue, so today's mission was one they'd rehearsed for many times. They had been in situations that were far worse than this and succeeded. Trey knew each man on the team was mentally and physically ready to get this job done.

Now they were in the darkened cabin of the helo, flying into the night over Quintana Roo, a state in Mexico that was a combination of thick jungle and tourist hotspots. Like him, each man was going over in his head what they knew. Hector Lopez Garcia, leader of the cartel, owned a massive *finca* — country estate — deep in the heart of the Quintana Roo jungle. A helo with very sophisticated equipment had done a previous flyover and reported that it was protected by heavily armed manpower and surrounded by thick stands of trees and other jungle growth.

'No external electronic security,' the pilot had reported. *'Nothing showed up on our instruments and they're ninety-nine-point-nine percent accurate.'*

'I'm surprised,' Slade had commented.

'They don't need it. The cartel owns three hundred acres of pure, overgrown jungle with the main building itself square in the middle. By the time a person reached the house, everyone would hear them coming.' Then he'd grinned. *'Except you guys, of course. I think you invented the word stealth.'*

Trey knew that their training would definitely come in handy today. Intel had reported there were at least twenty heavily armed guards—*sicarios*—at the *finca*. Their orders were to get in, take out as many of them as they had to, grab the hostage and get the hell out of there. He was sure the cartel was egotistical enough to be confident no one could breach their security and make off with their prize. Trey grinned in the darkness. They hadn't met the men of Delta Force yet. And after tonight, they'd probably hope never to meet them again—at least any who were still alive.

When Slade signaled five minutes to drop, each of them went over their gear again, double-checking both their rifles and handguns. Then they were hovering just at the tops of the trees, at the spot that had been selected as the best for insertion. Someone tossed a rope from the cabin and one by one they rappelled down, fast and neat just as they'd done so many times. The moment the last man was standing and the rope pulled up, Slade signaled the helo to get gone. It banked and lifted away, off to where it would wait for the signal to return and retrieve them.

Once on the ground, they made their way as quickly and quietly as possible through the thick stands of palm, poinciana and Caribbean pine trees, as well as a wide variety of dense flowering shrubs. Dressed all in black, hands and faces also blackened, and with the stealth for which they were famous, they made their way through the jungle to the main house. Here was where it would get dicey, but they had gone over the plan so many times Trey knew they could all recite it from memory.

At the edge of the clearing, Slade held up a hand for them to stop and Trey pulled the thermal imager from a side pocket in his pants. It didn't take long for them to determine which rooms had people in them. Knowing Dana Roberts was a small woman and that there was only one other female in the house, they quickly pinpointed her in one of two locations.

"I count twenty bodies in the house," Trey whispered. "Not counting our target. How copy?"

"Good copy," came back all the whispered responses.

They had no intel on whether Hector Lopez Garcia himself was at this location or not, but the prevailing theory was no. In a way, they were glad. Retrieving the hostage was their primary mission. They didn't need any distractions. Capturing Lopez Garcia could be on someone else's menu.

Trey noted exterior lights on the corners of the roof, throwing circles of light onto the grass. Slade pointed and gestured for them to stay beyond the perimeters of the lights. Then he whispered into his mic.

"Sierra Team, move out."

Trey clicked his mic to show he understood, knowing the other team members were doing the same. Then, like a choreographed dance group that had performed a routine multiple times, they moved slowly toward the house itself, alert for any guards sure to be patrolling outside. Even as isolated as the house was, it was a given that the cartel leader would not leave the exterior unprotected.

Their orders were to pull out all the stops for the mission to succeed. If that meant eliminating every one of Lopez Garcia's men, they were prepared to do that. No one would be shedding any tears over the vicious cartel members.

They had barely moved into the clearing towards the house when two guards came into sight, one from each side of the building. They spotted the team and lifted their weapons to fire, but before they could shoot or give any kind of warning, Slade's gun spoke twice, followed by two rounds from Axel, who was next to him. The shots were so close together it seemed as if they'd all come from the same weapon.

"Two tangoes down," Slade whispered into his mic.

Stepping over the bodies, the team moved toward the house. At a signal from Slade, they broke through two large sliding glass doors, startling the people inside. Marc and Brock tossed smoke grenades into the room and as the men in there reached for their weapons, even as they were coughing and choking, the team disposed of them before the tangoes could get a shot off.

"Eight more down," Slade informed them.

The team spread out, moving from room to room, with Slade and Trey heading for the first of two rooms where they believed the hostage was being held.

"Sierra Team, this is Sierra One," Slade whispered. "Remember, we want Lopez Garcia, too, if he's here. Keep an eye out for where he might be hiding."

"This is Sierra Four. So far no trace of him."

"Damn fucker," Marc Blanchard, Sierra Three, growled. "I'd like to kill that motherfucker myself."

Everyone on the team knew that Marc had a hard-on for anything to do with drugs. They had destroyed his first marriage before it had even got started. And though he was very happily married now, he still hadn't forgotten the devastating effects drugs could have on people. He'd kill everyone in the cartel given the opportunity.

"We'll get our chance," Slade told him. "Meanwhile, let's find the package and get the fuck out of here."

They moved through the house, the team clearing it room by room, the sound of a gun battle as cartel members confronted them a continuous barrage of noise. Reports of tangoes down sounded in their headphones as they reached each room.

Trey's assignment was to cover Slade's six as they headed for the two rooms identified as probable locations for the hostage. It was a stroke of luck that when they burst into the first one they hit pay dirt, but what they saw pulled them up short. Dana was there, disheveled and with a bruise on one cheek, but doing her best not to look terrified. Trey was seized with a desire to kick the shit out of whoever had laid hands on her — most likely the man dressed in black pants and shirt who stood behind her, one arm around her throat, his other hand holding a gun to her head.

"Don't worry, Dana." Slade spoke to the frightened woman in a calm voice. "Everything's gonna be just fine. Trey, let the team know what's happening and get someone up here to cover the rest of the upstairs."

Trey clicked his mic. "Sierra team, we have located the package but need assistance. How copy?"

"Good copy," came back from everyone.

"Sierra Five on the way up," Axel added, followed by Brock, and Trey repeated the messages to Slade.

"Put down your gun," the man growled, "or I shoot her then you and your men. Do it now."

At his words, Trey shifted his position ever so slightly so he could cover the room. Axel and Brock had just reached the hallway behind him and stood with their guns ready.

"I think you might want to reconsider that." Slade spoke in his low, deceptive Texas drawl, one that often lulled people into a false belief that he wasn't so sharp or so aware of things. "I promise you I'm better at this than you are and, if I miss, the other members of my team won't. Unless you want to bleed out here on this nice carpet, drop the gun and let the lady walk over here."

The man snorted. "You do the walking, right out of this room, or she is a dead woman. Get out of here now. All of you."

"Now, see? I just can't do that."

The rest happened so fast Trey hardly saw Slade's finger tighten on the trigger. The man moved his arm slightly and the *crack!* of a shot and the collapse of the man's body happened in a nanosecond. Slade reached for Dana as the thug fell, and pulled her to him.

"Oh, my god!" She leaned against Slade, who put an arm around her to steady her.

"You okay?" he asked.

"I will be when we get out of here. We will, right?" She was pale and shaking, doing her best to hold it together, but when she looked at Slade, fear was still evident in her eyes.

"Count on it," he assured her. Then he clicked his mic. "This is Sierra One. Any sign of Lopez Garcia?"

All the responses came back negative.

"He's probably a hundred miles away. Forget him for now and let's get the fuck out of here."

At that moment they heard more shots, these coming from the stairs and the hallway. Trey turned to see Axel with a body at his feet.

"Nice going," he told the man.

"Need help in there?" He nodded toward the room.

Trey shook his head.

Just then two more men sprinted up the staircase. Axel and Brock turned, their Colt M4 Carbines spat bullets and two bodies fell backwards down the stairs, blood pouring from multiple wounds.

"Let's get the fuck out of here," Slade growled again. "I don't know how many more tangoes are still here, but we need to haul ass. If any of them try to stop us, eliminate them."

On the move now, he held Dana close to him with one hand while he grabbed his radio with the other to signal the chopper. "This is Sierra One. Need exfil now. Hustle it. How copy?"

"Good copy," came back the answer. "On my way."

They raced from the house, aware that more men were running into it from wherever they'd been. With the rest of the team laying down covering fire, they hustled into the back yard, Slade in the lead with Dana hugged close to him.

"I don't know how many idiots are still alive, maybe out at the front of the house, but you can bet they'll be after us any minute now," he told the team. "Let's take advantage of the little lead we've got on them."

They made their way quickly through the jungle growth the same way they had reached the *finca*. In moments they heard shouts coming from inside the *casa*, the sound of their pursuers evident in the screech of birds as their nesting places were disrupted.

"How many of those fuckers were there, anyway?" Marc snarled.

"More than we were led to believe." Slade scowled. "Let's move it."

Then they were back to the tiny clearing spot where they'd landed, the chopper hovering overhead, two men crouched in the doorway. One of them dropped the rope with a harness attached, and Slade made quick work of fastening Dana into it. A second rope was dropped at the same time and the team climbed as fast as they could. Slade was the last to ascend, and was halfway up the ladder when they heard shouting below and shots fired.

The team in the helo riding the opening fired back, but Slade signaled for the chopper to lift away with him still clinging to the rope.

"Haul ass," Slade shouted, when he was finally pulled in.

With everyone inside and in one piece, the helo banked away and rose into the night.

Trey leaned back against the helo wall and glanced over at Dana Roberts. He had to give her high marks. She hadn't freaked, hadn't screamed when the asshole had held a gun to her head or bullets had been flying all around her. Even now, seated on the floor of the cabin, surrounded by men in black clothing with black grease on their faces, lethal weapons strapped to their chests, she managed to hold it together.

She was almost but not quite his type. A little short, a little thin and maybe even a little young for his taste. But damn brave.

For fuck's sake, McIntyre. She's not here for you to ask out on a date.

Still, it bothered him that she seemed so familiar. An image danced just at the edge of his consciousness, but he somehow couldn't manage to pull it into focus. *Later*, he told himself, and focused on the here and now.

"I—I want to thank you all," she shouted over the noise of the rotors, her arms wrapped around herself.

Slade grinned at her, teeth white against his darkened skin. "All in a day's work."

Her laugh still had an edge of nerves to it. "I hardly think so. But in any event, I am eternally grateful to you. I wasn't sure I'd get out of there alive. I heard they asked my bosses for twenty million." She snorted. "I'm not sure they think I'm worth that much."

"They thought you were valuable enough to pull strings and get Delta Force involved," Slade told her.

"I'm sure they were concerned about the headlines if I got killed." She brushed a hand, still trembling slightly, over her face. "Anyway, thank you all so much. I will be forever grateful."

"We're just glad we could bring you back in one piece." Slade shook his head. "It's just too bad Lopez Garcia wasn't on the premises."

"The man is a ghost," she spat. "He has to be stopped, if that's even possible. And I'm still going to follow the story. The cartels have their hands in everything, everywhere. The Lopez Garcia cartel is nearly as big as Sinaloa, and once they get a toehold, you can't dislodge them." She tightened her hands into fists. "I've seen what they can do, how bloodthirsty they are, the control they can exert when they manage to insert themselves into businesses."

"Just make sure you get a good bodyguard," he suggested.

Trey studied her face in the shadow of the cabin. She looked so familiar to him, but he had no idea why. He knew he'd never met her before. It was possible she just looked like someone he'd met once upon a time. Maybe it would come to him after a while. Problem was, he was so footloose and fancy-free where women were concerned, determined not to put down roots of any kind. The number of women who had passed through his life could probably fill a catalog. Sometimes he felt a little guilty about it, but he was so not ready to settle down yet, despite the fact that in the past year three of his teammates had.

For a moment, he thought of the woman he'd met at the party the Huttons had thrown, one that they'd all attended. She'd dumped a plate of food on him, helped him clean up, fetched him a beer and they'd spent two hot and heavy days and nights together. He'd been with a lot of women—not something he bragged about—but they all paled in comparison to this one. The electricity between them could have lit up all of San Antonio, and the sex had just blown his mind. And unlike a lot of the women with whom he'd enjoyed recreational sex, Kenzi had been smart and funny and easy to be with. If he ever had the urge to settle down, this would be the kind of woman he wanted.

If.

Because settling down was the furthest thing from his mind. Delta Force was his significant other right now. When he was done here, there'd be plenty of time to explore more options.

So when their interlude—their very hot interlude—was over, he'd followed his usual pattern. Thanked her for a great time, told her how much he'd enjoyed himself and gotten the hell out of there. He hadn't even asked for her last name or her phone number, because that implied continuity.

But then, to his shock and dismay, it had taken him a long time to get her out of his mind. He still hadn't been able to fully, much to his irritation. Dana Roberts in some way reminded him of Kenzi and that was the trigger for this unwanted trip down Memory Lane. He wondered if they'd ever cross paths again. Should he have Slade ask the Huttons about her?

No. Big no. He didn't do anything more than long weekends. A week was stretching it.

At least until now, a little voice whispered.

How was it that damn woman had taken up space in his brain and refused to move out? He always walked away. *Always.* It was tacitly understood from the beginning. So why the hell was this one hanging around? He needed to do something about that.

They were going to San Antonio after this, with an open invitation to stay at Slade's ranch. But their lieutenant was still a newlywed, with limited home time. Those without women waiting for them would go into San Antonio and scare up some kind of action. And that was fine with him. He liked the city. There was always action someplace, and that was just what he needed now.

Before long they descended and were landing at Fort Hood. The men all waited while Slade helped Dana Roberts off the chopper and delivered her to the group of people waiting on the tarmac. He watched as a tall, older man pulled her into a hard hug, and he assumed it was her father. He could only imagine the relief he and the others waiting were feeling.

Trey deplaned with the rest of the team and spent the next forty-five minutes in a debrief. A driver from the base's transportation unit waited with a van to deliver the entire team to a nearby private airfield, where Teobaldo 'Teo' Rivera, Slade's ranch manager, was waiting with Slade's personal helo to ferry them to the ranch.

"We've got ten days," Slade told the team, "and a promise that it won't be interrupted this time."

"Yeah," Beau, code name Surfer, laughed. "We know how that goes."

"No, this time is for real. If we don't get a break, we won't be any good on the next mission."

Beau and Marc would be taking off to be with their women, and Slade's wife, Kari, would be waiting for him on the ranch. The three of them—Trey, Axel and Brock—planned to head to San Antonio, check into a hotel downtown in the city and see what they wanted to do from there.

The sun was up by the time they were in their rooms and the only thing they wanted at that moment was a shower and some sleep.

"Whoever wakes up first, text the others," he told the other two. "Slade scored tickets for the Spurs game tonight, if you guys are interested. Good game tonight with the Golden State Warriors."

Brock lifted an eyebrow. "How the hell did he get those? I'm a basketball junkie and those are two of the hottest teams in the NBA."

"Beau's lady is a sportswriter, but the two of them weren't interested in using the tickets." He grinned. "I do believe they had other things to do. Anyway, three is an odd number to get but she took them because she figured us poor single idiots might want to go."

"Hell, yeah." Brock looked at Axel. "What about you?"

The other man shrugged. "I'm okay with it. I'm not in the mood to troll the bars tonight anyway."

They agreed to meet in the lobby at seven, drive to the AT&T Center where the Spurs played and grab some food when they got there.

In his room, Trey stripped out of his clothes and stepped into the shower, letting the hot water wash away the dirt and grime of the mission and ease the tension in his muscles. Then he crawled into bed and set his mental clock for eight hours.

As he was falling asleep, the image of Dana Roberts flashed into his mind. Only this one was an older Dana, and there was a familiarity about it he couldn't put his finger on. His last thought was to wonder what the hell that was all about.

Chapter Two

Kenzi Bryant stepped out of her shower and wrapped a towel around herself. For the fifth time she wondered why she'd even agreed to go to the basketball game tonight. Sure, she was a Spurs fan, and these tickets were like gold. But lately her life had been one tense roller-coaster ride.

First, there was the business with her younger sister. Well, half-sister, but they never thought of themselves like that. She never could understand how Dana deliberately put herself in harm's way. What story could be worth risking her life for, no matter how many awards she won? Thank the lord the big media conglomerate she worked for had strings to pull to get the government to send a rescue team for her.

Had Trey been part of that team? Had he known it was her sister?

Come on, Kenzi. How the hell would he know that? He doesn't even have your last name. And wouldn't it just be too much of a coincidence for him to be part of the rescue team?

She had spoken with Dana four times since the rescue, trying to convince her sister to take some time off, maybe come for a visit.

'We haven't spent time together in ages,' she'd reminded her.

Dana had laughed. *'That's because you're even busier than I am, big sister. You've got your career on a fast track and you don't need to put a plug in it to hold my hand.'*

'Maybe I just want us to have some sister time.'

'I'll tell you what. You get past this client that's your ticket to a partnership, I'll finish this series, then we'll hang out and celebrate.'

'Promise?'

'I promise.'

'By the way, how is that hot soldier you've been rocking the sheets with?'

God, she'd been sorry she'd ever mentioned Trey to Dana. But they spoke so seldom, or at least that was how it seemed, and she'd wanted to share something personal.

'That's nothing permanent. You know me.' She'd hoped she had just the right casual tone. *'Anyway, take care. Please.'*

She'd better clear her mind of thoughts dealing with Trey. Her life plan did not have room at the moment for a relationship of any kind. *Another date? Forget it.* He'd probably forgotten about her, anyway.

'Picky, picky, picky,' Deandra kept telling her when she insisted there was no one who interested her.

She deliberately chose men who weren't looking for anything beyond casual, whether it was two days or two months. Trey had given off the same kind of vibes, which was how they had hooked up at the Hutton party and screwed themselves blind for three days. Then he'd been gone, his down time over, leaving her with hot memories. And that was all she wanted. Ever. *Right?* The chance she'd ever see him again was less than zero, which worked for her. She had professional goals to reach before ever letting anyone into her life for an extended period.

But when his leave was over and he'd returned to base, somehow he'd kept invading her dreams, uprooting her world in a way that other men had not. She needed to get past that, since she'd probably never see him again. After all, they hadn't made any promises to each other. *Right?* And wasn't that the way they both liked it? Wasn't that what made the connection work?

So why the hell couldn't she get him out of her mind?

Just forget him, she kept telling herself. Her focus was on her career and on making partner. Four years of undergrad and three years at a top law school were the first steps in her plan to become a top-notch corporate attorney. Being hired at the elite law form of Byrnes, Calhoun and Raven was a major step in that direction.

Being—hopefully—on the partnership track meant every day she was putting twenty-five pounds of sugar in a ten-pound bag. This firm was one of the wealthiest in the San Antonio area, with a staggering list of high-profile corporate clients. Twenty years ago, they had literally emerged out of nowhere and exploded onto the legal scene. Now, in addition to the three senior partners, there were ten juniors and twenty associates.

Being hired there right after graduation had been a real honor and here she was, ten years later, being considered for partnership over many of the other associates.

Today had been another tough, busy day at the office. She and one of the senior partners, Reed Calhoun, were deep into work on a project for a long-time client, Alex Reyes. They were creating a new and complicated corporate structure for the man's growing international business operations. Apparently, he and his family were looking beyond their cattle operations, extensive as they were, and the very profitable mineral leases on a portion of each ranch. Now they were planning to buy into or create related enterprises in Canada, Europe and Australia.

Sometimes, when she was checking incorporation and nonresident rules in the various countries, she wondered what it would be like to have so much money that she could invest it anywhere in the world she wanted to. *'You'd think,'* she often mused to Deandra, *'that after working for seven years in a firm that catered only to the very wealthy, I'd be used to it, yet it still dazzles me after all this time.'*

But this was the biggest project she'd worked on by far. Calhoun had even hinted at a trip to Europe to meet with some of the people who would be involved. Kenzi had made a note to herself to learn more about exchange rates of foreign currency and favorable trades, which was their current focus.

If only there wasn't something about their client that pinged her. The worst of it was, she couldn't say what. The man was the epitome of old San Antonio society and wealth, polished yet friendly, never condescending and able to put people at their ease. Rich and well respected. Yet something about him set off her internal sensors. She'd better deal with it before she did or said the wrong thing and ended up in trouble with the partners. All her sweat, hard work and long hours would be down the drain.

After an intense morning working with Reed, she'd spent the rest of the day with her paralegal to dial her into the situation and give her a long list of things she needed yesterday.

It's always yesterday.

Not that she was complaining. She thrived on the challenges of corporate work the way trial lawyers thrived on the cases they had, while others lusted after the glamorous life of trial attorneys. Structuring businesses to give them maximum protection and solidify operations actually got her blood going.

'But aren't you bored?' her friend Deandra often asked.

'Not even for a minute.' She'd grinned. *'You have no idea how exciting closing legal loopholes can be.'*

But what about Mister Tall, Dark and Dangerous?

The instant the memory popped into her brain she made a supreme effort to erase it. Too bad it lodged itself there and wouldn't go away, reminding her of the moment Mr. Hottie had come into her life.

She'd gone to the party hosted by old friends Natalie and Paul Hutton, intending only to put in an appearance for an hour then boogie out of there. But fate must have been having a good time with her that night. She'd been helping herself to *hors d'oeuvres*, turned, bumped into the person behind her and it was all over his shirt. It would always be one of her top five embarrassing moments, since the victim of her clumsiness had turned out to be one of the sexiest men she'd ever bumped into. *Literally.*

Even now she remembered being frozen in place while she'd stared at the six foot plus of muscular male with curly brown hair worn a little longer than most of the men she knew, a trimmed scruff-style beard and brown eyes like melted chocolate. A tiny scar, barely visible, curled at the end of his left eyebrow. For one of the rare moments in her life she'd been actually struck dumb, staring at him like a tongue-tied adolescent.

Then he'd grinned at her, and out of nowhere her nipples had hardened and ached and a pulse had throbbed low and strong in the wet channel between her thighs. For a frightening moment she'd wondered if she was going to have a spontaneous orgasm just standing there looking at this guy.

'Here.' His deep, raspy voice had echoed through her body. *'Let me help you.'* He'd taken the plate she was holding before it slipped from her fingers and set it on the edge of the table. *'I think I'll just go and clean up a little now.'*

Somehow, she'd found her voice and managed to reconnect her brain.

'I am so very, very sorry. I promise I'm not usually this clumsy.' If she could have melted into the floor she would have.

'But then we wouldn't have had a chance to meet.'

He winked, and she was afraid her panties would melt right there in the Huttons' dining room.

She had insisted on going into the little powder room with him to help him clean off his shirt, never stopping to think how it would look to others. Or to him.

'Please let me get you a drink,' she'd insisted, when she'd repaired as much of the damage as possible.

'Ah, sure. Beer is good.'

From the spilled *hors d'oeuvres* and cold beer they had dissolved into a weekend with sex so hot she was afraid they'd melt the bed. For the first time ever, she'd been itchy to finish her work day and get home. When he'd left, he hadn't asked for her last name or telephone number. That wasn't usually the way she rolled, but okay. She'd deal with it. Anyway, her so-called relationships never lasted more than a few months. The men she met usually wanted more than she was ready to give, being too involved in her career to get tied up with some guy. She was up to her ears in the Reyes project, so she wasn't even sure she had anything to give to a relationship now, anyway.

Take it and enjoy it, she told herself.

But sometimes, in the dark of the night, when frustration grabbed her enough that she reached for her handy little toy, she'd call up his face while she pleasured her body and gave herself some very intense orgasms. Had she made a mistake not giving him her last name and cell phone number? There had been something about him that the other men in her life lacked. Was she too afraid to find out what it was?

It was important to her, however, to control every aspect of her life. She'd sensed with Trey that that would not be possible. In fact, she'd had an underlying feeling that any control would be in Trey's hands. And that had scared the hell out of her. She was a corporate attorney, for heaven's sake. A woman who controlled all aspects of her life. The last thing she needed was a battle-weary soldier who was the opposite of every man she'd ever dated.

But there had been something so totally masculine about him, so commanding, so take-charge. And the sex had just blown her mind, invading her dreams and driving her crazy with desire.

Forget it, Kenzi girl. Get dressed and try to have fun tonight. He's long gone and you don't need him.

And a good thing, because he would turn my well-ordered life upside down.

She looked at herself in the bathroom mirror and sighed. After the exhausting day she'd had, the smart thing to do would be to stay home, watch a sappy movie and enjoy some wine. But Deandra had scored tickets to the Spurs game tonight from her latest squeeze, a guy who worked in the team's office, and the seats were just too good to pass up. Besides, she'd been so tied up with the Reyes file for days that the words 'social life' had been wiped from her vocabulary.

She also had a hard-and-fast rule about never dating anyone from work. In the environment in which she labored, an office romance could be the kiss of death. Of course, that was even supposing there was anyone at the firm who made her hormones wiggle. But all that left her little time to spend with men who piqued her interest at all. Maybe she should have gotten Trey's last name. Or asked the Huttons to check with Slade.

And looked pathetic.

Get going. Get going. One night out won't kill you. It's just a basketball game with Deandra. Girls' night out. You might even have fun.

She'd arranged to meet Deandra in the lobby of the AT&T Center at seven-thirty. Traffic was already thick by the time she arrived, but she managed to find a place to park that wasn't in another county. They presented their tickets, took the escalator up to their level and stopped to get food and drink before taking their seats. They were the third and fourth seats in their row and she balanced her drink and food container carefully as she side-shuffled past the first two seats.

"Hope you're not planning to dump your food on me again."

The voice she'd been hearing over and over in her dreams broke through the noise of crowd chatter and startled her so much she nearly did drop everything. Shocked, she stared at the man occupying the seat next to hers as if he'd materialized out of a dream. Standing there dumbfounded, it took her a few seconds before she could form intelligent words.

"Trey?" She blinked, wondering if he'd disappear. How was it possible he was here? *No, no, no.* He was over in Afghanistan or Niger or someplace on the other side of the world. *Right?* Was her tired brain creating a mirage?

He looked as shocked as she felt, but then his lips curved in a smile she remembered so well.

"Fancy meeting you here," he chuckled. "What's that saying from *Casablanca*? Of all the gin joints in all the world... Here. Let me help you."

He took her drink cup and the cardboard box with her pizza from her unresisting hands while she settled herself into her seat, moving as if in a daze. Trey with no last name was certainly the last person she'd expected to be sitting next to at this game. A game she hadn't even known she'd be going to and had had to be talked into.

"I didn't know you were a Spurs fan." His warm, deep voice moved through her like hot molasses.

"I, um, oh, yes." Well! Didn't she just sound like the world's biggest idiot. "Uh, thanks for holding my food."

"Better in my hands than on my clothes," he teased, handing over the cup and box.

Heat crept up her cheeks as she remembered their initial meeting. She was acutely aware of Deandra's eyes on her, and busied herself settling her food so she didn't dump it. For sure Trey Gorgeous would think she was a klutz. But then her cheeks heated as she thought of the things they'd done where she hadn't been clumsy at all.

Stealing a sideways glance, she noticed the men in the two seats next to him watching them with undisguised interest.

"Aren't you going to introduce us?" the one closest to Trey asked.

He laughed. "Only if you promise to behave. Kenzi, meet Brock and Axel, the new guys on our team."

They nodded and murmured the usual "Nice to meet you" thing.

"Hi." Deandra leaned forward and stretched her arm halfway across Kenzi, nearly upsetting the pizza and soda. "I'm Deandra. Hall. Deandra Hall. My friend sometimes forgets her manners."

Kenzi would have poked her if her brain hadn't suddenly turned to mush. "Uh, sorry. Dee, meet Trey—" She stopped as she realized she still didn't know his last name.

"McIntyre." His grin was positively lethal.

"A pleasure to meet you." She nudged Kenzi, the look on her face saying *I can't wait to get you alone and ask questions.*

"Well." Brock winked. "Things just looked up here. Always better to watch a game with someone besides these two ugly guys."

Kenzi noticed Axel studying her face and frowning.

"Is something wrong?" she asked.

"Have we meet somewhere before?"

She shook her head. "No. No, we haven't. I'm sure I'd remember."

"Funny, I could swear—"

"Mexico." He snapped his fingers. "That's it. You look just like the reporter we pulled out of Mexico."

Trey was staring at her. "I kept telling myself that woman looked familiar. That she resembled someone I knew." He shook his head. "Yup. The resemblance is definitely there."

Kenzi's eyes widened. "You—You were with the men who rescued Dana?" How ironic and off the charts was it that Trey's team would be the one to rescue Dana? And that they both would be at this game tonight, in adjoining seats?

The world certainly works in mysterious ways.

Trey touched her arm. "Kenzi, it was our team that rescued her."

"Oh! Well. Thank you for that."

He studied her face. "So. Kenzi Bryant. Good to know."

Okay, now they had each other's last names. Somehow, to Kenzi, that made the whole thing more personal, more real. Not quite so much a weekend fantasy. Was she ready for that? Right now she was still dealing with the shock of seeing him sitting right next to her at the basketball game.

"Thank you." She blew out a breath. "For saving her."

Axel winked, breaking the tension. "It's what we do."

Kenzi just nodded, put her drink in the cup holder, her purse on the floor and settled the box on her lap.

"Would you, uh, like some pizza?" She looked at the man sitting next to her.

Somehow that broke the tension that had been wrapping around them.

The rest of the evening went by in a blur. She must have eaten her food because suddenly the box was empty and Trey took it from her and put it under her seat. The Spurs scored, and often, because the crowd was going wild. She knew she jumped up and cheered when everyone else did, but she felt as if it was all happening to someone else.

People were screaming and yelling, so she knew the game was exciting. Too bad her brain had gone to lunch so she had no idea what was going on. She couldn't seem to get past the fact that Trey McIntyre was here! At this basketball game, of all places. What were the odds? And why was it all she could think of sitting in the middle of thousands of people was how mouthwatering he looked naked and how great the sex with him was?

Then the game was over and they were making their way out of the arena itself and down to the lobby. She was acutely aware that Trey and his friends were stuck to them like glue, right behind them on the steps walking up to the concourse and on the escalators going down to the exit. Once they were outside, everyone stopped in the big area in front of the entrance.

Now what? Kenzi wondered. *Do we all shake hands and say what a great game it was?* An image flashed in her brain of the two of them naked on her bed, his cock buried deep in her body, his tongue dancing with hers. She had to squeeze her thighs together to contain the errant pulse that suddenly throbbed like a jungle drum.

Maybe just one more night with him. What could it hurt? And I could get him out of my mind, once and for all. Right?

"So." Trey stood with his hands in his pockets, a grin on his face but blazing heat in his eyes. "I guess we'll head back to our hotel. Can we persuade you two to join us for a drink?"

Kenzi looked at Deandra, who was doing her best not to grin.

"Sure. We'd love to. Right, Kenzi?"

"Uh, yes. That would be great." *Oh, my god.* She sounded like she was twenty years old.

"We came in separate cars," Deandra told them. "Kenzi, maybe Trey would like to ride back with you? The two of you can get reacquainted."

"Great idea," Trey said.

Almost before Kenzi could unstick her tongue from the roof of her mouth, everyone was climbing into cars, including hers, and heading back toward downtown San Antonio. She was still trying to wrap her head around the fact he was back in San Antonio—probably the main reason her conversational skills had deserted her and she sounded like the idiot of the year.

"If you'd rather just drop me at the door and head out," Trey said in his deep voice, "I'll understand. This all just kind of fell in your lap, and those guys can be a bit much. No pressure. Okay?"

But was that what she really wanted? To just say goodnight?

Go for it, the devil in her head whispered. *Give yourself a break for a change.*

"I'd, uh, like to have that drink," she told him in a soft voice.

He took one of her hands, lifted it to his mouth and kissed the knuckles. "Good. I'd like to have it, too."

They drove in silence for a while.

"Did you think it strange we never exchanged last names?" he asked.

"Yes and no," she said after a moment. "I don't think either of us was looking for something beyond that one weekend, so it really didn't matter, right?"

"Right," he agreed after a long moment. "Listen, I'm not a believer in fate, but what are the odds I'd be rescuing your sister in Mexico and we'd run into each other at this basketball game?"

Kenzi laughed. "Sounds like a cheap movie, right?"

"Well…" He hummed. "Maybe not so cheap."

"Okay." She laughed, despite a sudden attack of nerves racing over her skin like an army of ants. And what was that all about? She wasn't someone who ever, ever had that happen, not even when meeting with a client about a delicate situation. She turned into the hotel's parking garage. "Anyway, here we are, and I think I'm ready for that drink."

She turned off the engine but sat there a moment, wondering which of them would move first. The air was thick with an overabundance of sexual tension. When Trey didn't move, she climbed out of the car. She was barely aware of him doing the same, her mind being so busy with the whirlpool of thoughts. As she turned to walk away from the parking space, he was suddenly beside her, his strong hands gripping her shoulders as he pulled her body against his. Then his mouth was on hers and his hands sliding up to cup her cheeks and hold her head in place.

His kiss was as consuming as she remembered, hot and hungry and demanding. He swept his tongue into her mouth, licking and brushing and tasting every inch. She let her own tongue caress his, drunk with the flavor of him, closing her eyes and giving herself over to the pleasure.

He slid his hands from her face down over her shoulders and the line of her back until he cupped the cheeks of her ass, squeezing them. When he pressed her against him, she could feel the long, hard, thick line of his cock against her mound and in seconds her panties were soaked.

Only when they both needed to breathe did he lift his mouth from hers. When she opened her eyes, he was staring directly into them, the navy of his irises darkened almost to black.

"We, uh, should go in," she reminded him, without answering. "The others will be looking for us."

"Fuck the others. I want to take every advantage of my good luck here."

"I, um…" *God in heaven.* Why was she so tongue-tied?

Then he sighed. "You're right. We should do the polite thing, even though my cock is telling me otherwise." He stroked her cheekbones with his thumbs, and when he spoke, his voice was rough with need. "Come on. Let's go have a drink. But then, after that...Kenzi, stay with me tonight."

Kenzi knew she should tell him she had to go. That tomorrow was a busy workday. That...that a million things. But she knew just as she stood there that she wasn't going to pass up the chance to fall into bed with this man again. Fate had put them together. Who was she to argue?

"Come home with me instead," she whispered. "More private."

Chapter Three

Making polite conversation had been an exercise in discipline for Trey. And making excuses to get out of the lounge where they'd been drinking didn't fool anyone. He didn't care. The extreme coincidence of sitting next to Kenzi Bryant at a Spurs game was a sign. Hell, no matter how much he'd tried to forget about her, it had been impossible. Much to his dismay, he'd been dreaming about the woman ever since the short time they'd spent together and waking up every morning hard as a rock. As much as he'd tried his best to make her just another face in his life, she'd crept into his dreams way too often.

It was true that three of his team members, including his team leader, Slade Donovan, had found women who fit perfectly into their lives. Trey was convinced, however, that they were anomalies. He'd seen many more relationships crumble under the weight of the demands of Delta Force. He wasn't about to do that to himself or some woman. Why, then, had Kenzi Bryant haunted those dreams all these weeks? And why, now that they were shockingly and unexpectedly together — however it happened — was he determined to wring everything out of every minute he could?

Enough with this crap. Enjoy the moment.

Sitting in the cocktail lounge of the hotel and making small talk, Kenzi wondered if anyone could read the looks they kept giving each other. He was grateful neither of the other men made any wise remarks when he and Kenzi left after one drink. Especially when neither of them gave an excuse, just said goodnight and walked out.

"Well, that was awkward," she joked once they were in the car. "I'll bet your friends will be all over you with questions tomorrow."

"Not if I tell them to shut up. We give each other grief, but we also respect each other. If I tell them it's off limits, they accept that."

Sexual tension hummed between them as they rode to her house. It seemed neither of them needed words to acknowledge what they were going to do. But the moment they were inside her place, it was as if a tiger had been let loose. All restraint was off.

He pressed Kenzi against the door, cradled her head between his hands and took her mouth in a hot kiss that singed every nerve in his body. Her lips were just as sweet as he remembered, and now the faint taste of peaches in her lipstick mixed with the distinctive flavor of the amaretto she'd been drinking, like an erotic cocktail. Thrusting his tongue into her mouth, he licked every inch of the slick flesh. He held her head in place, turning it this way and that to give him the best access.

She was just as ravenous, threading her fingers in his hair to hold his head in place as she pressed her mouth to his just as hard. When she slid her tongue over his in a hot, erotic dance, every muscle in his body tightened, his cock got even harder — if that was possible — and a demanding ache gripped his balls.

Sliding his hands down from her face, he grabbed the hem of her embroidered T-shirt and yanked it up. His palms molded to her breasts as if they'd been made just for them, the warm mounds a perfect fit. Even through the silk of her bra he could feel the rigid points of her nipples and he squeezed them, hard, between thumb and forefinger.

Kenzi moaned into his mouth, the sound so sensual he nearly came right then and there, out of his mind with need. He unfastened her jeans and yanked them down her legs, along with her silk panties. His hand shook as he unzipped his own fly and freed himself. In seconds he'd lifted one of her legs to wrap it around his waist, opening her sex to him.

He trailed his lips along the line of her jaw and down the delicate column of her neck, all the while reaching between them to touch the lips of her pussy. *Slick! Wet and slick!* The words pierced his brain and ramped up his hunger. Kenzi was pushing herself as close as she could get, trying to rub her clit against him wherever she could make contact.

Shit!

He wasn't going to last another two minutes. With frantic haste, he reached into the pocket of his pants and found his wallet, hands shaking as he dug out a condom and ripped open the foil. Somehow, he managed to sheathe himself without tearing the latex. Cupping the cheeks of her magnificent ass to hold her in place, he pressed the head of his shaft against her opening, took a deep breath and thrust inside her.

Oh, sweet holy Jesus!

The feel of her tight, wet sheath wasn't just as good as he remembered — it was better. Her inner muscles clamped around him, squeezing him, and he was sure his eyes crossed. Every nerve was on fire, every part of his body focused on the unbelievable pleasure of being inside her. Holding her in place, he steadied them both, took another breath and began the steady in-and-out glide that would help them reach a shared orgasm that would shake them out of their minds.

Nothing had ever felt this good in his life. Every fiber of him was engaged, his brain totally disconnected as pleasure consumed his body. In and out, a steady rhythm, he did his best to slow things down, but it was a lost cause.

"Hurry," she urged, loving her hips with his, using the leg wrapped around him to anchor them together.

In what seemed like seconds, the familiar feeling was building deep inside him, drawing an answering response from her. He slammed his body into hers, holding her tight while she rode his cock. When the orgasm broke, it exploded like fireworks. Their bodies shook while he pulsed inside her and her hot pussy spasmed around him again and again.

When the last drop emptied into the sheath, he leaned against her, touching his forehead to hers, struggling to breathe and hoping he didn't fall down while he was holding her. In slow motion, he eased her leg from around his hips so she was standing on two feet, although standing might have been an exaggeration. He thought it was a damn good thing the door was there to hold both of them up.

At last he caught his breath, cradled her face and placed a gentle kiss on her lips.

"I didn't mean to savage you like a caveman." He smiled.

She lowered her gaze in a strangely shy gesture. "I wanted it, too."

He chuffed a laugh. "I seem to lose my control where you're concerned. How about we move to someplace more comfortable where we can take our time?"

"Yes." The word drifted out on a breathless note. "I can go for that."

Somehow he managed to juggle sliding out of her, pinching the condom closed so nothing leaked and kicking away his shoes, jeans and boxer briefs, which he left in a pile with her clothing. Then, divesting them of the rest, he carried her to the bed, yanked the covers back and placed her gently on the sheet. He'd taken her hard and fast and rough against the door, so hot for her body that restraint hadn't even been in the ballgame. Now he wanted to shift into slow gear and make sure he pleasured her properly.

He spared a long moment to appreciate the sight of her spread out on the bed like the most delectable feast in the world. His mouth watered just looking at her. As much as he'd tried to wipe her from his mind, just as he had the other women he'd spent time with, the memory of her clung stubbornly to his subconscious. Now he looked his fill at her gloriously naked body, round breasts with their dark nipples, the nest of dark curls at her mound the color of rich bourbon, a little darker than the thick tresses on her head. At her long legs that he wanted wrapped around him again.

God! How had he ever thought a few days with her would ever be enough? Even now, only moments after an orgasm that had rocked his body, his cock was hardening again in anticipation of what was to come.

Kenzi looked at him from beneath thick eyelashes that formed a curtain for her honey-gold eyes. When she ran her tongue in a leisurely swipe over her lower lip, Trey was afraid he'd come just from that alone. He reached down and grabbed his wallet from where he'd dropped it on the floor, and retrieved three condoms from it.

"Either you're very optimistic," Kenzi teased, "or you have impressive stamina."

"I don't want to run out." He winked and dropped the condoms on the nightstand.

Then the time for teasing was past. He knelt between her legs, took a long moment just to appreciate the exciting, sexy, incredible woman stretched out before him, then began to kiss his way up her body. Her skin had a delicate floral scent to it that made his senses stand up and shout, the aroma so erotic he took his time working his way up from her slender ankles. The taste of her skin was tantalizing, like the appetizer before a feast, and he licked and nibbled slowly, moving from one ankle up an elegant leg and down the other. His problem, he realized, would be maintaining his self-control. He was gripped by an intense urge to devour every bit of her at once.

He forced himself to move quickly from her sex, not pausing or he'd lose himself there and miss the other areas of pleasure. With the tip of his tongue, he traced from her navel up to the valley between her breasts, then paused to bite softly at each taut nipple. When Kenzi grabbed his head and tried to push it lower, he laughed, a low, guttural sound. He wrapped his fingers around her wrists and forced her arms to her sides. Then he held her captive like that while he sucked her nipples, grazing them with his teeth and taking little nips of her firm breasts.

Beneath him, her body was writhing, her hips pushing at him, her legs hooked over his. The pulse at the hollow of her throat pounded and her breathing was fast and choppy. He loved the low, sexy little hum she made as he teased and tormented her. Then, when he knew he was reaching the end of his own rope, he slid down her body, lifted her legs over his shoulders and used his thumbs to open her sex to him. Her glistening pink flesh made his mouth water and the scent of her musk had him craving a taste of her. He'd need all his control not to rush things here.

Using every bit of his learned discipline, he tamped down the orgasm that wanted to rush through his body right then. This was for her. He took long, slow licks of her tempting flesh, flicking his tongue over her swollen clit and using the tip to trace the rim of her opening. The feel of her heels as she dug them into his back in an effort to lift herself closer to him made him even harder, if that was possible.

He used his big body to hold her in place, knowing that would increase her desire even more, while he licked and teased over and over, alternating with tiny bites of her swollen bud. She pushed against him as hard as she could, the sounds of need becoming one long moan as he took her higher and higher.

"Please, please, please," she begged.

He groaned his pleasure then thrust his tongue inside her, sliding it in and out while he pinched and tugged on her clit. Sliding one hand beneath her ass, he eased a finger into the cleft and pressed hard against her opening there.

And she exploded on his tongue, her hips pushing at him, heels pressing into him. Spasms racked her body as she came hard, her liquid pouring into his mouth. He relished its tart-sweet taste, thrusting in and out of her hot flesh, his hands gripping her hips to hold her in place as her thighs pressed tight against him.

Slowly the shudders rippling through her subsided and the tension in her body eased. When she was limp beneath him, he moved up to cup her face and press his mouth to hers so he could share her taste with her. Her face was flushed, her eyes glazed with passion, her brandy-colored hair swirling on the pillow like strands of silk, and he thought she looked absolutely gorgeous. Of all the women he'd been with—and if he took a moment to reflect, there had been a damn long list of them—none had ever touched him the way Kenzi Bryant did. Nor had the sex ever been so intense and incredible.

What's going on here, anyway?

"Okay?" he asked, touching his lips to hers.

"More than." Her lips curved in a sexy smile. "How about you?"

"Just great."

He shifted so he lay next to her, on his side, and rolled her so she was spooned against him. Her breathing was still choppy and, when he cupped her left breast, he could feel the rapid beat of her heart beneath the skin. The curve of her ass was soft against his cock, which was already hardening again and ready for action.

"I think I feel something nudging me," she chuckled, and did a teasing little wriggle of her butt.

"It'll do a lot more than nudge you if you don't keep still," he warned, and gently bit the lobe of her ear.

"Really," she drawled, and did it again.

"Keep that up and I might have to spank you."

She stilled against him, and he wondered if his teasing had gone too far.

Then she wriggled again. "Promises, promises."

"Be careful who you tease, woman." He nipped her earlobe again. "I might have to make good on that, then fuck you senseless."

For a long moment she lay quiet, but then she turned in his arms, rolled to her knees and pushed him flat on his back.

"In that case, I should get my licks in first." The smile she gave him was positively wicked.

He lay there, wondering what she had in mind, and telling himself how lucky he was that this woman had dumped a plate of food on him. None of the women he'd been with in a long time were as unrestrained and playful and responsive as she was, without demanding anything in return. Even the ones who said they only wanted something quick and dirty clung a little too long when he got ready to walk away.

In the back of his mind, a little thought tried to climb to the surface. *What if he doesn't want to walk away this time?*

Then she wrapped her slender fingers around his shaft, slid the other hand between his thighs and cupped his balls, and his brain shut down completely. Heat shot through his body and he clenched his fists as he reached for some measure of control.

Her fingers were whispers of contact as she stroked him from root to tip, a gentle glide up and down. He forced himself to lie still, eyes closed, giving himself over to the magic of her touch. Every nerve in the skin sheathing his cock was alive and dancing in response and blood pounded in his ears.

"Close your eyes." Her voice was commanding yet soft.

He wanted to keep them open, to look at her while she pleasured him. He loved the sight of her on her knees next to him, the curve of her back as she bent over his shaft, the fall of her hair like a cascade of aged brandy. *Jesus!* When did he get so fucking poetic? Was he losing his mind?

Just then she closed her mouth over the head of his dick, ran the tip of her tongue over the soft skin of the head then slid her lips down to take all of him in her mouth. *Holy shit!* If his eyes had been open, he was sure they'd be crossed. Her lips were gentle but firm, and as she moved them up and down, she added a swipe of her tongue. The tempo increased, the friction of her hand on him making every nerve come alive.

He clenched his fists and gritted his teeth, trying to make the sensations last as long as he could, but the familiar tightening of the muscles at the small of his back was the signal that he was close to orgasm. Kenzi seemed to sense it, because she increased the pace even more and began a rhythmic squeeze of his balls.

Then he exploded into her mouth, his body jerking as his cock pulsed again and again. The sensation of his cum sliding onto her tongue made him come so hard he thought the top of his head would explode.

At last she loosened her lips on his shaft and stroked his balls instead of squeezing them. When she had sucked every drop from him, she slid her tongue from root to tip one last time and released him from the grip of her mouth. She peppered his cock and balls with soft kisses before at last sitting back on her heels.

When he opened his eyes, she was watching him, her lips curved in a smile of satisfaction.

"Pretty proud of yourself, aren't you?" he teased, his voice low and gravelly.

She nodded. "Damn straight. Be honest and tell me you respond like that all the time. Or even often."

He had to take a moment to catch his breath. He'd thought his head had exploded when he took her against the door, like some rutting animal, and had come like a maniac. But this made everything else seem mild by comparison. He lifted one hand and brushed the silk of her skin with gentle strokes, his fingers following the curve of her body.

He glanced down to where his cock lay limp against his thigh. Well, it had certainly had a workout. He sifted his gaze to her face again, caught up in the desire still flaring in her coffee-colored eyes.

"I think you're gonna kill me," he chuffed.

"That would never do." She kissed his limp cock then his mouth. "I should probably give you time to recharge."

"I think we can both use it," he reminded her and pulled her down so she was lying next to him.

Her body was soft and warm against his, her curves fitting perfectly. He was almost embarrassed to think about the amount of sex he'd enjoyed in his life, and how he'd always separated himself from it emotionally. He had the uncomfortable feeling that might not be possible this time and he wasn't sure what to do about it. Maybe this was all she wanted, too, and that would solve the problem.

Maybe.

What he did know was that he was nowhere near ready to walk away from this.

Chapter Four

"I know the way around your kitchen," Trey murmured into the crook of her neck. "How about I fix some coffee for us while you hang out in bed?"

She chuckled. "Are you hoping to get lucky again?"

He pressed a soft kiss to her lips. "If I got any luckier I'd need oxygen. But right now, I'll settle for caffeine."

Kenzi curled her hands around the mug he had brought her, sitting cross-legged on the bed and sipped the hot liquid, more wide-awake than she would have expected after a night of the most intense sex she had ever experienced. Her body had been used in the most exquisite ways and she was sure she had exceeded her allotment of orgasms for the week, if not the month. Who knew that this very sexy Delta Force soldier she had taken home for a weekend would turn out to be the man of her dreams? At the very least, of her erotic dreams.

Over the rim of her cup she watched him with his own coffee, drinking in the sight of him. He had pulled on his jeans to answer the door and they hung low on his hips, unzipped, exposing his perfect abs, flat stomach and just a hint of the thick, curly hair on his groin. Hair she'd run her fingers through again and again before closing them around his very impressive cock. Last night had been...memorable was too weak a word for it.

She wished that her job, the one she loved so much, the one that was going to make her a corporate star, would disappear for just a few days. What was that all about? Her job was everything, right? From the day she'd started law school it had been her entire focus. *So what's the deal here?*

She swallowed a sigh. "I have to go into the office today."

Trey frowned. "On Saturday?"

"Some things don't play by a calendar. The firm is doing a new project for a client and I've been given the main responsibility for it."

He quirked an eyebrow. "That's a kind of a big deal, isn't it?"

She nodded. "It is. The client is the head of a large cattle and mineral operation that's expanding into other areas. They're setting up a new international finance corporation to manage the money for the new divisions."

He frowned. "Sounds complicated."

Kenzi grinned at him. "I like complicated. Anyway, Alex Reyes has been a client of the firm for many years — I think their first major one, as a matter of fact — and provides a lot of billable hours with the work we do for him. Reed Calhoun, the senior partner who handles him, practically kisses this guy's ass to keep him happy."

"So, this *is* a big deal for you, right?"

She nodded. "It can be huge. I've been an associate for six years and Calhoun hinted I'm sort of on the partner track."

"And that's an even bigger deal. Even an idiot like me knows that much."

She frowned. "I don't exactly see you as an idiot, Sergeant McIntyre. You don't get where you are or do what you're doing without brains."

He placed his cup on the nightstand and sat down next to her, stroking her arm.

"Just yanking your chain, sugar. Don't take this the wrong way, but you're about ten cuts above the women I usually spend my fun time with."

She frowned and set her own cup aside. "Don't you take this the wrong way, but I'm guessing that's a deliberate choice on your part, so you don't have any regrets about walking away."

"I might not get away so clean this time," he whispered.

Kenzi wasn't sure she wanted him to explain. She treated relationships the same way, here today and gone tomorrow. But Trey McIntyre was beginning to wriggle past her Do Not Pass Go sign and she wasn't sure how she wanted to handle it. Especially now that she was working on a high priority case with Reed Calhoun and saw partnership signs in her future.

He brushed his mouth over hers, a feathery touch. Just the contact of his lips was enough to start the pulse throbbing low in her belly again and her nipples hardening. She needed to get in the shower and get out of there. A quick stroke of her fingers on his cheeks, then she pushed away from him.

"I could do this all day, but I really do need to get to the office. Time to shower and get dressed." She pushed herself off the bed, pulling the sheet to wrap around herself. Otherwise she was afraid she really wouldn't get out of there.

"Do you have plans for the day? Transportation? What's on your schedule?"

And what, she wondered, had become of her friend Deandra last night? She didn't think the woman was into threesomes, but one never knew. Guilt nudged at her for leaving her friend that way in the bar with the two other guys. She checked her cell for a text. Nothing. Her friend knew how to take care of herself, but still…

"The guys and I have one vehicle between us, a loaner from Slade's ranch. I need to see what's on their schedule for the day. How about dropping me back at the hotel on your way to the office?"

Kenzi chewed on her bottom lip for a moment, forehead creased in thought. "If you want to — and only if you want to — you could take my car and drive me to work, then do whatever you like to kill time. Maybe have breakfast with your friends? I should be finished by one o'clock. If you come pick me up, we can have lunch on the Riverwalk and do…whatever."

Heat flared in his eyes. "I'd say *whatever* sounds pretty damn good."

It sounded good to her, too. She had no idea how long his leave was this time, but she hoped it would be long enough for them to satisfy the intense craving they seemed to have for each other, and have some fun when they weren't wearing themselves out in bed.

"Well, then." She glanced at the bedside clock. "Let me get moving here."

"Okay. While you do that, I'll text Alex. I'm sure he's still asleep, but he'll get this when he wakes up." He tapped in the message on his phone. "Or not. Otherwise I'll wake him when I get back."

"Do you want to shower before we leave?"

A hungry look flashed in his eyes. "With you? Anytime."

Now it was her turn to laugh. "Not right now. Mine will be for cleanliness. I'm on a tight time schedule here, sad to say. No extra time for fun."

He was beside her in an instant, cupping her cheeks in his warm palms, his face so close to hers she could feel his breath on her skin.

"I can't wait until we get to the fun part."

He traced the seam of her lips with the tip of his tongue, nudging until she opened for him and he could slip inside.

She closed her eyes and gave herself over to the pleasure of it, reveling in the taste of him and the softness of his lips. When he drew back, she blinked to see what was wrong.

"You need to get going," he told her in his rich, deep voice, "and if I don't stop now, you might not get to work until Monday."

Kenzi sighed. "Don't tempt me."

Then she pushed away from him and grabbed her clothes from where she'd tossed them the night before. She just hoped she'd be able to concentrate at work this morning. She breezed through her shower, dressing and makeup in record time. Hair pulled back in a clip, pearl studs in her ears and she was ready.

Trey ran his eyes over her slowly when she emerged from the bedroom. "Lady, you look good enough to eat."

As if they had a sensor attached to them, her nipples hardened and peaked at once.

"Say that too often and I'll need to take another shower—an ice-cold one—to be able to concentrate at work." She eased away from him and grabbed her purse from the little table in the hall. "Let's get going. The sooner I get to the office, the sooner I can be done for the day."

"I'll vote for that."

The law offices of Byrne, Calhoun and Raven were in a building in downtown San Antonio. The partners had deliberately chosen it years ago because of its proximity to the Riverwalk, to hotels where they could house out-of-town clients, and to an abundance of activities and gourmet restaurants. It was also close to the county courthouse, which made it convenient for the clerks to file papers.

"I should be finished pretty close to one o'clock," she told Trey. "The client isn't going to be there, so it's just me and Reed Calhoun, the senior partner who represents him. In fact, it should be pretty quiet, so we might even finish early."

"Just text me when you're ready. You know—Damn!"

"What's the matter?"

"You didn't even get anything to eat. My bad."

"I'm good. Mr. Calhoun always has a tray sent in from the bakery near us. My problem will probably be eating too much." She slid out of the car and reached in back for her purse and messenger bag.

Trey came around to get in behind the wheel, but before he did, he tilted up her chin and brushed another one of those teasing kisses on her lips.

"See you later."

Then he climbed into the car and pulled away.

Before she headed into the offices, Kenzi texted Deandra. She at least wanted to know the woman was safe and sound. Somewhere.

You doing okay? Sorry to do a fast exit last night.

The answer came back at once.

Safe at home with only a tiny hangover. But you? I want details, girl.

Same goes. Later.

Reed was waiting for her in the conference room when she got there. He preferred working there rather than his office, because the table was bigger and he liked to spread things out. Kenzi grinned when she saw the tray of pastries set out on the credenza next to the coffeemaker.

"Good morning." Reed looked up when she walked in. "Thanks for coming in on a Saturday."

"The work never stops just because it's the weekend," she told him, repeating something he often said himself.

He smiled. "I think I've heard that before. Okay. Get yourself fixed up and let's go to work."

* * * *

Trey was sliding his key card into the slot of his hotel room door when the screeching sound of a radar warning came from on his cell phone. He fished it out of his pocket as he walked into the room and looked at the screen. A text from Axel.

You still alive?

Trey grinned. Instead of answering, he knocked on the door to the room across from his. Axel yanked it open.

"You're alive!"

He nodded. "And kicking."

"Brock and I were about to get some breakfast, but we didn't want to leave you alone and hungry if you wanted to join us."

"I'm fine," he snapped, then took a deep breath. He was suddenly very protective of his situation with Kenzi — unusual for him, but he didn't want to piss off his teammates.

"Okay, okay." Axel held up his hands. "I'll just ask again. Want to grab breakfast?"

"Yeah. I'm starved. Give me fifteen to shower and shave and I'm ready."

"Just knock on the door. I'll text Brock."

They ended up at a little restaurant down the block from the hotel, one that the desk clerk had recommended when they discovered the one in the hotel had a long line ahead of them. Trey was waiting for one of the others to make some smart comment about where he'd been, and when no one did, he thought they'd decided to mind their own business. But when the waitress had filled their coffee mugs and taken their orders, Brock shattered that hope.

"So." He leaned forward. "Interesting lady you've got there. Sharp. How long have the two of you been together?"

How to answer that? "We're not exactly together."

"Just friends?" Brock persisted. "With benefits?"

That was what it had started out as, just like every other hookup since he'd become part of Delta. He had realized this morning, to his discomfort, that that had changed somehow between the last time he and Kenzi had been together and last night. *Well, fuck.* That wasn't in his life plan at all. Nor did he think it was in hers. That was one of the things that made being with her so enjoyable.

"We met a while ago. Before you guys joined the team, we spent some down time at Slade's ranch and he dragged us along to a party with him."

"Yeah, we heard about that." Axel grinned. "That must have been quite some party. Slade's married and two of you are engaged. You next, Storm?"

He shook his head. "Never. This is one time I don't follow the leader."

But a strange feeling washed through him. He dismissed it as hunger pangs, but was it? Was Kenzi Bryant the one woman who could change his mind? *Not a chance,* he told himself. He was married to Delta, at least for the foreseeable future.

Neither of them said a word about Deandra, for which he was thankful. He was sure Kenzi would ask him and he was happy to be able to tell her his team mates hadn't exchanged dirty remarks like horny teenagers.

"By the way," Axel said, buttering a slice of toast, "I was watching the news earlier. Our friend Hector Lopez Garcia is in the headlines again."

"Yeah?" Trey stirred creamer into his coffee, grateful for the change of subject. "Anything dealing with our little visit to his compound in Quintana Roo?"

Axel shook his head. "Not since Dana Roberts' employers put out the big story about her rescue. My guess is Lopez Garcia is not anxious for anyone to know what a disaster the whole thing was for him. No, this is about a major drug bust just over the border in Texas. And I mean major."

"Like what?" Brock asked.

"The DEA got a tip that two semis would be hauling cocaine, meth and fentanyl hidden in crates of goods from a factory in Mexico. They pulled the trucks over once they crossed the border and discovered fifty tons of meth, with an estimated street value of four billion."

Trey whistled. "Holy shit. Are they sure who it belongs to?"

"Oh, yeah." Axel grinned. "The factory that produced the goods hiding the shit is owned by a corporation that they traced back to him."

"How did they do that? I thought these guys had very complex setups."

"That is a complex setup." Axel shook his head. "The crates are specifically designed to conceal the drugs, often stored in false walls and bottoms. This shipment came from a factory in Tegucigalpa owned by a relative of one of Lopez Garcia's lieutenants."

"Uh-huh." Brock smirked. "On paper, anyway." He leaned forward. "Axel and I actually did three cartel-related missions, and I'll tell you, Storm, these cartels are set up like the most complex corporations. They've got attorneys and accountants who keep things humming and make sure nobody smells their real purpose for existing."

"They seem to be getting more arrogant and confident lately," Axel added.

"Which is probably why they're getting harder and harder to catch," Trey commented.

"Our former team leader told us the DEA has let a lot of stuff slide so they can use the cartel members as informants."

Brock snorted. "Like those guys will feed them real information. They're all laughing up their butts at us. Take my word for it. I sense the government thinks because it has El Chapo in custody and are putting him on trial, Sinaloa will fracture without his leadership. Just look it up on the web. It's so big, and has so many 'lieutenants,' it just keeps on rockin' and rollin'."

"It's frightening, is what it is," Axel added. "You think about the power these guys have and the brutality of their organizations. I can promise you, someone's head will roll, literally, for this bust."

"They used to smuggle cash over the border, too," Trey added, "but they got caught so many times that they're changing their method. Now they clean the money through a complicated network and it shows up as legitimate income."

"Ha!" Brock took a swallow of coffee. "Legitimate? That's a fucking joke."

"I read somewhere that the cartel leaders are setting up dummy corporations," Axel went on. "And the money ends up in so-called legit enterprises. At least on paper."

"Takes a lot of smarts to put together situations like that," Trey pointed out, "and not leave any kind of trails. Or at least disguise them very well."

"Funny," Axel said, breaking his slice of toast in half. "You think of these guys as illiterate thugs, but then you look at the scope of the operations they run and the millions and billions of dollars that pass through their fingers undetected and for the most part untouchable, even if you know where it is. You either have to be incredibly smart to set up an organization or be savvy enough to hire people who are. Or maybe both."

"The assholes guarding Kenzi's sister weren't all that bright," Slade told them, "but no one ever accused Hector Lopez Garcia of not having a brain. Scuttle butt says he's rapidly gaining on the Sinaloa organization, but he's doing it so far under the radar we can't verify it."

"Yeah?" Brock hiked an eyebrow. "Why the low key? I mean, he'd have to go a long way to do that. Sinaloa, the big kid on the block, is in every country of the world and has enough people involved in it to fill their own country. You think Lopez Garcia is just trying to stay off their radar until he makes some kind of big push?"

"Maybe." Trey shrugged. "If you remember the briefing for the hostage rescue, the brass has managed to get that information. Very quietly, Hector Lopez Garcia has expanded far beyond the borders of Mexico. He's in Central and South America, the Caribbean and now is looking to set up distribution in Europe. The DEA has someone feeding them information." He snorted. "I hope the guy's life insurance is paid up."

"I know he's active in South America," Axel told them. "But I only learned that because Brock and I were part of a unit that worked with the Colombian military to neutralize a threat."

Trey frowned. "It's my understanding that the military, like the government, is pretty damn crooked."

"Not as much as they used to be. When the Medellin cartel was flourishing, and bringing more than four hundred million dollars a day, they owned everything and everyone. When Pablo Escobar was killed, for a while the Cali cartel swept in and took over, but then they fractured and spawned a number of smaller groups. Colombia had elections, new people were in power and they've been working to eradicate the cartels as much as possible."

"But nothing happens in a vacuum," Brock pointed out. "Miguel Gallardo, Mexico's first major drug lord, had an arrangement with Pablo Escobar. When the Medellin cartel began to disintegrate, Gallardo was ready. After him came Aviles, the originator of the Sinaloa cartel, then it was off to the races."

"It's insidious," Trey agreed. "There's not a country in the world where one cartel or another doesn't have a foothold. I need to talk to Kenzi about her sister. If Dana persists in doing her series on the cartels and how they control governments, she'll continue to put herself in danger. The next time we might be retrieving her body."

"Amen to that," Axel said. "And speaking of Kenzi—"

Trey held up a hand. "Which we weren't and aren't going to. Off limits, guys."

The two men exchanged glances, then Axel shrugged.

"Okay. I get it. It's your business."

"Unless"—Trey grinned—"you want to talk about her friend last night. I hope you didn't do anything to make Kenzi cut off my balls."

Brock chuckled. "We figured you'd be the one cutting off ours if we made a misstep." He exchanged a glance with Axel. "We behaved ourselves. She's bright and fun and she seemed to have a great time. I have no idea if she's into either of us, but we didn't want to fuck things up for you and Kenzi."

"Thanks. Appreciate it. I'll let you know if Kenzi says anything."

"Where is she, anyway?" Axel asked.

"She had to work this morning. Said she'd be done around one. I've got her car so I'll pick her up. I thought I'd take her to lunch on the Riverwalk. Maybe one of those outdoor places, since it's so nice today. What are you guys up to?"

"We thought we'd do the tourist thing and get in some sightseeing. We were waiting to see if you were hooking up with your lady for the day or wanted to come with."

"Normally I'd be happy to look at your ugly mugs for the day, but not this time." He finished his last swallow of coffee. "Okay. Let's get our checks and get out of here."

Chapter Five

Kenzi was more than glad when Reed Calhoun leaned back in his chair and heaved a sigh.

"I don't know about you, but this stuff is beginning to make my eyes cross. I say we hang it up for the day and pick it up again on Monday."

"I was afraid I was the only one whose brain was getting scrambled." She rubbed her forehead. "We've done complicated before, but this one really pushed the envelope. Am I sticking my nose where it doesn't belong if I ask why this complex structure?"

Reed shook his head. "Not at all. It took a while for me to figure it out myself." He raked his fingers through his close-cropped greying hair. "I should give you a little background on Alex Reyes first."

"I know he's been a client of the law firm for a long time."

"He has. He owns a ranch just outside San Antonio in the Hill Country that's been in the family for a long time. Four generations ago his ancestors came up here from Mexico after a fight between two brothers over who had the inherited rights to the existing homestead. Land was a lot cheaper then, so they bought more than five hundred acres."

"Wow." Kenzi was impressed. "That was a good chunk of land. They must have had some bucks to buy it."

Reed smiled. "Yes, they did. They run Charolais cattle on it. I forget how large the herd is, but suffice it to say big hardly describes it. Additionally, there is a large chunk of land with significant mineral deposits. That's where we came in."

"How so?" Kenzi leaned back in her chair. She was enjoying the story, details she'd never heard before.

"Descendants of the original brother who stayed in Mexico decided that the ranch actually belonged to them, and they wanted their share of the mineral rights."

Kenzi's jaw dropped. "But that's absurd. Alex's ancestor bought it with his own money, right?"

"Well," Reed drawled. A corner of his mouth ticked up in a hint of a grin. "I suppose it depends on who you ask. Anyway, I had met him at a couple of major fundraising events, he had just fired the attorney he had, so we arranged a meeting. We've handled everything for him since then. You recall when I briefed you on this?"

"Yes. This firm is really set up for what he needs." Kenzi ticked things off on her fingers. "The Reyes family has really branched out in the last couple of generations as current descendants saw the wisdom in creating a consolidated entity. Real estate. Buying and selling herds. Land development. You name it. And now Reyes is branching out internationally."

Reed nodded. "Both he and his brother, Antonio, although he is the point person. That's why setting this up is so tricky. You can make or lose a mint in the exchange rate of foreign currency, not just with the United States but between the other countries. So, we're setting up this conglomerate to always give the most favorable rate of exchange. That's why one of the businesses will be to handle the currency."

'Whew!" Kenzi tucked her hair behind one ear. "It also means, with different regulations in different countries, we need to get it right the first time."

"That's the idea." He saved the document on his laptop and closed it down. "But like I said earlier, I think we've pushed as far as we can today. I need to ask *Señor* Reyes some questions before he leaves town for a couple of days and we both need to give our brains a rest. Let's let it rest over the weekend."

"I can't say I'm sorry to hear that." She shut down her own laptop.

"You know, Kenzi, I know I mentioned this before. The partners and I have our eyes on you. Once this project is completed, signed off on and in place, there just might be a step up the ladder in your future."

She tried to quell the little thrill of excitement that wriggled through her.

"You know I love this firm and always try to do my best for our clients."

"I do. We all do. And you have a sharp mind for complex situations like this. I promise we'll be discussing this before too long."

"Thank you for your faith in me."

Reed rose from his chair. "I'm going to make a couple of calls, but you need to get on out of here. You've given us enough of your Saturday. Is there someone exciting waiting to spend the weekend with you?"

How did she explain Trey to him? *A hot, sexy soldier who tunes up my hormones and makes me lose my mind in bed?* It wasn't as if it was anything serious.

"I, uh, have a friend in town for a few days. We'll probably hang out together."

"Good. Have fun. See you on Monday."

When she checked her phone, she discovered another text from Deandra.

Can you talk?

Later. Everything okay? Any bad news from last night?

After a moment a smiling emoji appeared followed by a response.

Smiled and laughed a lot. Fun guys.

She hit the button to call Deandra.

"Couldn't stand not asking?" her friend laughed.

"I know Trey will ask me if they behaved and if you'd like to go out with either of them."

"So men gossip, too?"

Now it was Kenzi's turn to laugh. "Of course they do, although they'd die if we nailed them on it. So, what do you think? What should I tell Trey?"

"If you can do it diplomatically, while they are both great, I think I'd have more in common with Brock. Not that either of us would be looking for more than a fun time."

"Then that's what I'll tell him. Gotta go. Catch you later?"

After she hung up she sent a quick text to Trey telling him to pick her up then headed for the elevator, aware that Reed was on his way to his office. By the time he reached the end of the corridor his cell was to his ear and he was already deep in conversation. If ever someone needed to relax, it was him.

She had just signed out in the lobby and stepped into the street when Trey pulled up to the curb, sliding the car into a parking space luckily just being vacated. She tossed her laptop into the back, hopped into the passenger seat and blew out a breath.

"Tough morning?" Trey asked.

"Mentally stressful, but only because what we're working on is so complex. I really feel honored he has me working on this with him." She undid the clip from her hair and raked her fingers through the loose strands. "He hinted there could be big things in store for me when we finish with this project."

"Yeah? That would be great, right?"

"You know it. Maybe a junior partnership. It would have to be non-equity because I don't have the bucks for the buy-in. At least not right now."

"Sounds exciting. You can explain all that to me over lunch. But first, this."

He leaned across the console, cupped her chin so he could turn her face toward him and pressed his mouth to hers. She opened for him at once, welcoming the smooth feel of his tongue and the flavor of him. He stroked the inside of her mouth then gently slid his teeth over the surface of her own tongue. Heat surged through her body, stiffening her nipples and igniting the pulse that throbbed in her sex. She heard someone moan and realized the sound was coming from her.

"Damn." Trey broke the kiss, lifting his head just enough so he could lock his gaze with hers. "For a minute I was afraid the car would spontaneously combust. Holy shit, Kenzi."

A soft laugh bubbled from her mouth. From the first moment they'd had skin-to-skin contact, the air around them had exploded like an electrical storm. "I was sort of thinking the same thing myself."

"Listen." He brushed a few strands of hair from her forehead. "My purely animal inclination is to say fuck everything else, take you back to your place and get us both naked."

"Sounds good to me." She licked her lips, tasting the flavor of the kiss. Then a low rumble in her stomach ruined the mood.

Kenzi giggled. "Sorry about that."

"No, no problem." Trey laughed. "But I think I'd better feed you first. Anyway, I planned to take you to lunch on the Riverwalk, ply you with drinks and good food." He lowered his voice. "Seduce all your senses."

"Mmmm." She licked her lips again. "Sounds very good to me."

"I checked at the hotel and they recommended La Casita, on the Riverwalk."

"Ooh! I love that place." And she did, with its colorful outdoor umbrella tables, the strolling mariachis and the servers in Mexican garb, but she frowned at him. "But, Trey, that place is pretty costly. I don't need expensive meals."

He stroked her cheek with the tips of his fingers. "Kenzi, I spend most of my time in a barracks or on a mission. Where else am I going to spend my money except on a beautiful woman?"

"In that case, what are we waiting for?"

La Casita, while accessible from the street, also had an entrance directly on the Riverwalk, a collection of shops, restaurants and attractions bordering both sides of the narrow San Antonio River as it meandered through the downtown area. It was always busy, the crowds an eclectic combination of residents, tourists and business people.

Trey parked in the structure wedged between the stairway down to the Riverwalk and a row of stores and cafes. The street entrance opened into the interior dining area, a nice blend of stucco walls and dark furniture, with tasteful prints and other artwork on the walls.

"Inside or out?" Trey asked as they approached the hostess stand.

"Outside. Definitely. I love it outside there, all the color and the sounds and the people."

The hostess smiled at them. "This way, then."

They followed her down a short flight of stairs to the outside area that was right on the walkway. Tables were shaded by colorful umbrellas and nearly every one of them was filled. While almost every place on the Riverwalk was busy on a regular basis, Saturday was the peak day of activity of the week. People, laughing and talking, moved along the path between the tables on their way from store to store, and at one end of the eating area the trio of mariachis was serenading a group of diners.

They scored a table at the railing, right next to the river. From here they had a great view of the flat-bottomed river barges loaded with tourists taking the sightseeing trips and feeding crumbs to the ever-present pigeons.

Kenzi raked her fingers through her hair, loosening it even more so it floated in silky strands to her shoulders. "I think the Riverwalk is my favorite place in this city. It always has such a happy feel to it."

Trey winked at her. "And I consider it part of my mission to make sure you're happy."

"So far you're doing a great job," she assured him.

"Yeah?" He winked. "Just wait until we get back to your place and you'll see how happy I can make you."

Heat crept up her body and every pulse point throbbed in response. She couldn't recall another man who'd aroused her the way Trey did, just with words and looks. She could hardly wait until they got home.

Steady, girl. Remember. Like everything else, this has a short life cycle.

And that was fine, but she planned to enjoy every minute of the best sex of her life while it lasted.

They ordered drinks — a frozen margarita for her, beer for Trey — and sat back to study the menu. With the warmth of the sunshine, the slight breeze from the ancient trees that lined both side of the river and the faint strains of the music, Kenzi felt the tension of the morning's concentration ease from her body.

She reached across the table and touched Trey's hand. "Thank you for bringing me here. This is just what I needed."

"I think they work you too hard at that office."

She laughed. "I'm sure they'd think they don't work me hard enough. Life in a high-profile corporate firm is always on fast forward. Our clients pay very big bucks and they want everything yesterday."

He studied her face. "And you love it."

"I do. It's what I wanted ever since I started reading books by John Grisham. And I've finally reached the point where I think pretty soon I'll be moving to the partnership level. I hope."

"They should be grateful to have you." There was nothing light in his tone, nothing teasing.

His words gave her a warm, tingly feeing. She couldn't remember the last time a man she'd dated had paid her that kind of compliment. What did that say about the kind of men she'd previously spent time with?

"I know you've spoken with your sister since she's been back," Trey said. "How's she doing? Still in New York?"

Kenzi nodded. "That's where the media conglomerate she works for is located and where her office is. That is, when she's not running around all over the world getting kidnapped and such. And she seems to be doing okay."

"I hope she's decided to walk away from that story on the cartel. Or at least dial it back for a while. We did a lot of damage when we rescued her. Combine that with everything she dug up and she's probably still on their radar."

"I only wish." Kenzi sighed. "She never listens to anyone. A big reason why she gets herself into big trouble while putting together the stories they pay her the big bucks for. She keeps telling me this will really establish her. The head honchos are talking about taking her series international and on both video and print."

Tray leaned forward, his gaze locked with hers.

"These are some dangerous men she's after," he told her in a hard tone. "I can't imagine any story is worth risking your life for this way. She should be grateful and give thanks that she got away this time. Next time she won't be so lucky. Can you try to impress that on her?"

"I'll do my best. But honestly, Trey, she's not one to listen to anyone. This is like a drug to her, which is why she gives me such high blood pressure when I think of what she's doing."

"Try," he urged again. "Okay? I'd hate to be taking you to her funeral."

Kenzi's stomach clenched at the words. Dana had always been the reckless one, and Kenzi tried not to think too much about what she was doing.

The waitress brought their drinks, along with the usual basket of warm tortilla chips, and Trey lifted his bottle of beer and touched it to her glass.

"Then we have a lot to drink to," he told her. "My guys behaving themselves and the success I know you'll have. I truly believe you can achieve anything you want to."

She actually felt herself blush, heat creeping up her cheeks and warming her skin.

"Um, thank you." She took a swallow of the cool, tangy drink.

"I think I'll drink to the Huttons, too," Trey added. "For having a great party and inviting you. And to Slade for getting the team an invite."

"It was lucky, wasn't it?" she grinned. "I almost didn't go."

"No kidding?" He lifted an eyebrow. "Then I guess luck really was with us that night." He lifted the bottle again. "To luck. All good, for a change."

Kenzi took a moment to study the man across from her as he pored over the menu. He had a lean build, but it was all muscle—developed, she suspected, from a combination of grueling training and even more grueling missions. She knew, having run her hands over every inch of his body multiple times. His high cheekbones were set off by a square jaw, accented by what she and Deandra called a trimmed, five o'clock shadow beard. A well-tended scruff, at least when he was not out in the battlefield. His hair was the color of aged brandy, and behind sinfully thick lashes, his caramel-colored eyes seemed to see everything at once.

Sex, she thought. Pure, unadulterated sex, that made her mouth water just from looking at him. There should be a law against it. She refused to think about what would happen when he left this time. She wasn't a plan-ahead woman in her social life. The priority of her career blocked all of that. But damn, she didn't think she'd be able to close the chapter on him as easily as she had on other men she'd been with.

Just enjoy it. Don't stress. You have enough of that in your life.

"Do I have dirt on my face?" Trey's voice, edged with humor, broke into her thoughts.

"What?" She blinked, then held up her menu, embarrassed to be caught staring at him. "No, it was the pigeon on the rail next to you that caught my eye."

Trey lifted an eyebrow. "Upstaged by a pigeon? Okay, if you say so." He paused. "I'm asking this just out of curiosity, but did your friend happen to mention if the idiots we left her with last night minded their manners?"

Kenzi grinned. "Oh, you mean if they acted like assholes. Well, you can rest assured they were on good behavior. She said the kids actually behaved very well. She enjoyed them both."

"I'd say mostly because they didn't want to piss you off."

"Me? Why would I get— Oh, because of us."

He nodded. "I'd hate to have to beat the crap out of them."

She thought for a minute, trying to figure out how to phrase her next statement.

"Problem?"

"No." She shook her head. "Just hoping Axel won't be upset when I tell you she thinks she clicked more with Brock. Not," she hurried to say, "that there's anything wrong with Axel. It's just—"

"Chemistry," Trey finished for her. "I get it."

"Yes." She sighed in relief. "She enjoyed both of them, although I think she has more chemistry with Brock. Will that be a problem?"

"Not at all. Axel will step back without an argument. I think he might be just as happy hunting in the local watering holes, anyway. Listen, I'm sure no one's looking for anything more than a great weekend here. They're all adults and can make their own choices. Tell her it's all good."

"I will. Thanks."

"How about texting me her phone number so I can pass it along?"

She sent him the info then took a bite of one of the tortilla chips and opened her menu. "So what appeals to you?"

"Probably everything. How about you suggest something from the menu? You're more familiar with what would be good, right? My knowledge of Mexican food is limited to tacos and burritos."

"Both of which can be a real treat if they're properly done. But let's see what we can find for you."

They placed their orders and were enjoying their second round of drinks when Kenzi's gaze landed on two men being seated at a table tucked at the side of the restaurant.

"There's my client over there," she told Trey, inclining her head toward the table. "The one in the grey suit."

"Isn't it a little warm for a full-dress wardrobe?"

"I think he lives in a suit, except maybe when he's home at his ranch." She frowned. "I thought he was out of town."

"Maybe his plans changed," Trey suggested. "Does it matter?"

She shook her head. "No, I guess not. I wouldn't say this to anyone except you, but there's something about him that turns me off. I just don't like him. And I can't even tell you what it is."

"How well does your boss know him?"

"He's been a client for years." She took a sip of her drink. "In fact, I think he was the first important client the firm acquired. I don't even know why I'm bothered by him. He's just paperwork to me. Reed handles him personally."

Trey took a swallow of beer and set his bottle down. "Just out of curiosity, what are you doing for him that required you to spend half of Saturday at the office?"

"A very complex corporate structure." She munched on a tortilla chip. "I don't know if I can explain it."

"Hey." He held up a hand. "I know about confidentiality. Don't sweat it."

She shook her head. "It's not that. It's just so complicated. He has a lot of businesses in this country beside his ranch. Which, by the way, has a whole section closed off where the mineral rights are being developed."

"Even a dummy like me knows there's a ton of money in that."

Kenzi reached across the table and placed her hand on his. "Don't keep saying that. You are far from a dummy, so don't say that again. Reyes has set up separate corporations for each of his activities. Now he's opening companies overseas, expanding into foreign markets. One of the major things to deal with is currency exchange. Moving money from one country to another. You want to make sure the exchange rate is always in your favor."

"Yeah, I can see that. I can also see what a headache it can be." He smiled. "Juggling their millions. Or is it billions?"

She shrugged. "To me it's just a bunch of numbers in a file. I let Reed worry about the actuality of it. I'm just involved in setting up the structure."

"Structure?"

"You know, the holding company that all the others fall under, their outlines, how business between them is conducted and how to manage the currency exchange."

The corner of his mouth kicked up in a hint of a grin. "Sounds fascinating."

Kenzi laughed. "I'm sure it's boring you to tears, but keep in mind that's what I thrive on. Creating these corporations in the best possible way for the client."

Before he could comment again, the waitress arrived with their food and they dug into it. Kenzi couldn't help glancing now and then at the table where Alex Reyes sat. The man with him looked equally expensive, although instead of a suit he wore slacks and a silk shirt. But the sunlight glinted on the gold watch at his wrist and the medallion he wore around his neck.

Sometimes she wondered, just for a brief moment, what it must be like to have that kind of wealth. Then she remembered the headaches that went with it and decided she had the better part of the deal.

"You know," she mused, "that guy with Reyes looks sort of familiar, but I can't figure out why."

Trey shifted in his chair as casually as possible to take a look at the man. "He looks expensive, just like Reyes."

Kenzi looked again, then shrugged. "Probably a business associate. The discussion they're having looks more like that than just two friends having lunch. I wonder what the subject is that kept him in town when he planned to be away."

Trey took another quick glance at the two men then turned back to his food.

"You said Reyes has multiple interests. Probably someone he has an important arrangement with. Do you know all his contacts?"

She shook her head. "But I'm sure Reed does. Oh, well."

"You know, now that I look again, there's something about him —"

She lifted an eyebrow. "Like what?"

"When we were prepping for the, ah, trip to Mexico, we were shown a lot of pictures. People we might see at the *finca*."

"What kind of pictures?"

"Mostly of Hector Lopez Garcia and his top lieutenants. But they threw in a number of others without identifiers, just people who might in some way be connected to the Lopez Garcia cartel. Not that we expected to see them at the *finca*, but the military wasn't taking any chances."

"For the mission to rescue Dana?"

He shook his head. "Not just that. There are a number of missions that come up regarding the cartels. It started when JSOC—Joint Special Operations Command—began rotating teams in and out of Colombia. On the face of it, we were tasked with training Colombia's top military, but sometimes those groups accompanied them on missions. We're always being prepped because you never know when one of those assignments will come up. And it's usually without much warning, so they want us to keep those images in our heads, in case we cross paths with any of those guys."

Kenzi shook her head. "Alex Reyes wouldn't be among them. Or, I'm pretty sure, any of his friends. The Reyes family has lived in the Hill Country for at least three generations. They're highly respected members of the community, both locally and statewide. And he wouldn't be sitting out here in public with someone if there was anything questionable about it."

"You said he's been a client with your firm a long time?"

She nodded. "And there's never been a sniff of any trouble around him or his family. Byrnes, Calhoun and Raven would never have accepted them as clients if there was."

"I'll take your word for it. You certainly know the background on them. Anyway, I'm probably just seeing bad guys everywhere. It goes with the territory. But if for whatever reason you have reservations about this guy, you should pass that along to the firm."

"First of all, Reed Calhoun would look at me like I'm crazy. Alex Reyes is so respectable he's the poster child for it. He night take me off this project." She sighed. "Or, worse yet, fire me for being suspicious of a client."

"Then do what you said," he suggested. "Look him up online and see if there's anything that makes you uncomfortable. Is there some reason that today you got a bug up your ass about him?"

She shook her head. "Just...something when I was watching him." She sighed. "It's probably just me. I'm tired and see things that aren't there. But I will do a search."

It was unfortunate she had a mind that fastened on to things and didn't let go. In the years since she'd joined Byrnes, Calhoun and Reed, she had never had a hint or a sniff of anything on the wrong side of the ledger, ether of the firm or its clients. The partners themselves were so clean they squeaked. Icons in the community, members of every politically important board, supporters of community organizations — she couldn't see them even a tiny bit involved in anything seedy. Not for any amount of money.

But the brain that had gotten her though undergrad and law school with very high marks and earned her a high score on the bar exam left nothing to chance. It never hurt to collect information, just in case. Fiddling with her smart watch, she turned her wrist so the watch faced the table where the two men sat. As casually as she could, she pressed the button that would take a picture, capturing the image.

When they were back at her apartment, she'd do a search on her computer and see if anything matched. Maybe there would be a shot of Alex Reyes with the man and a caption would identify him as another respectable citizen. Then she could forget about it and kill the tiny flicker of unease Trey had ignited.

Chapter Six

"That was an extremely stupid thing you did."

Hector Lopez Garcia, one of the most powerful drug lords in the Western hemisphere, stood in the richly paneled office in his estancia and did his best to control his temper. Getting to where he was today had been far from an easy task. So much of the drug trade in Mexico had taken a huge leap forward in the 1980s with the rise to power of Miguel Angel Felix Gallardo, the country's liaison with Colombia's Pablo Escobar, leader of the Medellin cartel.

But so much had changed since then. A meeting had been held to divide up the country into regions, each controlled by a specific group. But, of course, people were only human, and greedy and always wanting more. Bloody fights over territory allowed people like Lopez Garcia, who had been a lieutenant in another cartel, to form his own group and carve out a piece of the country for himself.

In the ensuing years, new groups had come to power while others had failed, and killings and arrests often left vacuums to be filled. Little by little, Hector had chipped away at some of the others, reducing their power and strength, and until now he had been considered third in the power struggle and outreach. Wresting land in the state of Sonora from Sinaloa had only become possible when their leader, El Chapo Guzman, had been arrested for the third time. A bloody battle in the chain of command had followed and allowed him to claim a stronghold, a place to build from.

His goal was to occupy that top spot, but unseating the Sinaloa cartel, which was now an international force, would not be possible with his lieutenants doing idiotic things that brought them unwanted attention.

Like the one standing before him right now, the one he had summoned for an immediate meeting. Felix Santiago, his nephew and poor excuse for a lieutenant, glared at him.

"You said money is important. I had a chance to get some. Quick and easy. It was the smart thing to do. If we'd just killed the *gringa*, we'd get nothing for it."

Hector swallowed the growl that rumbled up in his throat.

"First, you did not get the money. Second, twenty million is a paltry sum compared to what our organization clears. Third, we have a specific pecking order in this organization. No one goes off on their own. Nothing gets done except at my direction. *Comprende*?"

"But—"

Lopez Garcia sliced a hand through the air to cut off his nephew's words.

"You brought us to the attention of people who don't need to stick their nose in our business, like the officials in the United States who would like nothing better than to put us all out of business. Third, you cost me the lives of sixteen of my men and four more are recovering from wounds. A fucking disaster, and a total disrespect for those men."

"If they were any good," Felix sneered, "they wouldn't be dead. Or wounded."

"Not for you to say." Hector's voice was like ice, a fact Felix seemed to ignore. "Finally, and perhaps the worst, you disobeyed a direct order. That is unforgiveable. I told you to get rid of that nosy bitch of a reporter and do it in a way her body would never be found. Was that too difficult for your simple little mind?"

Hector watched his nephew's face turn red as anger surged through him. He stood erect with his fists clenched at his sides, muscles in his arms bulging. If not for his sister, Luisa Elena, Hector would have disposed of his nephew long ago. The man was an idiot, had a short temper and too much arrogance for his own good.

"I analyzed the situation, saw an opportunity and jumped on it," he insisted. "You said you wanted me to show initiative."

"I also expected you to use your brain, never thinking you might not have one."

"I say again, I saw another way to score."

"And for your efforts," Lopez Garcia said in measured tones, "you got nothing except the deaths of several very good men and the attention of one of the deadliest divisions of the United States military."

"You don't know that," his nephew protested. "They could have just been a team of mercenaries hired by her bosses to retrieve her rather than pay the ransom."

Hector inhaled a deep breath and let it out slowly, grateful that he did not have a gun in his hands. "Because I pay a lot of money to the right people to feed me information, I was able to learn that the team that rescued the reporter is part of Delta Force, an elite special missions unit of the United States Army. Those *pendejos* don't shoot first and ask questions later. They just shoot. Which is why so many of my men are dead and the reporter is still alive. And why my house where you were holding her is no longer useful."

"It should not have played out that way," Felix argued. "We were prepared—"

"*Mierda!*" Hector spat the words out. "Bullshit! Quit lying to yourself. The reporter is gone, with all the information she acquired. You let your tiny brain take control of your tinier balls and now I have to clean up the mess."

"I'll clean it up," his nephew protested.

"You won't be around to."

Felix frowned. "What do you mean? Are you replacing me? But I am *familia*."

"Which is the only reason you lasted so long. But I have reached the end of my rope. I have sent my regrets to your mother."

Who, by the way, had cursed him more violently than many of his men, then broken down in tears, then spat on the ground and ordered him to leave. A breakdown in the family was sad, but this was not a business for the faint at heart. Additionally, he had the other branch of the family to consider, the one whose skirts needed to be hospital-clean. His cousins, who had built the structure the public saw, who by agreement had created a shield between them so they were free to conduct their public business while he continued to build his cartel and bring in more money than any of the other 'legitimate' businesses.

Long ago his great-grandparents and great aunts and uncles had created the solid structure for the cartel, appointing Hector's grandfather as the head of that area, with the two cousins leading the empire their great-grandfathers had put in place. One that was totally disconnected from the cartel yet provided a place to funnel all their cash and wash it so it came out clean.

And soon will bring all of us even more millions.

They had a plan in the works, and it was being organized in very careful steps, so it was important for him and his people to avoid doing things that brought groups like Delta Force into their country and onto their property. It was good for his people to have the reputation of being cold-hearted, to be willing to kill to achieve what they wanted, but not to be messy in their activities. Especially when it concerned the United States.

Right now, he didn't need any unwanted, unfavorable publicity, and his cousins needed to be able to finish their work without Hector's operation causing a disaster. If fucking Felix had just killed the reporter as ordered and disposed of her body, none of this would have happened. She would just be another missing person and there would be nothing to point a finger at the Lopez Garcia cartel.

He glared at his nephew, angry that he'd done something so stupid.

"What are you going to do?" Felix challenged. "Lock me in my room?" But even as he said the words, his face paled.

"Ah," Hector sighed. "If only it were that simple."

He pressed a button on the house phone and Pedro Gomez, his closest confidant and right-hand man, the one who had been with him since the very beginning, walked into the room. When he closed his fingers around Felix's upper arm and urged him toward the door, the younger man tried to jerk away. But Pedro's grip was like iron, his fingers digging into Felix's flesh.

"No!" Felix shouted the word as Pedro began to tug him from the room. "No, *Tio* Hector. I will make it up to you, I promise. Just give me a chance. *Please*."

"Don't demean yourself more by begging."

Hector spoke the words in a cold voice. Then he turned away, shutting his ears to his nephew's screams, grateful when the door closed, blocking them out. Sighing again, he walked to the bar against the wall and poured a strong shot of perfectly aged bourbon into a glass, dropped in one ice cube and tossed back half the drink. Still holding the glass, he walked to the big picture window that looked out on the acres of green rolling lawn.

He had worked hard for this estancia, with its lush acreage. For his stable of fine horses, his garage of high-dollar vehicles and the expensive jewels he showered on both his wife and his mistress. More blood had been shed—and continued to be shed—than in some official world battles. In many instances, the killing had become senseless, people slain with cruel heartlessness to serve as warnings to others and sometimes just for the pleasure of killing as brutally as possible.

But Hector liked to think he was not an animal, like many of his competitors. He had a brain and used it, so as vicious battles between cartels had continued to rage over the country, he'd made a decision. His family, after all, had been in Mexico for generations, raising cattle as their primary visible business. The drug business was seen as just another enterprise that would increase their income, one they kept well under the radar as they built their empire. Unlike many of the other cartels, they weren't looking for front-page all-out bloody war with the others. Little by little, they'd built their foothold until they were ready to put their expansion plans into place.

Hector had researched other geographical areas where they could get a foothold and expand their business. Rather than fight a useless and damaging war in an effort to take over more territory in Mexico, he'd developed a plan to spread his operation into the United States, Canada and Europe. Others were doing it, looking to move away from the sudden spate of crackdowns by the Mexican military, which Hector was sure were just for show.

There was untapped money in the billions around the world. Hector Lopez Garcia had his eye on that prize, saw it as his ticket to rise from being a midlevel Mexican drug lord to an elite worldwide distributor. An entrepreneur cloaked by so-called respectable businesses. Progress was slow, but steady, and he had a solid plan in place as well as people to structure it and manage it for him. He had chosen well, but his asshole nephew could have put a big crimp in it.

The last thing Hector needed was for the United States Drug Enforcement Administration to fix an eye on him, or the damned Department of Homeland Security—which insisted terrorists were being smuggled into the United State by the cartels—and start directing resources to shutting him down. *Or the Drug Enforcement Administration.* He had deliberately downplayed his place in the cartel battles.

It was important now for him to fly under the radar, to make sure the United States continued to focus primarily on the mammoth Sinaloa cartel and some of the others, along with the idiots who ran them. He wanted to be someone hardly worth their trouble, until he had all the pieces in place. At the right time he would emerge as the international leader in the drug cartel world, as well as an astute businessman with other enterprises. Those would bring additional capital as well as give him places to filter the drug money. Perhaps he would even relocate, maybe to Europe.

Right now, however, he had to control the damage that the high-visibility kidnapping had created.

He heard the door open behind him and turned to see Pedro Gomez re-enter.

"Is it done?"

Gomez nodded. "As you requested. Leon is handling the disposal."

"Thank you. This was a very difficult thing to do." He was not looking forward to the conversation with his sister.

"Will there be anything else?"

"Is Diego still here?" His top lieutenant, Diego Escamilla, had breakfasted with him earlier to discuss the situation.

"*Si!* Shall I get him?"

"Please."

Five minutes later, he was joined by the man who had been with him for nearly twenty-five years, helping him build the cartel from the bottom up. They had come a long way from those early days, and Hector trusted him with every fiber of his being.

"Are you okay, *jefe*?" was the first thing Diego asked when he walked into the den.

"As much as I can be." Hector sighed. "This was a most unpleasant thing to do. What hurts me more than anything is the trust that was broken, the deliberate defying of orders. And now I not only have had to break my sister's heart but also to drive a wedge right down the middle of the family."

"Her husband will help her through it," Diego assured him. "And the family will still be united, as it always has been and will continue to be."

Hector nodded. His brother-in-law was also a cog in the Lopez Garcia cartel machinery, and he hoped the man would really understand the cause of the tragedy.

"But the problem is still out there. The reporter is back in her own environment with whatever information she gathered up. We don't know how badly it will hurt us. And much as I don't want to step into the larger spotlight, if she discovered anything about our plans, that could be more devastating."

"I agree. But we are smart, right? The woman first, and any information she might have. Then, when we are in the position of power we are preparing, we can revisit the rest. Flex our increased muscle and show the United States military they cannot kill our people without paying a price."

Hector's mouth curved in a tight smile. "I knew I could count on you. Find me the girl. Woman, whatever she is."

Diego took out his cell phone and tapped a text message. "I will get with the men and we will follow up at once."

Hector smiled. He could always count on this man. "Of course you will. Meanwhile, we have plans to make." He waved his hand to indicate the papers spread out on his desk. "I would like to go over these one more time, scan them onto a thumb drive which we will lock away, then burn the papers. *Mi primo* will handle everything. And of course everything is indelibly inked right here."

He tapped the side of his head. His cousin was a brilliant businessman and strategist, but Hector was also blessed with a photographic memory. In case of emergency, when any hard copies of records had been destroyed, he had it all stored in his brain.

Diego nodded. "Then let's get to work."

* * * *

Kenzi loved her apartment. It was in an older complex in the city but it had many points in its favor. For one thing, it was close to downtown, so she was not always on an Interstate fighting traffic. For another, to compete with the many new communities popping up, the owners had renovated the units, so they had updated kitchens, floors that were tile but looked like hardwood, and in one bathroom a gorgeous shower while the other had a soaking tub. She was already dreaming about the tub when she headed for the bedroom, stripping off her clothes as she went. When Trey moved past her into the bathroom and she heard the water running in the tub, she had to smile.

"You must have read my mind," she called out to him.

"Or maybe you read mine. Taking a bath with you has become one of my favorite activities."

"Give me one minute," she said. "I just want to upload this picture to my computer and see if there's a match anywhere for this guy." She gave him a wicked grin. "It can do its thing while I'm doing nine."

When she had it set to go, she tossed her clothes into the hamper in the closet, then padded naked and barefoot into the bathroom, where clouds of fragrant steam were already rising from the tub and drifting up to wrap around her like a warm blanket. Trey turned to her, a hungry grin on his face. He had already removed his shirt, but he still wore his jeans, and was now tenting with a nice bulge at the fly. She had to stop herself from actually licking her lips.

She had certainly been with her share of men, not that she was indiscriminate. Far from it—she was very selective. She just never used the word 'relationship' because she didn't have time in her life for one. Her plan, to move from junior associate to senior associate to partner, was on a fast track and so close she was sure she could smell it. But staring at this man, she was shocked by the unfamiliar thought that struck her. What would it be like to have him in her life as something more than temporary? To plan for future visits, maybe even think about something long term?

Suddenly she realized that walking away from Trey McIntyre might not be as easy as she'd expected. *And what's with that, anyway?* She was a very smart corporate attorney, for the lord's sake. What was she doing on the verge of losing her mind over a battle-hardened soldier who was the antithesis of everything she wanted in life?

But he doesn't demand things of me. He respects my brain. He thinks about me in bed rather than himself.

She gave herself a mental smack. She had no business thinking about stuff like that at this point in her life. She had plenty of time for that later. Right now, she needed to concentrate on this moment and the pleasure they both enjoyed.

"I didn't realize getting into a nice hot tub took that much hard thinking."

His warm, teasing voice broke into her thoughts, bringing her back to reality.

"Just admiring the scenery," she teased.

By now the tub was full. She realized the scent was coming from the bubble bath he'd found and poured into the hot water. He had also turned on the jets. The spa tub had been another big selling point for the apartment.

"I'll give you plenty to admire as soon as you get that sexy body into the tub."

She took the hand he reached out and let him help her step into the bubbling water. As she eased down into it, the combination of the water pulsing against her skin and the aftereffects of the two frozen margaritas combined to ease away any residual tension from the morning's work.

She slid down in the tub, her eyes fastened on Trey, who popped the button on his jeans and was slowly sliding down the zipper. She hoped he didn't damage himself, because the swelling at his crotch had grown even more. Her hands itched to reach out and touch it, but she kept them beneath the water at her sides, waiting.

He stepped out of his jeans, leaving him only in his boxer briefs, before those were gone, too. She sucked in her breath at the sight of him, his cock heavy and thick, the head a dark purple, his balls resting against his thighs. He stood there like a symphony of muscle and sinew, a thin scar bisecting his right thigh, another on his left upper arm and on his right shoulder a tattoo of what he'd told her was the Delta Force insignia.

God! He's just such a magnificent male animal.

"Come on in," she invited. "The water's fine."

He eased himself into the tub behind, her, bracketing her body with his legs so her buttocks were pressed firmly against his shaft, capturing it in the cleft. At once the pulse in her core set up a steady throbbing, forceful enough that it resonated throughout her body, making it silently shriek in need.

Trey slid his hands beneath her arms and eased them around so he cupped her breasts, lightly pinching the tips.

"You have the greatest nipples," he murmured, his lips against her neck. "Firm and ripe and just made to suck and nibble on. And when I pinch them, I love the little gasp you make."

Proving his point, he squeezed each nipple and she sucked in a hard breath. Electricity shot straight to her sex, setting off another round of internal throbbing. When she clenched her thighs, the muscles in her buttocks tensed as well, squeezing Trey's cock in the hot cleft and eliciting another deep groan from him.

"You're killing me here. You know that, right?"

She laughed, a low, throaty chuckle. She loved teasing him. In addition to so many other aspects of their relationship — or whatever this was — she loved the fact that there was humor in it, even in the most erotic moments. She didn't ever remember feeling so comfortable with a man. She had to keep reminding herself not to get too comfortable with this. Like every other situation she'd been in, it would soon be over.

Any further thought disappeared from her brain as Trey teased her nipples, pinching and squeezing them and lightly dragging his fingernails over them. Those tight buds were exceptionally sensitive, and every time he stroked or sucked or teased them, heat raced through her body. Her clit tingled and again she squeezed her thighs together, doing her best to press hard on that sensitive little bud.

Trey put his mouth close to her ear.

"Keep doing that and I'll come right here, right now." He moved his hips a fraction, just enough to bury his shaft a little deeper in the warm cleft between the cheeks of her buttocks.

Kenzi wanted to get up on her knees, giving him full access, and beg him to thrust into her right then and right there. On the other hand, she didn't want to miss any of the good stuff that came before that. While she was attempting to have that internal discussion with herself, Trey coasted his hands down her body, over her stomach to her pussy where he paused to slide his fingers between the aching lips. Then he lifted her legs and placed one on either side of his, separating them so she was wide open. Shifting slightly, he positioned her so one of the jets pulsed directly onto her clit.

At once desire surged through her and the internal muscles in her sex clenched and vibrated. She wanted to press her thighs together, but Trey had cleverly positioned her so that was impossible. He banded one arm around her waist, pressing her body close to his, while he slipped his other hand between her thighs.

"Close your eyes," he murmured, his lips still close to her ear. Then he gently nipped her earlobe, something that always set off currents of electricity in her body.

She slid her hips back and forth in a desperate effort to signal to him that she needed more. *Anything more. Something more intense.* But Trey just laughed softly, held her even tighter against his firm body and continued to stroke her clit with the jets of water pounding against that swollen bud of flesh and into her open channel. The dual assault on her senses had her reaching for that orgasm, willing her body to climax.

Just then, when she was about to lose her mind and beg Trey to give her relief, it spiraled up from deep inside her, a rhythmic pounding that surged outward, finally reaching her sex. She jerked against Trey's body as her own shivered with spasms, riding his hand, silently urging him to thrust his fingers inside her.

But he wasn't finished yet. Still holding her against his body, he stroked her breasts, pinching her nipples then moving his hand downward again to tease her clit.

"I can't do it again," she whimpered, when the stroking of his clever fingers brought her right to the edge of release.

"Yes, you can. Come on. One more, then…" He licked the edge of her ear. "…then, I'm going to fuck your brains out."

He went to work again with his very talented hand, using the pulsing jets to best advantage and tormenting every inch of her desperate sex.

By the time he brought her to climax this time, she was shaking with need, the buoyancy of the water enhancing her rising desire. This time she only had to beg a little, because her body was primed. When he pinched her clit and one of her nipples at the same time, she exploded again, the water pounding against her open sex, Trey working every nerve in her pussy, knowing exactly where and how to touch her.

Kenzi closed her eyes and focused on the center of her body, willing it to give up one more orgasm that hovered just at the edge of exploding. Then it consumed her, igniting deep inside her, an orgasm that made the other two pale in comparison. The jet of water, Trey's clever fingers pinching her nipple, his tongue teasing her ear, were all a total assault on her senses that catapulted her into an erotic whirlpool. She shook with the intensity of it and her inner muscles squeezed and spasmed as the tremors raced through her with incredible force.

And just as she was sure she couldn't stand it one more minute, it began to subside. Trey stretched his legs out so she could close hers together and rest them on his. He tipped her head back against him and murmured gentle, soothing, yet erotically teasing things in her ear.

"I don't think I can move," she sighed. "I might have to spend the rest of the day and the night in the tub."

His sexy laugh rumbled up softly from his chest. "It might be a little drier in the bed, though. And I'm pretty sure I can move you without a problem."

"Well, you might be able to move me, but I don't think you'll get much response from me. It's your fault, though. You pretty much did me in with the tub."

"We'll see." He winked at her.

He rose with athletic grace, holding her in his arms, and hit the lever to drain the water. As he stood her on the bath mat and pulled a towel from the hook to dry her off, she marveled again at his strength and athleticism. His touch was so gentle yet at the same time sensuous. When he pulled back the covers and placed her on the bed, arranging her so her legs were splayed and her arms outstretched, she was shocked to find her body beginning to respond, to anticipate. She had never been this consistently and frequently responsive to any other man, ever. When he looked at her with his warm caramel eyes and ran his tongue over his lips, she wanted to pull him down and have him enter her right then.

From the look in his eyes, she had a sense he felt the same. Reaching into the nightstand drawer, he pulled out one of the condoms he'd stashed there and rolled it on with quick efficiency. He settled himself between her legs, lifted them and draped them over his thighs, then slid one finger into her, inhaling a breath when her wet flesh closed easily around it.

"Jesus, Kenzi. You're wet and slick again already."

"It's your fault," she told him in a soft, breathless voice. "It's what you do to me."

And that was just the damn truth. She couldn't remember a single man she'd ever been with who turned her on so much and so fast as Trey McIntyre.

"Here we go," he murmured as he slid his cock into her waiting body.

Here we go indeed, she thought, as he filled her completely. The feel of him inside her woke every one of her senses. She wrapped her legs around him, locking her ankles at the small of his back, pulling him in even deeper.

"That's it," he groaned. "Yes. Like that."

At first his body moved with the rhythm of a slow dance, hips setting up a controlled rhythm. But then, as if restraint had fled, he sped up the pace, increasing the rhythm, faster and faster. With each thrust, he scraped against that sweet spot, taking her right up that Ferris wheel again. She'd worried that she had used up all her orgasms, but she should have known better. Trey McIntyre could wring more orgasms from her than she'd ever thought possible.

Then she couldn't think anymore, because he was taking her on the ride of her life, a ride she didn't want to stop. *Ever.* Except it did, and as they exploded together, he pressed his mouth to hers in a kiss that scorched her to the soles of her feet.

She had no idea how long her body shook with spasms, only that at some point they slowed down, and Trey lifted his mouth from hers and dropped his head next to hers on the pillow. Ragged breathing sliced the air and she wasn't even sure whose it was, or whose heart was thumping so loudly.

Trey lifted his head and gave her one of his delicious smiles.

"I don't know how it's possible, but it just gets better every time."

She let out a long sigh and cupped her hand to his cheek. "It does, doesn't it?"

"Don't move. I'll be right back." With great care, he helped her lower her legs then eased from her body, pinching the edge of the condom.

"I keep telling you I'm on the pill," she said. "And we're both clean. We don't need those."

"Old habits die hard," he told her, "but maybe one of these days we'll get daring and try it bareback."

Daring, she thought. Just being with him was daring. But she smiled at the prospect.

It wasn't until the next day that she remembered to check the computer.

Chapter Seven

It was Monday morning and the team was having breakfast at Slade's ranch. For those coupled up — and Trey, to his shock and surprise, counted himself in that group — it was an opportunity to discuss business while their women were working at whatever they did. With everything from attorneys to reporters to nurses in the group, those concerned counted themselves lucky to steal any time together.

Today wasn't it. Today the women were occupied with their various work, providing the opportunity for the group to meet. Teo had made a typical Mexican breakfast for them — huevos rancheros with ground sausage, breakfast burritos and refried beans. As usual, the men ate as if they hadn't had a meal for a year. Finally, when they had eaten their fill and were kicking back with some of Teo's excellent coffee, Slade took out his laptop.

"I've been surfing through the news websites," he began, "looking for articles by Dana Roberts."

"That's our rescue from the Lopez Garcia cartel, right?" Beau asked.

Slade nodded. "It is indeed."

"She happens to be Kenzi's half-sister and I wish to hell Kenzi could get her off that kick," Trey grumbled. "Getting kidnapped was bad enough. She's damn lucky we found her alive. I'd think she'd be taking a step back instead of walking right into the fire again."

"That would make sense," Beau agreed, "except that woman we rescued wasn't scared shitless by the cartel guys and doesn't look like much would make her step back."

"That's the damn truth," Trey agreed. "By the way, I don't know if it's connected or not, but Kenzi has a bad feeling about one of the firm's clients, a man she's handling with one of the partners. She ran a picture of him through the computer looking for articles but all she got was the usual bullshit about a solid fourth-generation citizen. I told her not to give up. I trust the sixth sense more than anything else. It's saved our asses more than once."

"Has she spoken to her sister about him?" Slade asked.

"I think she's calling her today, probably after work. In any event, I'm keeping a tight eye on her, just in case."

"Let me know if you need help." Marc Blanchard swallowed some coffee. "Nikki and I are still trying to recover from our little adventure. It didn't help that three days after it all settled down, we had to report back again. But I'm here if you need me."

"Little adventure?" Brock raised an eyebrow.

"Some people can't stay out of trouble," Beau Williams joked. "Blanchard took his girl to the lake for a week of fun in the sun and ended up in a nest of terrorists."

"You're kidding! Oh, wait." Brock snapped his fingers. "That's about the plot to bomb the rodeo, right?"

The story of the terrorist group that had tried to blow up the San Antonio Stock Show and Rodeo, and the part the team had played in it—especially Marc and his lady, Nikki—had occupied an entire evening's conversation before the team had gone back to base. Brock and Axel had not joined the team at that point, but Trey knew they'd heard the details. They certainly weren't a secret.

"Okay." Slade cleared his throat. "Back to the situation at hand. It wouldn't hurt to go through the after-action report on our hostage rescue in Mexico again. Nobody can say we don't take out the trash. We knew there were twenty people in the house, not counting the hostage. We took down sixteen of them and the fire team in the helo wounded the other four when they broke from the jungle and shot at us."

"I imagine Hector Lopez Garcia is not too happy with us," Trey commented.

"You got that fucking damn right. And that gives rise to some new situations, which I found when I was surfing Dana Roberts' articles. Damn! That woman sure is pulling the tiger's tail." He tapped a button on the laptop. "Although Lopez Garcia operates somewhat under the radar—which makes the kidnapping an anomaly for him—there is a strong possibility that he will want revenge for what happened. Actually, the DEA is surprised they didn't just kill her and bury her body someplace where she'd never be found. That's more the Lopez García style, or so gossip says."

"Wouldn't the kidnapping defeat the purpose of so-called low profile?" Marc asked. "I mean, is revenge really that important?"

"Yes, depending on the situation."

"They want Dana Roberts," Marc guessed. "Now. They want to rectify their mistake. Damn! She must have uncovered something very hot."

Slade nodded. "Which means whatever they think she learned is critical, and could be damaging to them."

"More damaging than their usual order of business?"

He nudged the laptop to Beau, who was sitting next to him. "This is just one of her stories she's filed on Lopez Garcia. Gather round and read it. You'll see she doesn't pull her punches and she goes to any lengths to verify her information. And apparently now she's back in New York, she's hard at it again."

"I admire her grit and determination," Marc said in his taciturn voice, "but is it really worth risking her life?"

"Apparently."

Trey cleared his throat. "Let me talk to Kenzi tonight after she speaks to her sister and get her take on it. She knows her sister better than any of us."

"Do it," Slade told him.

"Then what?" Beau asked.

"Then we figure out how to get her some bodyguards. She can't run around unprotected."

Beau frowned. "Shouldn't her bosses be doing that?"

Trey shrugged. "In a normal situation, yeah. But nothing about this seems normal. Anyway, if they want to handle it, okay, but we need to make sure they get the right people."

"Agreed." Slade picked up his cell phone. "While you all finish looking at Dana's article, I'm going to call

Mike Elliott and give him a head's-up. He's who I'd want watching my back if I didn't have you guys." He looked across the table at Trey. "What time are you picking Kenzi up tonight?"

"She'll text me, but she said it would be close to seven. Long day working on the stuff for this particular client. I could call her and ask about Dana, but I'm pretty sure she would have mentioned something. I hate to call her at the office with this big project going. Besides, she'd wonder why I'm calling in the middle of the day to ask her this. I'd rather wait until I can ask her in person."

"It can wait until tonight. But we need to impress her with the importance of the situation without scaring the crap out of her."

Trey snorted. "Believe me, she knows the situation. She was frightened as hell for her sister. It won't be a problem."

Beau frowned. "I'd feel a lot better if we could handle this ourselves, but I understand why that's not possible. That said, Mike's guys are the best available for this."

By the time everyone had digested Dana Roberts' article, Slade had set things up with Mike Elliott and had him ready for when Slade gave him the signal.

"I tell you, this whole thing makes me uneasy." Trey rubbed his jaw. "As much about Kenzi as for Dana. I don't want her to get dragged into this."

Slade nodded. "I hear you."

"I'm surprised her bosses don't have her on a short leash," Brock mused, "considering she's still a high-profile target for the cartel."

Trey snorted. "If she's like her sister, trying to tell her what to do is a waste of breath. And I mean that in a respectful way."

"Okay." Beau nodded. "So now we're on top of it. Slade, you called Mike and read him in. Trey, you'll talk it over with your lady tonight. Then we go from there, right?"

Everyone nodded.

"Fine." Slade closed his laptop. "I think I'll call Kari and see if she can hook me up with someone who's got information on the cartel."

Slade's wife was an assistant prosecuting attorney in Bexar County, where San Antonio was located. Trey knew she was plugged in to a lot of sources. The question was whether she could tap into any of them without compromising her position. He watched Slade punch another number in his cell and figured they'd find out sooner rather than later.

* * * *

Kenzi rose to refill her coffee mug again from the single-serving machine on the sideboard. The remnants of the pastries Reed had ordered to be sent in that morning lay on a tray, nothing left but a few crumbs. Kenzi knew she always worked better when she had something sweet for energy, but she hadn't realized that Reed has the same craving.

He laughed when he saw her glance at the tray.

"My partners say my habits haven't changed since we were greenhorn attorneys living on cheap pastries and not much else. It gave us plenty of energy in those early days, but then we always had that damn sugar crash at midnight."

"I know what you mean," she told Reed. "I also started out at the bottom of the ladder."

He cocked an eyebrow at her. "But you came here as a first-year right after law school, didn't you?"

She nodded. "But I was pinching pennies. Trying to handle student loans. Buy a car. All that stuff." Then she grinned. "But then you made me your associate and things looked up right away."

"I'm glad. You've made yourself a valuable part of this firm, and your work on the Reyes corporation structure is outstanding." He winked. "We have big plans for you once this comes together."

She couldn't help the little skip in her pulse or the frisson of excitement that raced through her at his words. She'd known for months that she was right at the line to move into junior partner, but it hadn't been until they'd begun work on this new project for Alex Reyes that Reed had mentioned anything. Now he'd brought it up twice. Her invisible antennae were vibrating. She couldn't wait to tell Trey.

Wait. Was she allowing herself to get too excited about him? To project into the future when neither of them had discussed such a thing? In fact, it had been quietly understood from the beginning that when this was over, it was over. But thinking down that road gave her a suddenly tight feeling.

"You okay?" Reed asked. "You just got a strange look on your face. Everything okay?"

She gave herself a mental shake and carried her coffee back to the table.

"I'm fine. Truly. Let's get back to this." She sat back down in her chair, set her mug on the table and woke up her laptop. "Okay, we've got the basic structure down, but I think I have some questions." She looked at Reed. "Just so I understand where I'm going with this when I get back to my office and start the integration."

"Fire away. I'll answer what I can."

Why is his phrasing giving me a sudden twitch? Supposedly there was nothing she couldn't delve into. *Oh, well, maybe it's my imagination.* This was, after all, a complicated situation.

"Okay. The income from Alex's ranch—mostly the minerals—goes into a separate account for him and part of it goes to his brother's account in Mexico City, right?"

Reed nodded. "That's because when Alex's grandfather decided to move up here from Mexico after he married a girl from San Antonio, income from the huge ranch operation in Chihuahua was used to buy his land and set him up with stock. He had a generational grace period before he had to start repaying the money. But then they got into some joint operations so complex they took me, a law clerk and two associates to straighten out. That was before you joined the firm."

"Yes." She nodded. "I see he's been a client for nearly twenty years."

"That's a fact. He was one of the first golden hens who came to us." Reed took a swallow of his coffee. "The firm was finally taking off and the three of us had been invited to a formal event by a high ticket, highly satisfied client. He introduced us to Alex, who asked us to handle a small project for him. Testing us, I think. In any event, he liked what we did and recommended others."

"So, let me see if I understand this." She frowned at her screen, looking at the list she'd made, trying to get it all straight in her mind. "The two ranches, including the mineral output on both of them, are shared as one big corporation?"

"That was the optimum solution. The two branches of the family operate as one unit and it seems to work very well for them."

"Okay, but now they want to expand to other countries, right? They're opening bank accounts in Canada, Portugal, France, even Russia and Australia."

"All perfectly reasonable," Reed assured her. "Some of the biggest cattle ranches in the world are located there and the Reyes family is hoping to buy into one of them to expand their footprint. As well, they're looking at other foreign businesses to invest in, and they obviously need bank accounts in those countries."

"Why don't they just operate out of a Swiss bank, like a lot of corporations do?"

Reed chuckled. "I suggested that to Alex and he said he liked doing his banking where he could control the rate of exchange. In other words, keep his money in one bank until the rate was favorable enough to shift it to another. That way he makes money on his money."

"And it all flows through this very complicated new corporate structure we're setting up for him, right?"

"Actually, we're setting it up for the Reyes family, and their current corporate structure will be absorbed into it."

"Good lord." She stared at the screen again. "That will end up being an obscene amount of money."

Reed nodded. "And it's up to us to create a structure so that it's all appropriately protected. Us putting a system in place so that when they move the money around, they will always be able to take advantage of the best rate of exchange. Plus, we need to be sensitive to the tax situation. It doesn't do much good to make a lot of money if you're paying it out in taxes, especially in more than one country."

"Well, it seems to me we're heading in the right direction."

Still, she couldn't take her eyes from the screen. Something was twitching in her brain, something she couldn't put her finger on. And she wasn't about to bring it up to Reed Calhoun. She was probably seeing shadows where there weren't any.

"Don't sweat it," Reed told her. "You've got half a dozen key points you need to focus on right now while I prune and massage the rest of this. That's enough of a headache for you. Alex wants to meet with us next week to review where we are. I told him you were working on it full time and we'd be ready for him. I know he wants to move forward with his projects, but not until he has a proper structure for them. I gather he has some projects on hold until everything's in place, so we need to work toward that deadline. Are you good to go?"

"I am." Kenzi nodded. "I'll get back to work on this right away." She shut down her laptop and began gathering her file folders.

"Good. I'll be gone for the next three days, but I'm confident you've got enough of a handle on things that you'll be good on your own. We'll reconvene when I get back and make sure all our ducks are in a row before the meeting. And of course, you can text me if you have pressing questions, and I'll get back to you the minute I can. Work for you?"

"It does. And thank you for giving me this opportunity."

"Oh, it's my pleasure." He grinned. "You've got a sharp brain and understand things like complicated corporate structures and client confidentiality. And the clients like you. Yes, I'd say when we get Alex taken care of, there's a big change in your future."

"Thank you." *Damn!* She actually felt herself blush. "See you when you get back."

But when she was back in her office, setting things up to work, she wondered why Reed had bothered to mention client confidentiality. That was one of the first things everyone had drilled into them when they came to work at the firm. Had she given him the idea she didn't respect it?

Or — and a chilling thought popped into her mind — was he giving her a subtle warning that there were things in the Reyes project that she might be tempted to share with someone? What would that be? And who would she talk to?

She'd go through everything with a fine-tooth comb this afternoon. Then, tonight, she'd bounce it off Trey. Surely no one was more tight-lipped than members of Delta Force.

Chapter Eight

Kenzi was tired, stressed and feeling as if she'd worked ten weeks instead of ten hours. She wanted a hot shower, a soothing drink, a simple dinner and hot sex — and not necessarily in that order. Her day had been long and intense as she'd wrestled with the ins and outs of the new, multi-faceted corporate structure she was helping Reed Calhoun create for Alex Reyes. This wasn't the first one she'd worked on, but it was definitely the most complex.

There were still things about it that bothered her, but she just couldn't put her finger on them. She downloaded some material on rates of exchange in the currencies they'd be working with and also on cooperative cattle ventures. She knew nothing about the latter, but if they were going to be an integrated part of this conglomerate, she needed to know what she was talking about. In the email Reed had sent her at the end of the day there was also mention of a shipping company. Did that mean that now one was to be created for this purpose, again as a block in the structure of the corporation?

It also occurred to her that she hadn't spoken to her sister in a few days. Ever since the disaster in Mexico, she hadn't been able to stop worrying about her. Dana was smart, but she also tended to be reckless when she was on the trail of a story. Hence the kidnapping. If Kenzi had her way, she'd lock the woman up until she agreed to move on to something else, but she knew that was a pipe dream. Dana was her own person, and a damn good reporter besides.

Trey had spent most of the day at Slade's ranch with the team doing whatever. She knew they'd burned some time using the target range he'd set up on the ranch, although lord knew, she figured by this time they were all expert marksmen. But it was good for them to hang out with nothing to put pressure on them.

She had texted Trey to pick her up at seven, much later than she'd hoped to be finished, and when he called to tell her he was ready any time she was, the deep sound of his voice flowed over her like warm molasses. She wanted to pull it around her like a quilt fresh from the dryer and rub it all over her skin.

"Let's just order something in tonight," she said as she buckled her seat belt. "I don't think I could stand to sit in a restaurant. Besides, I have something I want you to run your very sharp brain over."

"Oh?" Trey reached over and cupped her chin, tilting her face toward him. "I think it can wait. You look stressed and exhausted. I prescribe a hot shower, a slow massage and a stiff drink."

She laughed. "I had something like that already in mind."

"Then let's get to it." As he pulled away from the curb he asked in a casual voice, "Heard anything from your sister lately?"

"Just a couple of very brief calls. Why? What's up?"

"You know we all had breakfast at Slade's this morning, right?"

She wrinkled her forehead. "What does that have to do with my sister?"

"We went over the details of the kidnapping, reviewing the after-action report. And before you say anything, it's something we always do. Anyway, Slade pulled up some of her articles on the cartel and we reviewed them, just to get the full picture of why she was a target for them. Kenzi, I'm not sure if you know this, but she's really sticking her toe in the fire. She ought to back off and let the government do its thing. The Lopez Garcia cartel may not be the top dog in Mexico, but it's just as vicious as the others. They just fly under the radar a little more."

"First of all," she huffed, "Dana says the government can't seem to get its thing done. Everyone writes about the bigger ones, like Sinaloa. She told me she's got a sixth sense about Lopez Garcia, that there's something there no one is seeing and she wants to find out what it is. Secondly, my sister never waits for anyone or anything. A news story is like, if you'll pardon the expression, crack cocaine to her."

"She won't write about anything if she's dead," he pointed out.

"I know, I know. I haven't heard from her for a couple of days. Maybe I'll call her and see what she's doing right now. Try to talk her out of the most dangerous things." Then she laughed. "Except I know that would be a fool's errand."

At that moment her cell phone rang with an unfamiliar ringtone. She pulled it from her purse, but when she looked at the screen, she didn't recognize the number, so she let it go to voicemail. Almost immediately she got a notification of a text. Reluctantly she looked at it, then blinked.

It's me, Dana. Answer the phone when I call back.

"Well, that's weird."

"What is?" Trey asked.

"A text from Dana to answer when she calls again. Why is she calling from a strange number?"

"Maybe she had to change her phone because of the whole cartel story," he suggested.

"Damn. I know you're right in what you said. I wish she'd get off that kick. What if next time they don't screw around and just decide to kill her?"

"That's a very real possibility." Trey's voice had a harsh edge. "Someone should talk some sense into her. They didn't do much damage to her this last time, but it wasn't a good situation."

Before Kenzi could respond, her phone rang.

"Is there some reason you're using a different phone number?" she asked at once.

"Hello, Dana. I'm so excited to hear from you. Thank you for calling."

Kenzi huffed a sigh, "Okay. Hello, Dana. I'm so excited to hear from you. Thank you for calling. Now tell me why you have a different number."

There was a pause, and Kenzi could visualize her sister trying to come up with the right explanation.

"My editor thought it would be best," she said in a slow voice. "You know, in case anyone had my phone number from before."

"You mean anyone in Mexico. Right?"

Pause. "Or perhaps here in the States."

"In the States?" Kenzi fisted her hand in her lap. "Dana, what the hell is going on? What are you getting yourself into here?"

"He's still having fits over the kidnapping, but he hasn't pulled me off the story. This is still the same project, the Lopez Garcia cartel, but I've got some new angles. A new lead. And my editor wanted me as invisible as possible while I chase them down." She gave a nervous little laugh. "He's even hired a couple of bodyguards for me."

"Bodyguards?" Kenzi exploded. "Dana Roberts, what the hell are you up to now? Are you out of your everlovin' mind?"

"I assure you, my mind is working just fine. I didn't tell you about the bodyguards before because I was afraid you'd come to New York and lock me away. My boss hired them as soon as the military delivered me back to New York. They've been shadowing me day and night since then."

"You still should have told me," Kenzi protested. "And by the way, you should get out of any line of work where you have to have two men with guns taking care of you."

Trey nudged her shoulder. When she glanced at him he mouthed, *"Ask her the name of the agency."*

"I'm going to see this story through to the end." Dana's voice was laced with steel. "This is the biggest thing I've ever written, and no one is going to scare me out of it."

"Do you know the name of the agency your boss used to hire these bodyguards?"

"Agency? I have a card here. Wait a sec." Pause. "Here it is. "Gillette. They're based in New York. Why?"

"Just making sure they got someone top notch."

"Oh, no worries there. But, Kenzi, listen." Now there was a touch of excitement in her voice. "I'm following up on a new lead that might break this story wide open. And guess where it's taking me?"

"I hope to god not to Mexico again."

"You won't believe this. To San Antonio!"

Kenzi sat up straight. "Here? You're coming here?"

"Yes. And I'm flying in on a private plane the security company owns. You know. Just in case. They think going commercial leaves me too exposed."

Kenzi didn't want to ask just in case what. "So what prompted this trip?"

"I am only telling you this because I know everything stays with you." Pause. "A contact managed to make a connection for me with a cartel member in San Antonio who wants out. Is ready to dish for me in exchange for protection. Maybe a new life."

Kenzi snorted. "Which he'll need if the cartel finds out he's spilling secrets. So I'm guessing this would be one of the distributors?"

"You know I can't say," Dana admonished.

"Okay, then tell me this. Where are you staying?" She was torn between wanting her sister safe and not have anything interrupting the few days she had left with Trey.

"Don't worry, sister dear. I won't be busting in on you and your hunk. I'm staying in a condo owned by a friend of the man who owns the security agency. And the bodyguards will be with me at all times."

"Honey, I am really worried sick about you and the chances you're taking."

"We're all being smart about this, I promise you. And I will make time to see you, but in a secure location. For sure while Trey is still here so he can see for himself you aren't in any danger."

"I'm sure he'll appreciate that." She tried to keep the sarcasm out of her voice. "When do you get here?"

"Tomorrow morning. Wheels up at eight o'clock, which gets us there about nine-thirty your time. We're landing at a small private airport. Tonight, I'm locked up tight with my bodyguards."

"Do they stay in your apartment with you?"

Dana laughed. "You mean in my overpriced one-bedroom apartment? I don't think so. But they check every inch of it every night before they spend the night watching the building, and I have a special phone to signal them with if there's trouble. Then, in the morning, the new shift comes on."

"So, they stay up all night to watch for trouble? They won't even be awake to guard you when you leave."

"A different shift handles the daytime hours. They'll show up at seven in the morning and we'll leave for the private airport. It's all good. I promise to call you as soon as we land so we can set something up. Okay?"

"How about a text when you get ready to leave. Please? Just to ease my mind?"

Dana chuckled. "Yes, Mom. I'll send you a text. Love you, big sister."

The line went dead. Kenzi just sat there for a moment, trying to control both her temper and her fear.

"Problem?" Trey asked. "That was your sister, right?"

"Yes." She sighed. "I never know whether to hug her or smack some sense into her."

"Still on that story, right?"

There was something in his tone of voice that made her slide a glance at him.

"She is." She repeated what Dana had told her. "I'm worried, Trey. She's wading in dangerous waters again."

"You have no idea."

She frowned. "Is there something I should know that you're not telling me?"

"Yes. I was planning to go over it with you anyway. Let's wait until we're inside your place. You can take your shower, I'll fix a drink for you and let you know why Dana won't be all alone out there in case she gets into more crazy shit."

He wants me to wait? Is he crazy?

"Why can't you tell me now?"

"Because we're already home and we shouldn't discuss this in the parking lot."

Kenzi looked out of the windshield and realized that she'd been so preoccupied with her sister's situation, she hadn't even been aware they'd arrived at their destination. She tamped down her irritation and unfastened her seat belt.

"Fine. Fine, fine, fine."

Trey locked the car and came around to where she stood, cupping her chin to tilt up her face.

"And I meant it about the shower. Get comfortable because I know you'll have a lot of questions. Okay?"

She huffed anther sigh. "Okay, but I have something to talk to you about, too. I guess this will be the quickest shower in history."

So much for long and leisurely. Whatever Trey had to tell her, she wanted to hear it now. And she would also use him as a sounding board for her own tangled and probably absurd thoughts.

In less than fifteen minutes she was washed, rinsed and dried, her hair pulled back in a ponytail and her clad in her favorite at-home outfit — yoga pants and an old Houston Texans T-shirt. Trey was waiting for her in the living room, his cell phone pressed to his ear.

"Uh-huh. Uh-huh. Okay, good. Let me know what you find out." He disconnected and shoved the phone into his pocket.

"What's going on?"

"I gave Slade the name of the agency that's providing the bodyguards and asked him to check them out. He's got a friend who has an agency here in San Antonio that we'd trust with our lives. I don't leave anything to chance."

He picked up the drinks from the coffee table where he'd set them. She noticed he'd poured the same for her as he had for himself, Jack Daniel's, her go-to when she wasn't drinking wine.

"I figured you might need something a little heftier than your usual favorite shiraz," he told her, handing her one of the glasses. "Take a sip."

The aged bourbon had a delightful burn to it as it slid down her throat and she felt her jangled nerves begin to ease at once. Holding the drink, she sat cross-legged on the couch, looked at Trey and said, "Okay, give."

In a voice she was sure was supposed to project the feeling that everything was handled, he told her about the discussion that morning, as he and the team reviewed the information they had on Dana and what they themselves had. Kenzi stared at him, not sure which amazed her more—that her sister would put herself in the line of danger again or that Trey's team would choose to get involved in assuring her safety.

"But that's unbelievable," she finally managed.

He grinned. "Which part?"

"Mostly about your team getting involved."

Trey sat next to her on the couch, leaned over and pressed a light kiss to her lips.

"It's what we do, Kenzi. We take care of what's ours."

Her breath hitched a little. "What's yours? Trey, we hardly know each other—how can Dana or I be yours?"

He took her hand and rubbed his finger over her knuckles.

"I'm not sure I can explain it myself, if you want to know the truth. The word on this came down to us because we were the team that did the rescue mission. It's coincidence that Dana happens to be pursuing her story in the city we're in for the moment. The rest of it?" His smile was gentle and something indefinable flashed in his eyes. "Like I said, we take care of our own."

Kenzi drew in a breath and let it out slowly. She was both frightened and warmed by the sense of possession. Right from the beginning, although they hadn't had an actual discussion about it, there had been a tacit understanding this was all for fun and hot sex. Kenzi was immersed in her career and Trey was dedicated to Delta Force. But somehow, after the rescue in Mexico, the atmosphere between them had changed, and she wasn't sure if that was good or bad.

"Kenzi?"

She gave herself a mental shake. "Yes?"

"Before we get into what's on your mind, do you think you can call your sister back and find out what airport they'll be landing at?"

"Sure, but why?"

"I think we should be there when they arrive. Something about this whole thing makes my neck itch. I'll feel a lot better if I can get a look at these bodyguards myself."

"Okay." She blew out a breath and picked up her cell. "I'll try, but she might dig in her heels."

"Be inventive," he urged. "Use that brilliant lawyer's mind of yours."

"Yeah, well, I'm not so sure it's all that brilliant right now, but let me make this call first."

The phone rang twice before Dana answered.

"I'm not so sure the bodyguards will be all that happy with you guys coming to meet us," she said when Kenzi explained what was happening.

"Tell them it's your sister and a member of Delta Force. How much safer could that be?"

There was silence for a long moment. "All right. But be sure no one follows you."

"Jesus, Dana. Trey is the icon of stealth, okay? Now, give." She repeated the information to Trey. "Text me when you leave New York so we can judge your arrival. See you then, baby sister." She paused a moment. "Stay safe." Then she disconnected.

"Do you know where this is?" Trey asked.

Kenzi nodded. "We have a couple of clients who fly into there on their own planes. I've picked them up there before."

Trey chuckled. "I keep forgetting what high society your clients are in."

"Not just high society. It's their financial situation. Some of them could buy and sell San Antonio. I often wonder where they got all that wealth to begin with. Some of it goes back generations." She held out her glass. "Which brings me to my own subject. Another drink, please, so I can tell you what's dinging my brains and you can explain to me how I'm seeing shadows where there are none."

When Trey handed her the glass with fresh liquid in it, she too a healthy swallow and let the familiar taste and feel soothe her. *Sort of.*

"You know I'm working with one of the senior partners on this big project for a long-time client of the firm, right?"

Trey nodded. "Yeah, the one you're putting in all the extra hours on."

"That's it. He's the man I pointed out to you at the restaurant the other day."

"The one you took the picture of? Did you get anything when you ran a computer search?"

"Just the usual business and society stuff. I had hoped to catch shots of him with some possibly shady characters, but either he doesn't associate with them or he's very good at keeping his skirts clean. But I haven't given up."

"Tell me about him. I will say he looked respectable when I got a look at him the other day, but we both know appearances can be deceiving."

"And I may just be letting my imagination run away with me, because there hasn't been anything overt to trigger this." She paused, figuring out how to phrase this. She didn't want Trey to think she was seeing bogeymen where there weren't any, or that her sister's situation was coloring her thinking. "He owns a huge ranch in the Hill Country just outside the city. Besides the capital, he's leased out the mineral rights to almost a quarter of the property."

"Sounds like a smart thing to do. Even a grunt like me knows there's a ton of money in that."

"He has some other small businesses, too, that he runs with his brother, who still manages the family ranch in Mexico. In Chihuahua."

Trey lifted an eyebrow. "I admit I don't know all that much about it, just from what I've gathered listening to Slade about the area, but that doesn't seem to me to be uncommon enough to raise flags."

"I know, I know." She took a sip of her drink. "And he is one of the pillars of Texas society and the business community. Still, he's expanding into all these overseas investments, opening new businesses, buying into others." She shrugged. "Maybe I just watch too much television."

"So, you're what, thinking this is all a coverup for some deep, dark criminal operation?"

Kenzi gave a breathy little giggle. "Sounds stupid, right? I told myself the same thing. My imagination is probably working overtime because of Dana and her story. Criminals don't use our law firm. They can't take the chance they'd reveal something by accident."

"Was there anything particular that kicked your brain in this direction?" Trey asked.

She shrugged. "Probably just the fact that with Dana's kidnapping and her boss hiring bodyguards, and all the current publicity on the growth and strength of cartels, it's all at the forefront of my mind. And my concern factor ratcheted up several notches after I spoke with Dana."

"I can understand that."

"And now with Dana coming to San Antonio and having some secret meeting…" Kenzi treated herself to a healthy swallow of her drink. "Crazy, right?"

Trey set his glass on the coffee table. "In my line of work, I've learned never to write anything off as crazy."

"So, you think it might not be so farfetched? That I'm not making up some nutty scenario and should just forget it?"

"Sure as hell if you do, it will come back to bite you in the ass." He grinned. "By the way, biting your ass is something I very much look forward to."

He reached out for her and tugged her so she was sitting in his lap. In spite of the fact that her mind was in a turmoil, the contact sent shivers of heat racing over her skin.

"Is that what you have in mind?" she teased, trying to erase the worry that had just popped up out of nowhere.

"I think it might help you think of something else besides what's got your brain in a turmoil." He pulled her against his hard body and took a gentle nip at her earlobe.

"At least you don't think I've lost all my marbles." She leaned into him, feeling the hard thickness of his cock beneath her ass. "I think I might just do a little more research on *Señor* Alex Reyes." She wiggled her butt. "Just not right now."

"Good." He put his mouth close to her ear and slid a hand up to cradle one breast, lightly pinching a nipple. "Because I plan to work up a real appetite for dinner."

"Me, too," she whispered, the pulse in her sex coming to life as he eased her top over her head.

Chapter Nine

Hector Lopez Garcia sat back in his armchair, feet up on the ottoman, and pulled on his cigar. A snifter of brandy sat on the little table next to him. Through the big picture window, he watched the sun setting, casting its warm glow over the manicured lawn and the carefully trimmed shrubs. He loved this time of day, when he could relax and enjoy his brandy and cigar, with a pastoral setting stretching away from the house.

His daughter Maria sat on the patio, sitting in a glider with her boyfriend Emilio, the son of a lieutenant in his cartel. It did not do for children to marry outside their environment. While he tried to keep the more graphic side of the business away from the women and children, there were just too many chances for things to blow up if they moved outside the cartel structure. Whenever it had happened, disaster had followed.

But Emilio was a nice young man who was being groomed to move up in the organization, probably one day to be a lieutenant himself. His parents had taught him to respect women and to wield authority in a proper manner, so Hector had every confidence that Maria was in good hands, with a man who obviously loved her. She and her mother were already deep in discussions for the wedding six months from now. It gave him a warm feeling knowing she would be settled and well cared for.

Plans for everything seemed to be moving ahead on target. Smooth, with no bumps in the road. The way he liked. Even the unpleasantness with Felix and his sister's reaction to it had faded. She was a smart woman, his *hermana*, and she had sadly accepted the truth of the situation. But an unsettled feeling still plagued him.

It was all because of that damn fucking reporter. If Felix had just killed her the way he'd been ordered to and hidden the body, none of this would be happening. Her bosses would be very reluctant to send another reporter down here to stick their noses into his operation. Other news sources would back off, at least for the moment, giving him and his cousins time to put every particle of their plan in place. And no one would connect all of them in any way. Then, no matter what they looked for, it would all be so well hidden beneath the surface that they'd never find anything.

He blessed the fact that he had relatives who could move in a world that gave them access to all levels of society and of business. He, *El Lobo*, bore the brunt of the bad publicity, but that was expected. The others, they were the ones who took his plan and now were creating a mammoth structure that would bring them billions, all perfectly legal.

At least at a superficial glance.

He allowed himself a momentary smile at the realization that success was so close at hand.

Except for the fucking reporter.

And now he had received word that there was a rat in the wolf pack, a nasty animal who had the balls to think he could turn on them and get away with it. Thank god someone had discovered this and given him the word. The problem was, his snitch wasn't sure which of three people it actually was. But, as always, he was able to put a plan in place to discover it. Then he would kill the betrayer and the reporter at the same time, and he would bury her so her bones would not be found for at least a century.

As he drew on the cigar, the cell phone next to his brandy snifter rang. The ringtone let him know it was Diego, the only person he currently trusted to handle everything for him. If not for Diego, he would have been totally unprepared for the disastrous situation at the *finca* and its fallout. Those in the public eye with no visible connection to the cartel handled the legitimate businesses, the paperwork, the structure. Hector, for his part, was responsible for the nitty gritty, on-the-ground activities, particularly if someone tried to block them in any manner. Diego was in charge of overseeing the mechanics and overcoming objections in whatever way was necessary.

Hector picked up the cell and tapped the Answer icon. He hoped this wasn't bad news. He'd had enough of that for a while.

"*Hola, mi amigo.* Please tell me that today you have good news for me. That all is well and moving along. Have you got eyes on the reporter yet? She's such a public person, it should be easy."

"We know she is in New York at the moment, and unfortunately digging deeper into our organization."

Hector frowned. "Surely a woman who is supposed to be as smart as this one has learned we have put a price on her head? And yet she still moves forward. Is she crazy?"

"You know how these people are, *jefe*. We've run into it before. And not just us."

"Are you telling me we have not been able to get close to her and take her out, once and for all?"

Diego's sigh traveled across the connection. "You'd think with as busy as the city is and as much crime as they have, taking someone out in New York would be easy enough, especially in a way that the body just disappeared. However, it is impossible to get close to her, even when she is entering or leaving buildings. The employer has hired full time bodyguards."

"Damn." Hector thought for a moment. "What about when she's home? Is she alone?"

"Not without those two people keeping an eye on her and her place. It is impossible to get close to her without causing a problem." There was a pause. "And I have more bad news. I mean very bad, so please brace yourself."

"What could possibly be worse than this woman who is determined to destroy an organization it took generations to build?"

Diego's sigh reverberated through the connection. "Our contact who is feeding us the information on this reporter tells us the traitor is going to be meeting with the reporter."

Hector clamped down on the cigar so hard he almost bit through it. He yanked it from his mouth with a vicious tug and jammed it into a crystal ashtray.

"*Que chingados?*" *What the fuck?*

"Indeed."

"Just who is this traitor and how is this happening to something we have constructed so carefully over many decades?" Hector demanded. "Everyone knows that being a traitor means death, so who is willing to take that chance?"

For just that moment, he felt like the wolf he was compared to, in full alpha mode, ready to rip someone's head off with his teeth. He could not believe that anyone valuable enough for a reporter to meet with them was about to betray him. *What could convince them to do this when they know the penalty for such an action?*

"Well, that's the problem, *jefe*." He cleared his throat. "We don't know exactly who it is, but as I said, we do have an idea. If my plan works, we should be able to identify this person and take care of two problems at once."

"I'm listening." Hector treated himself to a long swallow of the brandy. A little sip would do him no good at all under the circumstances.

"I have learned that tomorrow she is flying into San Antonio and tomorrow night she will meet with this traitor. Supposedly that is when he or she is going to spill all they know about the cartel."

Hector uttered every curse word he knew under his breath. "And does this piece of shit know about all the aspects of the organization?"

Hector was sure Diego knew exactly what he meant—the very public face that was never connected with the cartel operation itself.

Another pause. "I am sorry to say, but I believe he or she does."

Hector ground his teeth, then took a deep breath and let it out slowly. If he wasn't careful, he'd give himself a heart attack here. But there was so much at stake, more than ever before.

"And you don't know who this is."

"No, *jefe*. While, as I said, I have been able to narrow it down to three, I don't have a positive identification yet, ashamed as I am to tell you."

"You aren't the one to be ashamed," Hector growled. "You are the most reliable person in the entire cartel. Have we not been together since we were children?"

"*Si*," Diego agreed.

"Have we not, together, taken our organization and grown it while the others were all fighting the Sinaloa cartel and lost as many people as they killed?"

"*Ay!* It is so." Diego's sigh was audible over the connection. "Bloodshed has always been their only answer."

"While we used it when it would do us the most good," Hector reminded him. "I assume you have a plan in place for this? You always do."

"You are correct. I will be at that meeting with Julio and Erik, and we will take care of both of these pieces of garbage at the same time."

"Tell me again when that will be."

"As I said, the reporter arrives in San Antonio in the morning and is supposed to meet with the snitch that night." He chuckled, but it wasn't a humorous sound. "Money can buy you any information, you know."

"How do you know where they plan to meet?" Hector wanted to strangle the people who had created this situation.

"I don't at the moment, but I have made arrangements to find out. Trust me on this. I just don't want to say anything until it happens and maybe jinx myself. But if everything works, all I need is to be there when they are together. I'm on it."

"Fine." He paused. "But I want you to change the plans a little. Before you kill them, bring them here. I want to see them for myself before we take their lives. And this time I will make sure things are done right."

"Of course, *jefe*. I will call you tomorrow and bring you up to date."

For a long time after the call disconnected, Hector sat in his chair, thoughts racing through his mind. Who in the fucking hell could be crazy enough to talk to a reporter about the Lopez Garcia cartel? Was this someone, god forbid, who knew about the other side of the business as well, and could connect the two? The one they'd spent generations creating without a hint of scandal or criminal activity? Didn't he know what the retribution would be? Hector hoped that whoever it was had the foresight to stash their family away someplace under different names where no one could find them.

He could not afford for this whole thing to go up in flames, not when they were on the verge of a massive expansion that would bring in billions instead of millions.

Fuck, fuck, fuck.

* * * *

Trey looked at the woman lying naked beneath him on the bed and wondered exactly when this had morphed from fun and hot sex to...well, something else, although he wasn't sure exactly what. His original plan had been to take her home from her stressful day at work, order dinner and fuck her brains out. And his along with it.

But the phone call from Dana had altered the atmosphere. He could easily see how tense she was about it. While her cheeks had been flushed with need, worry and uncertainty had swirled in her eyes. Between worrying about Dana and her unease about the client she was working with, he could tell Kenzi's stress level was off the charts. And for the first time in — well, maybe ever — he wanted to make it his mission to wipe away that stress and take her to a place where nothing but pleasure existed. Taking a deep breath, he reached for every bit of self-control to keep his hormones and his lust in check.

Bracing himself on his elbows, he brushed the hair back from her cheeks and studied her face. *God.* He could look at her forever and never get tired of it. With a touch soft as a breeze, he brushed his mouth over hers, then stroked his tongue over the satiny feel of her lips. With a little nudge, they opened for him and he slid his tongue inside, swirling it in the hot well, tasting her. She met him willingly, running her tongue over his and sucking it deeper into her mouth. His cock swelled even more and he sent it an urgent message to stand down for the moment. He didn't want to rush this.

Lifting his mouth from hers, he trailed his lips along the line of her jaw, pausing to nibble at her earlobe before moving along the slender column of her neck. She moaned and shifted beneath him, rubbing her body against his. The soft roundness of her breasts imprinted itself on him, tempting him, so he shifted a little to lower his head and capture one hard nipple with his lips. When he drew it into his mouth, he grazed his teeth over the pebbled surface. Her little gasp made him even hornier. He was going to need every bit of self-control to keep himself in check while he drove her crazy.

He teased the nipple with his teeth and tongue, licking and nibbling until it was fully engorged. Then he shifted to the other one and gave it the same treatment. Kenzi moaned, a soft sound, winding her fingers in his hair to hold his head in place.

When her nipples were puffy and swollen, her body shaking with arousal, he eased slowly down her body, stringing kisses along the valley of her breasts until he reached her navel. He paused long enough to pay full attention to the little indentation and the curled flesh outlining it before moving even lower. When he reached the position where her pussy was directly aligned with his mouth, he lifted her legs and rested them on his shoulders, effectively spreading her wide and exposing every inch of her to him.

For a moment he could do nothing but just stare at the glistening pink flesh, so wet and tempting. He took a slow lap at the slick surface, tasting her essence and swallowing it into his body. *Jesus!* It was always like this, better than even the finest liquor he'd ever had. And the moment he had that taste of her, his entire body went on full alert, hungry and demanding for every inch of this woman.

He glided his tongue in slow sweeps over the smooth flesh, lightly brushing her already swollen clit. Each time he did, a little gasp rushed from her mouth and she tightened her grip on his head. He had her arranged so that he held her in place and her movement was limited, just the way he liked it. In the short time they'd been together, he already knew her body so well that he recognized the sounds she made and the movements signaling the rush of her orgasm.

And she exploded, capturing her juices in his mouth as he drank from her and continued to torment her slit. She shuddered against the pressure of his body and the little sounds and cries he'd become familiar with vibrated through him and aroused him even more. She was just so fucking responsive, more than any other woman he'd ever been with, holding nothing back.

He stroked with his tongue, swirling the tip around her clit, her body shivering with aftershocks. He placed slow kisses on the lips of her sex, then scattered a line of them up her body to her mouth, where he pressed his lips to hers, sharing her taste with her. When she opened her eyes, he smiled at her.

"Good?"

"Better than good." Her mouth curved in a tiny grin. "But you know that, right?"

"I know that we aren't even close to being done," he teased. "That's what I know."

Then he began the process again, tracing her jaw and the column of her neck with the tip of his tongue, cupping her beasts to bring the now fully engorged nipples to his mouth, where he bit then lightly and dragged on them with his teeth. The pulse at the hollow of her throat increased in its tempo, fluttering against the skin there. He pressed a soft kiss to it before lapping his way down her body again. This time when he reached her sex, he bent her legs at the knees and spread them as wide as he could before feasting on her drenched sex.

He realized he was addicted to her taste and wasn't sure if that was a good or bad thing, but what he did know was that before this ended, he had to have as much of her as he could get.

This time he took the tip of her clit between his teeth and teased and scraped it, tugging it then licking it while he slid two fingers into her soaked passage. When she clenched her muscles around them, his cock flexed, and he sent it a stern message to stand down, if that was even possible. His goal was to give her as much pleasure as she could handle—maybe even more.

Adding a third finger to the other two, he stretched the walls of her passage and plundered them, sliding in and out with first a rapid stroke, then a slower one, then fast again. She rocked his hand, riding it, delicious little sounds coming from her mouth. When he sensed she was cresting again, he increased the pace and pinched harder on her clit, and she exploded. Digging her heels into his back, she clenched down on his fingers while shudder after shudder gripped her body and she poured herself into his palm.

A last, when the tremors had subsided, he slid his fingers from her tight sheath and held his hand in the air. With his gaze still locked to hers, he licked each finger slowly until he'd swallowed every drop. Then he moved up her body until he could slick his tongue over her lips then press a light kiss to them.

"You're delicious," he told her. "I could eat you forever."

Her mouth turned up in a shaky grin. "Promise?"

"Right after I fuck you until you can't breathe."

"I think I might already be there."

He shook his head. "Not even close."

"I might need to stop and take a breath here," she huffed.

"No stopping, no breathing." He planted a kiss on her mound and dragged the tip of his tongue through her slit. "Just feeling and having orgasms."

He reached over to the drawer of the nightstand where he had taken to keeping condoms. Pulling out a string of three, he ripped one off, tore off the foil and rolled on the sheath with hands were shaking unbelievably hard. When he was fully suited, he knelt between her thighs and lifted her legs over his shoulder, Then, cupping the cheeks of her ass, he thrust inside her tight, wet heat.

Holy shit.

He closed his eyes and reached for every ounce of control he had. Then, focusing solely on giving pleasure, he began a slow glide in and out of her welcoming body. The tight clasp of her internal muscle squeezing his cock nearly drove him out of his mind. The pull and drag were so erotic he nearly came right then. But this wasn't about him, no matter how aroused he was. This was about Kenzi right now. *Just Kenzi.*

He kept up a slow but steady rhythm, sensitive to her body's reaction. Then she wrapped her legs around him and pulled him close and tight to her.

"Faster," she urged. "Harder."

"Thought you didn't have another one in you."

She gave a hysterical little laugh. "Only you could do this to me, hotshot. So do it. Now."

"Yes, ma'am."

He picked up the pace, driving into her harder and faster, scraping the sweet spot with his dick each time he eased back, then filling her again. Then his control shattered, he thrust faster and harder, and the moment he felt the walls of her sex begin to spasm he let go. She clenched around him, her inner walls pulling and dragging and squeezing him as her orgasm gripped her, milking him of every drop of fluid until he was drained.

He collapsed forward, barely catching himself on his forearms so he wouldn't smother her. Her breath was choppy and her heart beat against his chest. Fighting for control of his own respiration, he peppered her cheeks and forehead with light kisses, inhaling the wonderful scent of her.

They lay like that for what seemed like endless minutes, but he had no desire to move. It was different tonight, and not just because he had a mission to wipe everything from her mind but sex. Something had shifted between them and, for a moment, it scared the shit out of him.

At last, knowing they couldn't stay like that forever, he eased himself slowly from her hot, wonderful body and headed to the bathroom to dispose of the condom. When he walked back into the bedroom, she was lying on her side, facing him, a smile curving her lips, a satisfied glow on her face. The tension from earlier in the evening was gone.

My job is done.

He climbed up behind her, spooning her supple body, banding his arm around her narrow waist and cupping a warm breast with his palm. They lay there like that for a moment, everything rippling through his brain. He hoped the incredible sex had taken her mind off the dangerous situation her sister was in. He couldn't believe the woman was actually coming to San Antonio to meet with a member of the cartel that had kidnapped her and had now put a price on her head. *How stupid is she, anyway?*

And he wasn't sure he trusted bodyguards he knew nothing about. He'd be sure and quiz them thoroughly in the morning. He knew Slade would have Mike Elliott check them out upside down and sideways. It wasn't so much that he gave a rat's ass about Dana, but he didn't want Kenzi worrying herself sick about her reckless sister.

But, at least for the moment, Kenzi was in a good place — stress-free.

While he was mulling all this over, the woman in question wiggled her sweet ass against him.

"Better cut that out unless you're ready to go another round."

She laughed softly. "Maybe tomorrow night." She was silent for a long moment. "Trey?"

"Uh-huh?"

"Thank you."

"For?"

"For being you. For…you know…everything."

He hugged her and gave her breast a gentle squeeze. "For you? Anything. Oh, and by the way, it was my pleasure."

And isn't that just the damn truth?

Chapter Ten

Trey slept tentatively, his body attuned to Kenzi, so when she slipped quietly out of bed, he opened his eyes, reached for his cell phone and glanced at the time.

"A little anxious today, are we?" he teased when the readout said five-thirty.

"More than a little." She found her big T-shirt she slept in—when she slept in anything—and pulled it over her head. "I'm going to fix coffee. You can go back to sleep if you want to."

He laughed. "You're kidding, right?"

"No, I'm not. Just because I'm antsy doesn't mean you can't sleep a little longer."

He climbed out of bed and grabbed his jeans off the chair where he'd flung them the night before, yanking them on with one swift pull.

"We'll both get coffee. I'm pretty sure we'll need it today."

He followed her into the kitchen, where she had her snazzy new one-cup coffeemaker set up, and leaned against the counter while she filled mugs for both of them. He would have offered to do it, but the nervous energy buzzing around her was almost visible. He was damn sure she needed to something to occupy herself.

"At least come sit at the table to drink your coffee," he urged, and pulled out a chair and dropped into it.

Kenzi sat down close to him, placing her cell phone on the table. She was so filled with nervous tension he could practically see her vibrating. She took a sip of her coffee, then looked up at him and managed a tiny grin.

"I'm a mess, right?"

He set his mug down and took her free hand. "Understandably so, but at this rate, you'll wear yourself out by eight o'clock."

"Have you heard back from Slade about the bodyguards?"

"No, but I will. He might still be trying to connect with Mike. But I promise we'll know something before we leave to meet your sister. Any word at all from her?"

"Not yet." She looked at her cell. "But it's only six o'clock— Oh, wait. They're an hour later so it's seven there. Dana said they'd be landing about nine-thirty. It's not even a real airport, just a hangar and a runway on some uber wealthy rancher's property. He lets certain people, the ones who for various reasons want to stay under the radar, use it to avoid the major terminals."

"Well, then, it sounds like a good place for them to be landing. Give me the info so I can program it into my cell."

He was just setting it up to get directions when Kenzi's cell rang with what he'd learned was Dana's ringtone.

Kenzi answered right away. "You all set? Good to go?" She listened, nodding her head. Then the muscles of her face tightened. "Wait. What? Speak up. Why are you whispering? But you— Did you— Okay, okay. We'll be there before the plane lands and Trey will be with me, but let's let that be our secret. Don't worry. Uh-huh. Uh-huh. Okay, that's good. Remember, your bosses have their own agenda. Okay. See you soon."

She disconnected and sat there, nibbling on her lower lip.

Trey frowned. "What's the deal?"

"She was calling me from her bathroom, whispering. I don't know why she didn't text like I told her to. She wanted to let me know they were getting ready to leave the apartment. I had told her not to tell the bodyguards we'd be there waiting for her. Well, you heard what else I said, about her bosses having their own agenda. I'm sure they want to keep her safe, at least until she finishes this investigation and the series of articles."

Trey nodded. "Still, I don't trust anyone but people I know."

"Well, you can size everything up yourself when they land." She checked the time again. "I need to call the office shortly and let them know I won't be in this morning."

"What do you plan to tell them?"

"That I have a family emergency, which is actually the truth. I just hope it doesn't turn out to be a dire one."

He badly wanted to pull her onto his lap, rub her back and see if he could relieve some of the tension. He didn't think, however, she was in any mood to be soothed. He fixed another mug of coffee for her, although he was pretty sure the last thing she needed was more caffeine.

He finally coaxed her into the living room with him and onto his lap, where he sat with her until the ringtone on his phone went off just before seven. He looked at the readout.

"Slade."

"Looks like everyone's up early today," she commented, her lips turned up in a hint of a grin.

"Are you kidding? This is late for him." He hit the Accept button. "Got something for me?"

"Only that Mike Elliott says Gillette is a top-notch agency with an impeccable reputation. By the way, he was busy with a client emergency, which is why he just got back to me."

"No problem," Trey assured him.

"You're going to be at the airport, right?" Slade asked.

"Yup."

"Okay. I think I'll ride into town with Kari today, drop her off at work and meet you there. Always helps to have another pair of hands." He paused. "And a gun."

Trey's tension eased a little. "Thanks, Lt."

"And just to be on the safe side, so we know what we're dealing with, I'm going to call Mike back and ask him to have Gillette check on the two guys assigned to Kenzi's sister today. You can't be too careful."

He thanked Slade again, gave him the airport information and disconnected the call.

"Well?" Kenzi was studying him, her brow lined with worry.

He repeated the conversation to her. "That's just who he is. And I'll be glad to have him for backup. You know, just in case."

"I just hope this all turns out to be just my imagination."

"You're dealing with cold-ass killers here," Trey reminded her. "You can't leave anything to chance."

At eight o'clock Kenzi called her office, told them she had something in the nature of a family emergency, and she would not be in that morning. Maybe not even that afternoon, but she'd let them know.

"Lucky for me Reed Calhoun is out of town," she told Trey. "I can always bring the work home tonight to finish it if I need to."

Trey tried to get her to eat some breakfast, but the most she'd choke down was a piece of toast. Finally they showered and dressed, Kenzi in jeans, a T-shirt and blazer rather than one of her usual professional outfits, and they headed out to the airport.

Mountain Ranch Airport was a miniscule facility just outside the city proper, right at the edge of the Hill Country. It was tucked into a parcel of land in the middle of the vast ranches that made up most of the area. According to what Trey had found out when he'd done a search for it, the facility was owned by a private corporation and only people who had the permission of the owner could land or take off from there. Arrangements had to be made in advance, although in cases of emergency, there was a special number to call. When Slade had checked it out with Mike Elliott, the man had told him it was mostly used by millionaires who had their own planes. Gillette, it seemed, had permission because they had once done a job for the owner.

Trey headed out of the city proper on Interstate Highway 10. They passed shopping centers and residential communities, emerging eventually into the landscape of small Texas towns. They pulled off at the exit indicated by the GPS voice and followed a two-lane country highway bracketed on both sides by rolling pastures dotted with herds of cattle. At the next prompt they turned left and drove along a dusty road toward what looked like a Quonset-hut style hangar, with a long runway leading up to it.

"It looks pretty deserted," Kenzi murmured.

"I don't think they provide a welcoming committee," Trey commented. "From what Slade told me, it's pretty much come as you are. There should be a vehicle here waiting for them, but maybe it's around the other side or inside."

He pulled onto the tarmac and drove around to the front of the building. Luckily — and unexpectedly — the door to the hangar area was rolled up, ready for the plane that was expected.

"This way they won't see us on their approach," he said. "In fact, we'll pull way into the back and with luck they'll think the car belongs here."

"I saw an SUV parked out in front," Kenzi said.

"I'm assuming that's the car Gillette ordered for the people on the plane." He drove their vehicle to the rear of the metal building and parked it against the curve of the wall. Then he moved with Kenzi so they were partially concealed by the car, and settled in to wait.

Five minutes later they heard the sound of another vehicle approaching, and a pickup pulled into the building and drove back to where they were. When Trey saw Slade's tall figure unfold itself from the driver's seat, he breathed a sigh of relief. Not that he wasn't capable of handling this himself, but Slade was the best backup anyone could have. And if they had trouble, he had the contacts and the strings to pull. And he was, above all else, the ultimate leader.

Kenzi was strung so tight she was almost vibrating, but she managed to smile at Slade and shake his hand.

"It's all under control," he assured her in his deep voice.

"That's what Trey keeps telling me, but I can't help worrying."

"And with good reason. But like I said, we're good to go."

Trey settled his hand at the base of her spine and stroked his fingers against her taut muscles, even as he waited on full alert. Ten minutes passed, minutes that he was sure seemed like an hour to Kenzi, before he heard the faint sound of an airplane engine in the distance. "Someone's coming in."

"That has to be them," she murmured. "Right?"

Slade nodded. "Unless there's a runway around here we don't know about, I'd say yes. Take a deep breath, Kenzi. We want them in the hangar and out of the plane before we let them see us."

Through the open door they could see the twin-engine plane touch its wheels on the runway and taxi up to the building. The pilot cut back on the engines as they moved closer, maintaining just enough power to get them inside and park the plane before he shut them down. In a moment, a door slid up on the side of the plane and a flight of stairs popped out.

A tall man in a dark suit jogged down the steps then turned to help Dana, in jeans and a tailored shirt. Trey had expected her to be in business attire, but then he realized he had no idea what she'd wear to a meeting with a 'source'. Right behind her was another suit, almost a twin to the first, walking more closely on Dana's heels than Trey would have liked.

The man in front stopped, held out his hand to help Dana down the last couple of stairs and waited until all three of them were standing on the concrete. Before they could head outside, Trey stood and eased out from behind the car, Slade right behind him. Despite him trying to push her back, Kenzi moved up, as well.

"Hold on a minute," Trey called, moving forward.

All three people stopped, the men staring at him. Before anyone could do anything, the pilot appeared in the doorway to the plane.

"Who are you people? This is private property."

The first man off the plane stared at Trey. "What the hell is this? We were assured no one else would be here. This is a matter of safety. Miss Bryant, you should get back in the plane, right now."

But Dana didn't move, just looked at Kenzi and Trey as if waiting to take her cues from them.

"We're all good," Slade added. "This is Miss Bryant's sister. She wanted to surprise her."

"Yeah? Miss Bryant, is that right?"

Dana nodded, and swallowed, visibly. "Yes, that's right. And I know these men."

"I still want to see some identification."

Trey and Slade pulled out their wallets and flipped them open, showing their military ID cards.

The lead man frowned. "Military, huh?"

Trey just nodded and they stashed their wallets.

"This is just a friendly gathering," he told the men with Dana.

Even at first glance there was something about these men that set off alarm bells. Theoretically, they were professional. Bodyguards. As such, they were sure to be armed, and neither he nor Slade was looking for a gunfight, if they could avoid it.

"Then you should have made arrangements, not shown up here like this out of the blue. You're lucky one of us didn't shoot you. What the hell are you doing here, anyway?"

"Miss Bryant wanted to surprise her sister," Slade told them. "She hasn't seen her in a while. It's all good. I assure you, we're as concerned for her safety as you are. She just wants to see Dana."

At his words, Kenzi, obviously unable to wait any longer, broke away from Trey and ran to her sister. The two women hugged, while the men with Dana moved to stand closer to her.

"You just surprised all of us," the lead man said, not looking any too happy about it. "Miss Bryant is under our protection, so I'll have to ask you to step away while we get her to our vehicle."

"Hey, it's just family," Slade said in a relaxed voice. "We were part of the team that rescued Miss Bryant and the sisters haven't seen each other since then."

Trey noticed that, at Slade's words, the man standing closest to Dana tensed, just a bit and not noticeable if a person wasn't looking for it. But Trey was on the alert for anything.

"That's right." Kenzi glared at the man. "I know she's in danger. That's why I wanted to see her with my own eyes."

"We still have our orders," the man insisted.

"How about if you show us your credentials?" Slade still maintained that easygoing tone of voice, but he had moved closer to the lead man, every muscle in his body on high alert.

"We don't have to do anything," the second man said, his tone belligerent.

Trey's ears detected a hint of an accent in the man's voice and his antennae were zinging away. Not that her bodyguards might not have an accent anyway, but with the Lopez Garcia cartel so front and center in this, it pricked his radar.

"Show him," the other man ordered. "Then let's get the hell out of here. We don't need amateurs screwing this up."

Amateurs? Trey clenched his back molars. *If only they knew.*

The first man pulled out a badge wallet and flipped it open, showing his credentials. Trey moved closer to get a better look. The name on the Gillette Agency identification card read Paul Malone. The card, the badge and the wallet showed signs of wear, so not a new hire.

"I'm calling the boss and reading him in on this," the other man said. "He needs to be aware there's a wrinkle here."

"Show him your damn creds first, so we can get the fuck out of here."

The other man reached into his breast pocket for his badge holder. Trey noticed idly that both men wore shoulder holsters. *For easy access*, he figured.

"Here." He held it out. "George Ashford."

Trey studied it, then nodded, but that trickle of unease wouldn't go away. The man flipped the wallet closed and went to slip it back into his pocket. When he did, the sleeves of his jacket and dress shirt hiked up, revealing a tattoo that Trey was all too familiar with.

Cartel!

God damn it. Here? How the fuck has this happened?

He stepped forward so his body shielded the women and whispered to Kenzi, "Grab Dana and run to the back where the cars are."

"What the hell?" Malone asked, whirled and grabbed his weapon.

"Gun!" Trey yelled, registered that the women had done what he told them, and dropped to the floor.

Malone's bullet whizzed past him, but before the man could pull the trigger again, Trey fired twice. The sound of the bullets echoed in the vastness of the metal building as they both hit dead center of the man's chest. Malone fell to the floor, blood welling on his upper body, his eyes blank. Ashford had his gun out and managed to get one shot off before Slade hit him in his shooting arm. He screamed as he dropped the gun, Slade already there yanking both of the man's arms behind him.

"You should be careful about exposing your tattoo," he told Ashford. "We saw the same one on every single man we killed in Lopez Garcia's *finca* in Quintana Roo. Trey, get me something to tie this guy's wrists."

"*Madre di Dios! Chinga tu madres!*" Ashford spat on the floor. "Fuck you, asshole."

"What the hell is going on here?"

Trey looked up and saw the pilot standing in the open doorway of the cabin, staring down at the tableau. He and Slade exchanged glances, then he jogged quickly up the fold-out stairway to where the pilot stood.

"You've got one chance to tell me if you're with these guys," he told the man, pressing the gun to his temple.

"No. Please, No." He held up his hands. "I was just hired with the plane. That's all, I swear it."

"Take off your shirt," Trey ordered.

"What?" The man's eyebrows rose. "Take off my shirt?"

"Do you understand English? Do I need to say it in Spanish? Take it off."

The man started to protest again, then thought better of it and stripped off the garment. Trey had him turn completely around before he nodded to Slade.

"No tattoos."

"Lucky for him," Slade grunted. "Okay, tell me how these pigs came to be riding on your plane with this woman?"

The pilot tried to glower at him, but there was a trace of fear in his eyes that diluted the expression.

"Can I put my shirt on first?"

Slade nodded. "Let's have it. Do you know these men?"

"No." He shook his head. "I fly for Gillette Security. Agents on assignment, clients who need to move under the radar. Whatever they want. This is their plane."

"How long have you worked for them?" Slade demanded. "And what's your name?"

Kenzi and Dana had crouched behind Slade's pickup when the shooting started. Now, from the corner of his eye, he saw them move out from behind the vehicles and head slowly toward him, eyes averted from the body. They were smart enough to keep a good distance away from the wounded man, too.

"Marc Phillips." He finished tucking in his shirt. "I've worked for them for seven years. And by the way, this is a first for me. I'm used to the security agents being armed, but a shootout like this is a new one on me."

He jogged down the stairs to where Trey and Slade were now standing. The women stood off to the side, well away from the groaning and cursing man on the floor. But just in case, Trey planted himself between them and him.

"Have you flown these men previously?"

Marc shook his head. "Never saw them before, but Gillette has a number of agents. They showed up at the right time, with the right client and the right credentials."

"I need to make some phone calls," Slade told him. "I'm calling Joe Trainor at the sheriff's office. I think I've still got some chits to cash in from the bomb scare at the rodeo. Then I better call Mike Elliott and tell him to get hold of Gillette. They're missing two agents."

"And somebody better reach out to the guy who owns this place," Trey added. "He's in for quite a shock."

"Joe will help us with that. "

Slade pulled out his phone and walked a distance away as he dialed.

"If anyone's interested, I can make coffee in the plane's galley," Marc told them. "I'm sure the ladies could use a cup."

Trey glanced over at Kenzi, who nodded.

"That would be great."

Chapter Eleven

Trey wondered if Joe Trainor and his men had used lights and sirens to get there. He remembered where the sheriff's office was, and he knew how far out of the city they were, yet the men had gotten there in record time. With Joe were Detective Adam Gorsh and senior deputies Frank Novak and Ward Benton, men from the team they'd worked with on the bomb scare. They all shook hands with Trey and Slade.

Trey let Slade take the lead. He was, after all, the man in charge of their Delta Team and the one who had the relationship with the senior detective, just as Joe was in charge of the group from the sheriff's office. Trey was more than glad to let him do it. His entire focus was on doing what had to be done as quickly as possible, then getting Kenzi and Dana out of here and away from danger.

"Thanks for getting here so fast." Slade looked at Trainor and indicated the other men. "I see you brought the team with you."

"You didn't give me too many details to work with and I didn't want to be unprepared."

"Of course. Although maybe a little overkill, don't you think?"

A tiny grin teased the corner of Joe's mouth. "But you make things so interesting for us they didn't want to miss the excitement. Oh, and the coroner's on his way."

"Good."

"I need a doctor," the man on the floor spat. "I am shot."

"You're fucking lucky to still be alive," Slade pointed out, "so shut the fuck up. At least you're better off than your friend."

"You are all dead," he growled. "*El jefe* will make sure it is a slow, painful death."

"Only if he catches us first," Trey growled. "And that ain't happening."

"Okay," Trainor said. "So, what have we got going on here? You gave me the nickel version on the phone. How about filling in the details for me?"

While Ward Benton checked over the dead man, emptying his pockets, Frank Novak did the same with the fake Ashford, ignoring the man's groan and curses. Then he snapped pictures of both men.

"I'll send photos of these guys to the office," Ward Benton called. "Maybe we'll get lucky and they'll be in the files. I bet they've had their picture taken before at some time or other."

Joe nodded. "Let's hope."

"Want me to send it to the district DEA, too? Just in case, since there's a cartel story at the heart of this?"

"Yes. I think we can all agree that's what this is related to. Add a message to get it to Rod Bustamante. He's the agent I work with the most." Joe glanced at the women, then back at Slade. "I take it this was who you referred to in the phone call?"

Slade nodded and motioned the two women over to them. "Meet Kenzi and Dana Bryant. Dana's the reporter we rescued from the cartel in Mexico. Kenzi's her sister. We got involved today because she —"

"Was worried about her sister and wanted to meet the plane. She's with me." Trey stepped up beside Kenzi and put his arm around her, pulling her close to his body. He didn't know which was more surprising, his action or his words. Or who was more shocked by them, himself or Kenzi. "It was my idea to come here today."

Joe glanced at Kenzi then turned his attention to Dana. "So, you're the one getting ready to stir the cartel pot, right?"

"It's already stirred," she told him. "I'm just getting it to boil over."

Adam Gorsh chuckled. "That you are. Too bad it's so dangerous for you, because someone needs to do it. Those assholes are the blight of the earth."

"I imagine you know that all too well," Dana agreed.

Trainor looked around then back first at Trey then at Slade. "So you, what, decided to have a little shootout here?"

"Only when we discovered these guys were phony," Slade answered. "It happened it seconds. They pulled their guns first. We were —" He was interrupted by the ringing of his cell, and he held up a finger. "Hold on. This is important. I asked my friend Mike Elliott to call his contact at Gillette Security, see if they could tell him how or when the bodyguard switch was made, if possible."

As Slade stepped aside to take the call, two vehicles pulled up to the hangar, a van with the sheriff's logo on the side and an ambulance.

"Ah, good. The coroner's here." Joe inclined his head toward the van. "And I called paramedics for the piece of trash you shot. It pains me to give him any kind of medical attention, but the bleeding hearts are all over us if we don't. Let's deal with this first."

Joe introduced Slade and Trey to the new arrivals, then the coroner went to deal with the body while the paramedics attended to the man with the bullet in his arm. After having Frank Novak search the man again thoroughly for any hidden weapons, he had the deputy stand guard while the paramedics treated him. When they pronounced him ready for transport to the hospital, Novak handcuffed him to the stretcher and climbed into the ambulance with him.

"I'm ordering guards for the hospital," Joe said, pulling out his cell. "You need to hang out until they get there. We'll pick you up on the way in."

By that time the coroner was also ready to leave, the body securely tucked into the van.

"When can you get to it?" Joe asked.

The coroner shrugged. "You know how backed up we are, but I'm told it's a priority. No sweat. I'll do it right away."

"No, that's okay. He's dead, we know who shot him and we're pretty sure we know where he came from. Just slot it in as soon as you can."

The coroner nodded, then he and his assistant climbed into the van and pulled out of the hangar.

Joe turned to Trey. "Slade says you're friends with the woman involved here. Can you fill me in a little more? I want to call the guy who owns this place and give him a heads up." He shook his head. "He definitely won't be happy, I can tell you."

"Can't say I blame him. Sure. I'll tell you as much as I know, although it's really about the sister of the woman I'm, uh, dating."

Dating. He wanted to laugh. Was that what they called it when the focus was just no-strings fun and sex?

But before he could say anything, they were interrupted again, this time by the pilot hollering down to them that the coffee was ready. Telling him she needed to be busy, Kenzi volunteered to help him bring everything down from the plane. By the time Wade Benton had sent the photos of the two men to his office, coffee had been handed around and they were seated around a table.

"All right, Miss Roberts." Joe looked directly at Dana, so she'd know which Miss Bryant he was speaking to.

She wet her lips and took a breath, and Trey was damn sure she was trying to figure out how to color the story to keep her secrets. *Didn't the little scene that just played out have any effect on her?*

"The truth," Joe snapped. "You won't be doing yourself any favors if you try to lie to us. Lieutenant Donovan has already given us the outline of the situation."

Trey thought the woman looked like she wanted to strangle Slade. But she just nodded.

"Fine. What do you want to know?"

"Take me through your routine since your boss hired bodyguards for you. When and how they showed up, what they do when you're working, going places, at night. How this all works."

When she was finished, it was evident that Gillette had not assigned a regular team to her but rotated the guards, something they'd probably regret for a long time. That had made it easy for two strangers to pick her up for the trip without raising any red flags. And she'd been so busy in her brain trying to figure out how to ditch them before her meeting, and so used to their presence, that she hadn't noticed any of the small details.

Trey studied Kenzi while her sister answered questions, checking her out to make sure she was okay. The tension gripping her body was visible in the way she stood and the tight line of her jaw, but she was holding it together. He knew she was as worried about Dana as he was. Maybe this episode would convince Dana that following this story was way too dangerous for her, but he didn't hold out much hope. He figured she was like Kenzi in that respect, determined to follow through. Besides, she could be poised on the edge of international recognition if this story turned out to be as big as she thought. *Hoped.* There'd be no stopping her or getting in her way.

At that moment Slade's cell rang. He walked away from the group as he answered it, but then Kenzi saw him stop dead, turn and look at the group and hang up his call.

"More trouble." He looked at Dana, his face set in harsh lines. "Was there any reason why Gillette rotated your bodyguard teams?"

She shrugged. "Not that I can think of. The agency had explained in the beginning that sometimes they had to rotate agents. It didn't seem like there was anything wrong."

"Gillette Security said they just now found the bodies of their two agents in a car, parked behind Dana's apartment building," he reported. "The men had checked in at six this morning and were supposed to call again when they got to San Antonio. It's past time for them to check in, so when neither of them answered their phones, Gillette sent two agents to check out the situation. They drove to Dana's building and found them. They'd been shot and their throats slashed. Identification missing."

"Jesus!" Trey let out a soft whistle. He glanced at Kenzi and saw fear and tension grip her body.

"Uh-huh. They're all over it there, with the New York police."

"Dana, why wouldn't they check with you?"

"Two so-called bodyguards told me to turn it off until we landed. I should have told them to forget it." She bit her lower lip. "I'm so sorry those men were killed trying to protect me."

He glanced at Dana. "When we're done here, they suggest you call your editor. Gillette assured him you're still alive, but he's damned insistent he wants to hear your voice. He's going apeshit because he can't get hold of you."

Dana smacked her forehead. "Of course. Especially if he knows about the dead bodyguards. Let me get my purse. I dropped it by the truck."

"In a minute." Slade put a restraining hand on her arm. "They can wait a few while we figure this out."

Trey could tell the woman wasn't happy, but at least she just nodded and didn't try to give them a hard time. He hoped that seeing how close the cartel could get to her again would make her think twice about this whole series she was doing.

"The guy at Gillette said he'll call the owner of the property the airfield's located on, a rancher named

Craig Medina. He might have to track him down if he's not home. Guy's not going to be too happy."

Trey barked a laugh. "No shit. I'm sure he didn't bargain for anything like this."

"The cartel is sending a message." Joe rubbed his jaw. "From what you said, Slade, they've been watching her, trying to find the right opportunity to get to her again."

"We're damn lucky they didn't just kill her and be done with it." Slade's voice was like ice.

Trey couldn't help noticing Dana's face pale at the words, but she also didn't look like she had any intention of backing down.

Joe looked around the table at everyone. "You know this will bring the DEA back into it. If it has to do with the cartel, it's their bailiwick. Once the people at Gillette relay the info to the police there, they'll be on the phone to the local DEA office. Frank sent the pictures of these jackasses to the district DEA office as well as ours. We'll see who comes back with what."

"I know there's a big problem with drugs here," Slade added. "It's hard not to notice when you live here."

Joe snorted. "No shit. You have no idea." He looked over at Dana. "Lieutenant Donovan tells me you're supposed to meet with someone from the Lopez Garcia cartel on this trip who's going to spill the beans about whatever. That right?"

For a moment she sat there, not moving a muscle, her face set rigidly, looking at Joe then at her sister.

"Oh, for god's sake, Dana," Kenzi snapped. "Tell them. They want to break up this thing as much as you do."

"But every time the police get involved," she protested, "you put up every roadblock you can to keep me from getting my story."

"The police are trying to keep you from getting killed, Dana." Trey had to bite down hard to keep from smacking the woman, Kenzi's sister or not. "Didn't you learn anything when they kidnapped you?"

She sat up straighter in her chair and lifted her chin. "That's what the bodyguards were for. Besides, no one knows about the meeting."

"Clearly you're mistaken, or today's disaster would not have happened. Someone has found out about this."

"But I have to meet with this person," she protested. "It's my big break on this story." Then she said exactly what Trey had been thinking. "I'll be a top reporter on the international press stage if this turns out the way I think it will. I'm not giving that up for anything."

"Miss Roberts." Joe looked as if he'd like to strangle her himself. "That won't do you much good if you're dead. It's obvious to everyone here the cartel can get to you anywhere, and that they know about your meeting. They learned your routine, killed your bodyguards and I'm sure were waiting until tonight to take out both you and your source at the same time."

"So what am I supposed to do? If I don't show, this person will never set up another meeting."

"Okay." Joe leaned forward, pinning Dana with his gaze. "I think you need to tell me who this secret snitch is. This could turn out to be a wild goose chase and people have been killed for nothing. Or it could be a trick by the cartel to lure you away from your bodyguards so they could kill you. I don't think they'd be interested in hostage-taking this time."

Dana sat there, staring at Trainor, hands clasped tightly in front of her on the table. Trey thought she looked as though she wanted to punch someone. He was pretty damn sure she wasn't used to having her decisions questioned like this. He'd have figured, with what had just happened, she'd use some common sense and re-examine the situation, but apparently she had a recklessness that Kenzi wasn't even aware of.

"Miss Roberts." Joe's voice was soft but there was a definite undertone of anger. "Are you listening to what I'm saying? Two bodyguards are dead, and we just had another body and a wounded man carted out of here. We're done playing games here. Tell me who the hell you are meeting with tonight and where." He shook his head. "You know, I can arrest you on any number of charges and that would put an end to it."

"Dana, for god's sake, tell him," Kenzi snapped. "I don't want yours to be the next dead body I see."

"I don't have a name," she said at last, looking down at her tightly clasped hands.

"What?"

"Are you kidding?"

"What?"

"Say again?"

Trey, Slade, Joe and Kenzi all spoke at the same time.

Joe was about to say something further, but Slade held up his hand.

"Are you telling me this whole disaster is about a meeting you're having and you don't even have the person's name? You've flown halfway across the country to meet an unknown snitch who could just be setting you up?"

Trey didn't know who in the room was angrier at the answer. He sure was ready to throttle the woman. He couldn't believe they were going through all this for an unknown quantity.

"I've asked this person several questions," Dana told them, "all of which were answered correctly for someone who says they are close to a person in an elevated cartel position. People are afraid to give their names, ever, and I don't blame them. And I promised this person that if the info is worth it, my bosses would help get them away from the cartel."

"That's a hell of a lot to promise," Trey pointed out. "Especially when this person is still an unknown quantity."

"We need to get control of this situation before you go off to meet anyone." Joe looked at Frank. "Any word back yet on the photos you sent?"

Frank looked at his phone just as it beeped. "Coming through right now. Yeah, and your friend Rod is the one answering me. *Shit*. Both of those animals are soldiers in the Lopez Garcia cartel. Pretty high-placed ones, too. Rod asked if he could put double guards at all times on the jackass in the hospital. The cartel would have no qualms about trying to grab this guy and shoot their way out of the place."

Joe nodded. "Do it."

"He also said to call him ASAP. I think he means now."

"Text him back that I'll call him the second I'm done here. Miss Roberts, are you sure you don't know who this person is? It's obvious the cartel is prepared to go to any lengths to find out who it is and eliminate both of you. I've had far too many reporters play dumb on identity and it always comes back to bite them."

Dana bit her lip. "I wish I knew. I promise you that. But this person demanded total anonymity."

"God damn it." He ground out the words. "You went to all this trouble, put yourself and whoever in danger and you don't even know who you'll be talking to? How do you know the information will even be any good? How do you know it's not a trap?"

"Because the cartel could have killed me at any time," she blurted out. "They didn't have to murder my guards and go through this elaborate charade. This person sent me enough snippets for me to know there is something big going on within the Lopez Garcia cartel, something that would blow things wide open, and this person is courting danger by meeting with me."

"And why do you think he or she is willing to do this?" Joe Trainor's voice was calm and even, but Trey heard the undertone of anger. "They have to know they're putting themselves in considerable peril."

"I asked, and the only I answer I got was that this has to be stopped." She lifted her hands and dropped them. "I've met with people when I was working on stories who gave me even less to go on. If you don't take chances, you could miss out on the most important stuff."

"You shouldn't be out there wandering around," he told her. "I promise you, someone in the hospital has already passed the word that a cartel soldier has been shot and is under heavy guard. They'll wonder where his companion is. They'll put out the word to hunt for you."

Trey had had enough. He looked at Slade, who nodded. "Dana, do you have a phone number to reach your contact?" When she pulled it out, he went on, "Did you make arrangements to make at least one phone call or send a text before the meeting, just in case?"

She bit her lip again, looked from him to Joe to her sister. "Yes," she said at last. "I can send one text, with a code word so it verifies who I am. Then I can get a response and I destroy the phone."

"If you have to reschedule, how do you reconnect?"

"I'll get an email sent from a public computer. It comes to an account set up just for this." She tucked her hair behind one ear and Trey noticed the trembling of her hands. So, their cool cucumber wasn't quite as unbothered as she tried to appear.

"Okay. Call this person and say there's a glitch." He looked at Joe, who dipped his head in agreement. "There's no way to know what else the cartel put in place as a failsafe if their hit crew went down. Then we'll discuss your safety."

"But—"

"Do it, Dana." Kenzi leaned forward and touched her sister's hand. "He's right. You're the only sister I've got. No story is worth your life."

For a long moment, Dana Roberts, body tense, jaw tightly clenched, looked as if she was going to give them an argument. Then she blew out a slow breath. "Fine. But I'm not making the call sitting here. I want some privacy."

"Whatever works for you," Joe agreed. "How about over by the truck again?"

"I'll send the text first, and then I'm calling my editor, but I need my purse." She looked around. "When everything happened, I dropped it by the truck. I think."

"I'll get it." Slade retrieved it from where it had fallen and handed it to her.

Dana had just walked away toward the back of the hangar when an SUV drove in, fast, and rocked to a stop near the plane. A man in jeans, a tailored shirt and what Trey was sure, when he saw them, were the most expensive boots available, slammed the truck door and stormed over to where the group was assembled. His face was set in an angry expression and fire glinted in his eyes.

"I think this may be the owner," Trey murmured under his breath.

"No shit," Slade whispered back.

The man stopped close to Joe and Slade and looked around at everyone, a muscle twitching in is cheek.

"I'm Craig Medina and I own this place. Someone want to tell me what the fuck is going on around here? I got a call from Tony Gillette telling me there were dead bodies and a gunfight and what all else in this place. I did him a favor with this. What has he gotten me into?"

Joe held out his hand. "Detective Joe Trainor, Bexar County Sheriff's Office. If you'll have a seat here, I'll fill you in." When the man hesitated a moment, he added, "Please."

"Okay, but I'll stand, if it's all the same to you."

Joe gave him a condensed version of what had happened, hitting the high points.

"Wait a minute. Just wait a damn minute here. I've let Tony deliver his clients to this hangar before, so they can have the privacy they need. I do it with others of my friends. Am I now going to be involved with the fallout from this?"

"Not at all," he told Medina. "And no one is sorrier than we are that this happened on your property. But remember, your friend Tony lost two good men and the client is lucky to still be alive. Your name and the name of the ranch won't appear on any of the reports. You have my word."

Medina frowned as he let Joe's words register. Finally, he nodded.

"Okay. Who are all the rest of these people here? And by the way, I hope you don't take this the wrong way, but I'd sure appreciate it if you all got the hell out of here."

"We understand."

By the time Joe had finished the introductions, Dana was finished with her phone calls and her text. While Joe was herding everyone over to their vehicles, Trey pulled Slade aside.

"We need to get Dana out of sight. I'd like to take her out to your ranch, if you have no objections. Your name hasn't been involved in any of her activities. It's a very long shot that the cartel would have the names of the team that rescued her." He shrugged. "I just can't think of any place else safe to tuck her away, although I hate putting Kari in any kind of danger."

"Don't worry about Kari," Slade assured him. "Teo and all the ranch hands will be carrying, and I might call Brock and Axel to come spend a couple of days. No sense bothering Beau and Marc unless we have to."

"Agreed. Okay, let's get everyone out of here, figure out a place to huddle with Joe and move on."

"Sounds good to me."

Dana walked up to the two of them while Joe finished soothing Craig Medina.

"I'm done on the phone," she told the two men, "and—"

Trey held up his hand. "Not until we're out of here. Kenzi, you and your sister get in our car. I'll be there in a minute."

She opened her mouth and for a moment he thought she was going to argue with him. Then she just nodded and tugged her sister along with her.

"Okay," Slade told him. "Let me talk to Joe and we'll get this show on the road."

Preoccupied as they were, no one noticed the pilot, cleaning away the coffee things, taking out his phone and casually snapping a few shots. Before long, they'd pay a price for this lapse.

Chapter Twelve

Hector had just finished a long conference call on the upcoming expansion of the cartel and was enjoying a cup of *café con leche* when his phone sounded with Diego's special ring. His *baho jefe*, his underboss, would be calling with an update on that bitch Dana Roberts and her arrival in San Antonio. And, hopefully, information on who she was meeting, although they had that covered, too.

He punched the button to answer the call.

"Good morning, my friend. I trust all is well and going as planned?"

There was a moment of silence on the other end, long enough that Hector's hand tensed around the phone and a sour taste washed into his mouth.

"I'm sorry, *jefe*. It pains me to tell you that is not exactly the situation."

Motherfucker!

Now what? He had been assured everything was in place. The *gringa*'s bodyguards had been replaced and they had boarded the plane with her in New York. They would stick to her like glue until her secret meeting tonight with whoever had foolishly chosen to betray him. He was waiting with a mixture of rage and disappointment to see who the traitor was and would deal with that person in an appropriate manner, one that would send a lesson to everyone else. The man he trusted as much as his family had taken care of the arrangements, so how could anything have gone wrong?

He drew in a calming breath and let it out slowly. It would not do to lose control, not at this point with everything that was going on. They were so close to expanding the activities of the cartel, with a solid legal and financial structure to protect them as they moved into other countries and other so-called merchandise. So how, he wondered, had someone managed to throw a monkey wrench into such careful planning? It had to be the goddamn reporter, of course. From the moment she'd started in on her fucking stories about the cartel, she'd been a problem. *If only that goddamn Felix had killed her like he'd been ordered to, none of this would be happening now.*

"All right." With an effort, he kept an even tone in his voice. "Let's have it. What's going on?"

"Everything was fine until they arrived at the private landing spot," Diego told him. "Apparently the reporter's sister decided to be there to greet them, and she was escorted by two of the soldiers who rescued the reporter from Quintana Roo."

"What? How did they even know to find the location? And how did you identify them?"

"My best guess is the reporter told her sister, and the woman arrived with a welcoming committee."

Hector took a sip of his coffee, grimacing when he realized it had cooled too much to be enjoyed. Although right this moment, he was pretty damn sure he couldn't enjoy anything. *How is it turning to shit like this?* If he hadn't already had Felix executed, he would do so. Now. With great pleasure.

"Best guess? Diego, we are not in the business of guessing. It gets people killed, especially our own."

Diego's sigh echoed across the connection.

"*Si, jefe.*" He paused. "But you do understand I am getting this all second-hand, right? Because the location was known, things did not go as planned and the bodyguards are history. Gone."

"What do you mean, history?" Hector snapped. "Dead? Captured? What the fuck?"

As he listened to Diego relay the details, his hand tightened on the cell until he wondered he didn't crack the case.

"And you know all this how?"

"The bodyguards did not check in as they were supposed to when they arrived, so I called the Gillette Security office and pretended to be from her employers just double-checking the arrangements for the reporter. Making sure she arrived at her destination safely. Thank god the person I was connected with is an idiot, careless enough to give me the information I wanted. Roberto is dead and Ignacio is in the hospital under double guard."

Fuck, fuck, fuck.

Hector wanted to strangle someone. How was it that such careful planning could fall apart?

"You must get to Ignacio. Surely there must be someone who works at that hospital who we own. Get someone in there."

"I am pissed off that we even have to do this," Diego growled. "But yes, we must take care of him before the DEA sweeps him away. Although he will never give them anything, I assure you."

Hector tapped his fingers on the arm of the chair in irritation. "We cannot be sure of that. You know that as well as I do. We cannot take chances, not with everything that is at stake right now. Do whatever is necessary, but just get it done."

"I will, Hector. You have my word on that."

"Those were supposed to be two of your best men. How in the hell did this happen? I thought everything was going so smoothly."

"It is the soldiers," Diego spat. "If they hadn't stuck their noses into this, it would have gone off without a hitch."

"And how did they get involved?" Hector demanded.

Another audible sigh from Diego. "I have learned the reporter is sister to a woman who is hooked up with one of the two soldiers who showed up today."

Fuck again.

"Find out everything you can about the sister. I cannot have anyone throw a monkey wrench into things when we are so close to launching this new phase. Get me every single detail. I want to know where she disappeared to, who she is with and how these gringos are involved. If my source is right, these are some of the same men responsible for the slaughter in Quintana Roo. I will not have them interfering again."

"Yes, yes. Consider it done." Diego paused. "But now we have another problem. First, I have to find her. She has disappeared, and we have no way of knowing where she was meeting our traitor, only that it is tonight."

"It doesn't matter," Hector told him. "They'll change it. She'll call the snitch and relate what happened, and they will change both the place and the time. Reach out everywhere, find that woman and learn where the new meet is going to be. And when."

"*Si, jefe.*"

Hector disconnected. Only his rigid self-control prevented him from throwing the phone across the room. He was bothered by the fact that for the first time in his memory, Diego seemed slightly uncertain about doing what needed to be done. He sat in his chair for a long moment, running everything over in his mind. This woman had to be stopped and the traitor found and eliminated. There was way too much at stake to let it go.

Although the cartel had people everywhere, most of them were drivers or low-level guns. They had their network of distributors in San Antonio, as in other major cities, but he hated to call attention to them. He knew the DEA had eyes out everywhere, just waiting to pounce if something happened. No, he couldn't ask any of them to nose around, risking exposure and worse, outing the traitor to the Feds before the cartel could eliminate whoever it was, along with that fucking reporter.

He knew in his gut the sister would also be a problem. Her relationship to the situation might be peripheral, but he wondered if she even knew what her sister had been working on. If she'd guessed what the real purpose was. He had been assured that was not the case, but he knew first hand that blood was thicker than water. That if she guessed anything, knew anything that would help her sister, she would tell her. And all their careful planning would be for nothing. Eliminating both of them would cause a problem, but if done right, it could be managed. Desperate times called for desperate measures.

Knowing he needed to be prepared, he dialed a number he seldom used.

"I am sorry to have to call you," he said when the phone was answered on the other end, "but a problem has arisen, and I think we need your help to resolve it."

* * * *

They were all gathered around the table in Slade's kitchen. Brock and Axel had been only too willing to haul ass to the ranch and provide whatever help they could.

"Deandra said to do whatever was needed," he told Kenzi. "She's pretty cool, you know."

She had forgotten that the two of them had hooked up. She'd been so busy she hadn't connected with her friend but once since the day after the Spurs game. Hadn't even exchanged texts the way she usually did. She would have felt badly about it except Deandra wasn't one of those clingy friends who needed contact all the time. Besides, Kenzi thought, she'd probably rather spend all her free time with Brock.

"I'm glad you two hit it off," she told Brock.

"She said you've been friends for a long time."

"Since college." She grinned. "So if you don't treat her right, I might have to hurt you. Badly."

He laughed. "Duly noted."

Teo had made coffee and warmed a plate of flaky pastries, which hardly anyone seemed interested in.

Then he went off to make sure all the hands were properly armed.

Kenzi was working on her third cup of coffee and hoping she didn't get the caffeine shakes. She alternated between relief that Dana had not been harmed this morning, fear at the situation she was in and irritation—no, anger—that her sister was so focused on this story that she was willing to step into danger again. *How important can a story be to risk her life over and over again for it?* She had hoped the kidnapping would have been enough to scare the daylights out of her, but apparently not.

Dana had just received an email in response to her text and everyone watched as she pulled it up on her phone.

"Well?" Kenzi prompted. "What did he—or she—say?"

"Whoever it is, they're having second thoughts. This message wants to put the meeting off for two days. Apparently, word is already out about the shooting and my source is nervous." She glared at first Trey then Slade. "Damn it. If only you all had just waited to play cops and robbers until my meeting—"

Kenzi slammed her fist on the table. "If they'd waited, you could be dead. Those men had orders to kill you. Bet on it."

"You just don't understand." Dana's forehead was creased in frustration. "This is my ticket to everything. Major networks. Maybe even my own television show. You've seen how successful other investigative reporters have been."

"I'd like to think you value your life more than bright lights," Kenzi snapped.

"Listen." Trey leaned forward, looking directly at Dana. "You know how dangerous these guys are, and now you have an even bigger target painted on you, but if you insist on doing this, then you have to put your safety in our hands and do exactly what we tell you. This is what we do, Dana. Handle bad guys. Take it or leave it."

Kenzi set her mug down and looked at her sister. "He's right, you know. And speaking from a selfish point of view, since you're the only family I have, I'd like to keep you safe."

Dana sighed. "I hear you. I know you all think I'm nuts for doing this, but I've worked my ass off to get a story like this and I can't walk away from it."

"Then let these guys protect you. You won't find any better bodyguards anywhere."

"Okay, okay." She smiled. "Believe it or not, I'm not eager to get whacked. So where do we go from here?"

Before anyone could answer her, Kenzi's cell rang, and when she looked at the screen, it showed her office number.

"Excuse me. I've got to take this."

She punched Accept as she walked out of the kitchen, through the living room and onto the porch, where she perched on a chair.

"This is Kenzi."

"Oh, whew! I'm so glad you answered." Susan, her secretary, sounded uptight, unusual for her. Her ability to remain calm in the craziness of the office was what made her so valuable.

"What's going on? I've never heard you so wound up."

"Oh, god." She lowered her voice. "Hold on just a second. Okay, I'm in your office where I can talk. Lordy, Kenzi, Mr. Calhoun's on the warpath."

"About what? I thought he was out of town."

"He was. He is. But apparently Mr. Reyes called him about accelerating whatever you're working on, so he asked to speak to you. He went ballistic when I told him you were out for the morning."

"Damn." *What on earth is suddenly so urgent about a new corporate structure?* So it dealt with foreign countries — so what? They did those all the time.

"He wants you to call him and, as he said..." She paused for a moment. "Um, get your smart ass back here pronto. He's calling Mr. Reyes back to tell him you'll get on it ASAP. And, Kenzi?"

"Yes?" *Now what?*

"He said he's catching the next plane back here. He'll be in the office by four and he wants everything ready for him to look at."

A frisson of fear danced through her. What was so damn urgent about this, anyway? Another day or two wouldn't make a difference.

"Okay. I have to go home and change, and I'll be right in."

"Okay, but hurry."

She disconnected the call and walked back into the kitchen. Something about this project had bothered her recently, and she couldn't put her finger on it. But now, with this phone call and the summons, she was even more unsettled. What on earth could be so imperative about setting up a foreign corporate structure? *What am I not seeing here?* And, again, she wondered what it was about Alex Reyes that bothered her for no reason?

Trey looked up when she walked back into the kitchen, raising his eyebrows at the look on her face.

"*Problem?*" he mouthed.

She held out her hands in a helpless gesture, but mouthed, "*Maybe.*" Then she cleared her throat. "Sorry, but my office just called and I need to get in there. Reed Calhoun is on his way back from out of town. If he's cut his trip short there's something going on. Trey, if I take the car, can you get transportation?"

He pushed his chair back and rose. "I'll drive you. I—"

"No, it's okay. Really."

"I'm taking you." His voice left no room for argument. "Let's go. Slade, call me and fill me in. I'll be available while Kenzi is at her office."

Slade nodded. "Ring me when you get there. I'll have information for you by then."

Kenzi reached for her sister and pulled her into a hug. "You'll be safe here. No one can get to you."

"Not even the DEA? You and I both know they'll have a million questions for me."

Kenzi glanced at the men still seated at the table, tough warriors who didn't take shit from anyone.

"Unless you say it's okay, there isn't a chance in hell that will happen."

"I know I'm being a pain in the ass," she said in a low tone. "But this is a hot story and my big break."

"As long as you promise to do what this team tells you, everything will be fine. You'll get to meet your source with better protection than any private agency. You'll be safe here. No one will find you, and Slade has everyone weaponed up."

"But the DEA—"

Kenzi looked at Trey. "What do you think?"

"Slade, you want to bring her up to speed?"

Slade nodded. "I'm just waiting to hear back from my friend Joe Trainor. You met him earlier."

Kenzi allowed herself a small grin. "Ah, yes. The cavalry."

"He was on the phone with the DEA even as he drove away from the hangar. He texted he'd get back to us shortly. No one is doing anything until then, so we're on hold for the moment. Believe me, it's better for everyone that way. We'll do everything possible to make sure you get your interview, but not at the cost of your life. That's the deal."

Kenzi waited and when at last Dana nodded, she let out the breath she'd been holding.

"Good. Trey, let's get going then. I still have to change my clothes for something more office appropriate."

She fretted the entire drive to her apartment, her brain so busy with everything going on that she hardly noticed where they were until Trey pulled into the apartment complex. They were barely inside, the door closed behind them, when Troy put his hands on her shoulders and turned her so he could force her to look at him.

"Okay, I don't want to get into your professional business, but something's going on here. That call put you on edge, but you've been...uneasy about something at your office since Saturday. Can you spill it without violating professional confidence? I hate seeing you like this."

She stood there for a long moment, gaze shifted downward, every muscle in her body rigid with tension. At last she looked up at Trey.

"I must sound like a broken record to you," she said, "because I keep mentioning this with nothing to go on."

He cupped her chin and tilted her face up so he could look in her eyes. "Don't knock intuition, Kenzi. It's saved our asses more times than I can count. And this isn't the first time you've mentioned it."

"Silly, right?"

"Let's say I wouldn't discount it. You've got a sharp brain, Kenzi, and good instincts about people. Why don't I get Slade to ask Rod Bustamente, our DEA contact, if his name has ever popped up?"

Kenzi frowned. "You think we should? I don't want to put him in the crosshairs if he's nothing more than a wealthy asshole who irritates me. And the odd part is, the few times I've been in meetings with him, he's always been very courteous and pleasant to me."

"I'll say it again, babe. Trust your instincts. Now." He gave her a little pat on the ass. "Get yourself together and I'll take you to work. You'll get there before Reed Calhoun's flight even lands and have things well in hand."

"From your lips to God's ears," she tossed over her shoulder as she headed for her bedroom.

By the time they left the apartment, Kenzi had cloaked her unsettled feelings in a navy business suit with a short-sleeved gray sweater, navy business heels, her hair in a French twist and tiny gold studs in her ears. Conservative and discreet, she thought. By the time Reed Calhoun arrived at the office, she'd be knee-deep in her paperwork again, everything organized for him as if she hadn't been AWOL for a few hours.

"Have someone get you something to eat," Trey insisted when he dropped her off. "One doughnut is not going to take care of you for the day."

"I will. I don't know what time we'll be finished, but hopefully not after seven. I'll text you when we're getting close."

"Don't let Reed Calhoun get to you," he ordered. "I don't want to have to punch his lights out."

Kenzi actually giggled. "That would be a scene." Then she sobered. "You'll make sure Dana is taken care of?"

"You have my word. She couldn't be in a safer place or with better people. By the time I pick you up, I hope we'll have the information from the DEA and know what the fuck else is going on."

She unbuckled her seat belt and opened her door, but by the time she climbed out of the car, Trey was there, pulling her into his arms and hard against his chest.

"You take care of yourself." His voice was fiercer than she'd ever heard, and had an unfamiliar rough edge to it. A well of unexpected emotion rushed through her, and she wondered exactly what turn this relationship might have just taken.

"I promise."

"Okay. I'd kiss the living shit out of you, but I don't want to mess up your lipstick. Just remember I'm only a text away."

She was smiling as she rode up in the elevator, a smile that stayed with her until she entered her office and Susan came rushing in.

"Oh, thank the lord you're here. Mr. Calhoun called twice before he got on the plane and he did not sound like a happy camper. What on earth, Kenzi?"

Kenzi shrugged. "I wish I knew. What time does his plane land?"

Susan looked at her watch. "In another hour. I ordered a car to pick him up."

"He always takes only carryon luggage so he should be here right quick after that." Kenzi blew out a breath. "Okay. Can you call our favorite delivery place and ask them to send up lunch? Chicken salad on rye and iced tea for me." She fished in her purse and handed Susan some cash. "And get whatever you want for yourself."

"So, you need me to work with you?"

Kenzi nodded. "You bet your ass I do. As soon as lunch gets here, bring your laptop and come in here. And get someone to take our calls."

"Wow." Susan blinked. "This must be some damn important project."

"Apparently more than I thought," she muttered. "Okay. Order lunch while I get myself organized." She glanced at her watch. "Mr. Calhoun will be here in just a little over an hour and I want to be ready for him."

Her concentration was broken only twice during the afternoon, both times by texts and both from Trey.

Dana has nw metng set up with source. Details when I c u.

An hour after that her phone beeped with the second one.

Be sure u do not leave office w/o me.
What the hell? Had they received new information? Had Joe Trainor's DEA friend answered their questions? She did her best to quell the uneasy feeling that crept through her and focus on her work. She still wondered what it was about this particular project that had gotten Calhoun's shorts in such a bunch.

Chapter Thirteen

The two women worked steadily, Kenzi sending her notes to Susan and the other woman typing them into the format they used. Kenzi had almost everything ready when she heard a strident voice in the corridor that she recognized as belonging to Reed Calhoun, and gulped down the rest of her coffee before sending her current document to the printer.

"We finished just in time," she murmured to Susan. "Thanks for all your help. Let's get all this cleaned up."

Susan closed her laptop and gathered the reference books they'd been using into a pile. Kenzi saved her final document, stacked the printouts already finished and grabbed the last document as the printer spat out the final pages. A single loud knock on the door and Reed Calhoun strode into the room. His mouth was set in a grim line and his eyebrows were drawn together in a scowl.

Susan hurried out past him as he came to stand next to where Kenzi was seated.

"I called the office this morning," he barked, "and was told you were out until early afternoon. I thought I made it perfectly clear that Alex Reyes was a top priority and the work needed to be done. Did I not leave explicit instructions for what I wanted while I was gone?"

Kenzi nodded, forcing herself to remain calm. This was a side of Reed, usually the epitome of calm and collected, she'd never seen. *What in all that's holy is so urgent and important about this project?* It wasn't the first corporate structure they'd put together and certainly wouldn't be the last.

"I had some family business I had to attend to," she told him in what she hoped was a calm, measured voice. "I apologize, but I got here as soon as I wrapped it up." *Liar!* "Everything that you asked for is ready, and it looks good. We're right on target."

God! I certainly hope so.

"Then get your laptop and bring it and your printouts to the conference room with you. We'll work in there."

Kenzi grabbed everything and hurried down the hall while Reed Calhoun made a stop at his office. She barely made it to the conference room before he strode in and settled himself at one end of the table.

"Okay." He looked at Kenzi. "Let's have it. Where do we stand with everything?"

"Right where you wanted to be," she assured him. "Let me walk you through everything."

At the end of two hours she had explained it all to him in great detail then sent the finished document to him at his computer. He'd be able to access it from anywhere with his personal code.

"Can I get you more coffee?" she asked, carrying her mug over to the machine.

"No, thanks. I think I'm about coffee'd out." He studied her carefully when she sat back down at the table. "Thank you for getting this done so quickly. Sorry I was a bear before, but Alex is really pushing to get this done fast. He's escalating the timeline to take advantage of some new opportunities. I don't want to take the chance on screwing up."

"It's none of my business," she said slowly, "but did something happen to make this so urgent? This kind of corporate structure is complicated with all the foreign banks and regs involved. Surely he knows that."

Reed nodded. "Of course he does. As I understand it, some new opportunities have arisen that make it imperative to get this in play sooner rather than later. The international marketplace is getting more crowded every day and he doesn't want to lose his edge."

"Yes," she agreed, "it is a busy place out there. It's interesting that he's expanding beyond cattle and minerals into things like electronics and leather goods. And that he's chosen to do it overseas."

Reed shrugged. "Labor's cheaper, costs are less. Plus he can take advantage of the ever-changing rate of exchange." He studied her intently. "Is there a particular reason you're asking?"

"Oh, no." She made herself smile. "Just curious. I guess I'll just wait for you to review all the documents and let me know if we need to make any changes. I added a page to the first one with the list of reference sources I used."

"Very good. That will help when I go over it with Alex." He looked at his watch. "Who, as a matter of fact, I am having dinner with tonight in one hour. Damn. This day certainly went by in a hurry."

"Then I'll let you get back to your office and do whatever you need to." She gathered her laptop and the folder with her notes.

She was more than ready to be out of this room. Somehow, she'd shifted from the excitement of working with one of the senior partners to a tension that gripped her entire body. She hoped it didn't show, or that at least he'd just chalk it up to the demands of what she was doing.

"Kenzi." His voice stopped her as she reached for the doorknob.

"Yes?"

He studied her face, and she was amazed to see a slight tic near his left eye. This was the most self-controlled man she knew next to the Delta Force team.

"I'm sure this is a stupid question," he said in a slow, tight voice, "and please don't be insulted by it, but you don't discuss this stuff with anyone, do you?"

What the hell? No one had brought anything like that up to her since the day she'd been hired here and signed the all-encompassing confidentiality agreement.

"Of course not." She tried to sound insulted he'd even ask. "I knew about confidentiality before I even graduated from law school."

"Of course you did. And I apologize if I insulted you. But this project just happens to be…particularly sensitive. We're taking our client into new territory. It's a very aggressive move on his part, there is an enormous sum of money involved and he is understandably highly focused that there be no problems that can trip him up. You understand, right?"

"Our fifteen years of experience with him should give him a feeling of security, don't you think?" *Lord.* Why didn't she just shut the hell up?

"And it does. But new territory is always somewhat nerve-wracking. He'll be here tomorrow to review it, so I want to make sure every T is crossed and every I is dotted. You'll be here first thing in the morning?"

Kenzi frowned. "Are you planning to include me in the meeting? He doesn't usually want to meet with anyone but you."

"Yes, and this will be the same. But I'm taking the file home to review one last time. If there are any changes to be made before or after he arrives, you'll be doing them."

Her nerves twanged at the thought, but she curved her lips in a smile and nodded. "Absolutely. Um, if we're finished for the day, I think I'll get out of here."

"Good idea." He rose and walked toward where she stood. "Go home and relax. See you tomorrow. Early, so we can tweak it in any way if we need to. At our meeting tomorrow, I'll be reviewing everything with him so I can get him to sign off on it. Then I'll move forward with filing all the appropriate papers."

"Of course. No problem."

By now the first pings of a headache were pinching the nerves on one side of her head. As soon as she was back in her office, she texted Trey.

Come get me now.

Okay. About 20 mins.

Twenty minutes? He must not still be at Slade's place, and she wondered where he was.

She locked down both her desktop and laptop for the night and put away the folders on her desk. Then, just to be safe, since suddenly this project had taken on a weird new feeling, she locked her office.

"I'm out of here," she told Susan when she stopped at her desk. "And you should be, too. We're done for the day and it's late."

"Is everything okay?" Susan whispered the question.

Kenzi made herself smile. Whatever was going on, she didn't want Susan to be a wreck over it.

"It's fine. Mr. Calhoun is happy with the documents, so we're good as gold."

"Whew." Susan let out a slow sigh. "In the five years I've worked here, I don't think I've ever seen or heard him angry the way he was today."

Yeah, Kenzi could relate to that.

"I think he has a lot on his plate right now. And you know Alex Reyes is one of the firm's oldest clients. In fact, I think he was one of the first, and actually opened a lot of doors for Mr. Calhoun."

"No wonder he's so important. Okay, I'm getting out of here. You have a good night."

Kenzi took the elevator down to the ground floor and stepped outside. She still had about ten minutes to wait for Trey, but it was nice out, the sun shining, plus it was a good opportunity to do one of her favorite things — people watch. And lucky for her, there was a little wrought iron bench just to the right of the building entrance, one of the many unique artifacts and decorations in the downtown area.

Sitting there taking in the colorful sounds and sights around her usually relaxed her, especially after a tough day at work. But today nothing seemed to do the trick. Between worry about Dana and the escalating cartel situation, and Reed Calhoun's odd behavior, she felt as if she was one big nerve.

If only she could figure out what it was about Alex Reyes that made her so uneasy. She'd scoured the Internet for every scrap of information on him, and apparently he was exactly what he appeared to be—a very wealthy fourth-generation Mexican landowner in the upper echelon of Texas society with a brother who ran mirror businesses in Mexico. The two of them had won many awards with their unique breed of cattle. Not only that, they were great philanthropists. Something else they'd won awards for.

So, what was her problem?

Maybe, when they got home, Trey could pull out a few of his tricks and soothe every one of her frayed nerve endings.

As she shifted in her seat, a group of people exited her office building, among them Reed Calhoun and a man who looked vaguely familiar. Whoever he was, even at that distance she could see he wore an expensively tailored suit and the sun glinted on a ring that she was sure was gold. She wished she could dredge up an identification in her overworked brain, but nothing popped up. They walked to the corner and waited for the traffic light. Neither of them looked happy, and whatever they were discussing made Reed scowl.

She was aware not every conversation Reed Calhoun had was pleasant. She'd seen him in arguments before, either with clients—although not too often—or with people he felt were screwing his clients over. Did it have to do with the work for Alex Reyes or did she just think that because the project was at the top of her mind? The fact that the man was obviously Hispanic should mean nothing, since sixty-three percent of the San Antonio population fell into that category.

Get over yourself, Kenzi. Not everything has to do with Reyes.

At that moment, the light changed, the two men stepped onto the crosswalk and Trey pulled up to the curb. She climbed into the front seat but even as she fastened her seat belt, she craned her neck to see if she could still catch sight of the two men.

Trey turned his head to look at her. "You look like you're carrying a heavy problem."

She sighed. "Probably just making worries where there aren't any."

"What's going on, babe?" Trey asked, studying her face.

Kenzi turned back. The men had disappeared.

"My boss came out while I was waiting. He didn't see me, thank goodness, because he was with some man that he was arguing with. If you knew Reed Calhoun, you'd know that's out of character. I've seen him do it in the office but never, ever in public. With anyone. And he looked really mad. And his attitude in the office today was way out of character, although he did apologize."

"Maybe whatever got his shorts in a twist earlier today still had a grip on him."

"Maybe." She chewed her lip. "I'm probably wrong, but the man with Reed reminded me of the man we saw Alex Reyes having lunch with on the Riverwalk. Remember?"

"I do. You think it is?"

She sighed. "I don't know. I just caught a sideways glimpse of him in a crowd of people. God. I'm giving myself a headache over this thing, and probably for nothing."

"I believe I have a cure for that."

He leaned over and kissed her, a hot, open-mouth contact that made her nerve endings sizzle. She slid her tongue over his for a moment, swallowing his taste before he lifted his head and shifted into drive.

"Wow!" She licked her lips. "That did it all right. Too bad you can't be my chauffeur every day."

"I can certainly fit that bill while I'm still here," he teased.

His words jolted her with the reality that all this was temporary. Of course it was, and she'd known it from the first night she'd taken him home with her after the Huttons' party. That was a big part of the attraction. Her career came first. She was very specific about that. They could have a good time together and when it was over, no regrets. Getting together with him when he was back for ten days was like the frosting on the cake.

Of course, he'd had the same rules and regulations. He wasn't looking for anything that would detract from his commitment to Delta. Maybe some of his teammates had found the right woman and were making it work, but that wasn't where his head was.

Good.

Fine, even.

Absolutely.

That was his plan and he stuck to it.

So, when had the situation changed? And how was she going to handle it? More importantly, how was he?

"If your brain was burning any hotter," Trey teased, "I'd have to stop for a fire extinguisher. What's going on?"

Kenzi rubbed her forehead, hoping to ease away the headache lingering there.

"It's probably just me. This thing with Dana is making me see shadows everywhere, but…"

"But you still think there's something off with this client you're working on."

"Yes, and I can't even tell you why. I'm telling you, Trey. I just feel something's going on with Alex Reyes that Reed doesn't want to discuss." She chewed on her bottom lip. The whole situation was disturbing her more and more. "God. I know I keep repeating myself, but I've never seen Reed Calhoun in a fit the way he was today just because I took the morning off."

'I'd say you might be reading something into it that's not there, but even in the short time we've known each other, the sharpness of your mind amazes me. So if you think there's something off, there's a chance you might be right."

"If only I could figure out what," she groaned. "Okay, give it. Why didn't you want me to leave the office except with you?"

"Because Slade and I are convinced the cartel now has all the details of what went on this morning. There was an attempt made on the guy under guard at the hospital. A nurse was knocked out and her scrubs taken from her body. It's a damn good thing one of the guards on the room has a photographic memory. He knew the fake nurse was just that, because he'd been introduced to everyone who had access to the room."

"Holy hell." Every one of her muscles tensed. "How did they find out?"

"Not difficult. The cartel has people everywhere, including spies they pay off to feed them information."

She shuddered. "It chills me to think of how much they insinuate themselves into our daily life."

"No kidding. But that's one of their specialties. They either pay people or threaten them or their families. Whatever works best." He pulled into the parking area at her apartment complex and slid into a spot. "How fast can you change?"

"As fast as you need me to. Why?"

"We're going back to Slade's ranch." He turned off the ignition. "Dana's there, although she resembles a caged wildcat."

Kenzi chuffed a laugh. "I'll bet. She's not good at being contained or told what to do."

"If she wants to stay alive, she'll give up fighting us. Anyway," he went on, "she's received an email from her contact, so we have some planning to do. And Slade met with Joe Trainor again this afternoon, so he has stuff to share."

The muscles in her stomach knotted. "Why do I get this feeling I won't like any of it?"

"Just keep in mind that we have things under control."

"Ha! With my sister involved? Not likely."

Trey laughed. "She definitely has a mind of her own. Okay, let's get moving."

He hustled her out of the car and into her apartment in record time, locking the door the minute they were inside. "Make it quick, okay?"

Kenzi stared at him. "Are you afraid someone's watching us?"

"With the cartel involved, I'm considering every possibility."

The knot in her stomach tightened again. "What happens when you guys have to go back to base?"

"That's one of the things we're talking about at Slade's."

Kenzi stripped out of her business clothes and changed into jeans and a blouse in record time. She slipped her feet into sandals, brushed her hair and pulled it back into a ponytail.

"I'm ready," she told Trey, hurrying back into the living room.

He looked at his watch and actually grinned at her.

"You should get some kind of medal. None of the other women I knew could make it in under thirty."

"Maybe you hung out with the wrong women," she teased.

The smile disappeared from his face and an expression she couldn't decipher washed over it. Heat and hunger blossomed in his eyes for a scant moment, then it all disappeared.

"Maybe," he said in a soft voice. "Just maybe." Then the Trey she was used to was back. "Let's hustle it, babe."

When they got back in the car and pulled into the street, he turned the opposite way from the road that would take them to Slade's place. She watched him check both the rear view and side view mirrors as he wove through the residential streets around her apartment community. In a few moments he picked up his cell from the console and punched a button on it.

"Looking clear?" he asked whoever answered. "Yeah? Okay, good, but I'm going to do a little more maneuvering before I get on the highway. Okay. Gotcha. Thanks."

"Who was that?" she asked.

"Brock. He and Axel are my shadow car. I wanted to make sure no one was keeping eyes on us and-or following us."

Kenzi tried to keep her jaw from dropping. "You really think the cartel would have someone watching me? Why, for god's sake? I'm nobody to them."

"You are the sister to the reporter who is endangering their operation and working to expose everything. Plus, you were at the hangar this morning when two of their men were shot and their plans for Dana went up in smoke."

"Damn." She leaned her head back. "So, what do we do now?"

"Now we go to the ranch. Teo, Slade's foreman, is grilling steaks for dinner. Kari Donovan is home by now and hopefully she's managed to soothe Dana's nerves. We'll have dinner and figure out what to do next. Especially since Dana has a new time and place for her meeting."

When at last they reached the Donovan ranch and Trey pulled into the gravel parking area, another car parked beside them. Kenzi recognized Axel and Brock as they climbed out of their vehicle.

"Nice job, guys," Trey told them.

"You were clean," Brock assured him. "There were a few cars on your tail out of the apartment community, but most of them turned off into side streets. The couple that hung in there got left behind with Trey's maneuvers. It's all good and we're happy to help."

Kari Donovan grinned at Trey when he got to the screen door and grabbed him for a hug.

"Never a day without excitement for you guys, right?"

"I think we could do with a little less when we're on leave," he teased.

"And that's my fault." Dana had appeared from inside the house, with Kari close behind her. "I'm sorry to get everyone involved in this."

"Stop it," Kenzi said, although she wanted to throttle her sister herself. "It is what it is. Now the plan is to help you get your work done and keep everyone safe."

"Damn straight," Brock agreed. He and Axel had come up on the porch behind everyone.

"So, let's get you all inside," Kari told them. "I've got the bar all set up and some snacks while Teo grills the steaks."

"You were clean on the way here?" Slade asked.

Trey nodded. "As a whistle. Brock did a good job."

Kari made sure everyone had a drink of some kind as they seated themselves in the living room. Slade chose to stand, rather than sit. Kari was sure it was so he could see everyone at once.

"Okay," he began. "Updates. I drove into the city to meet with Joe Trainor today. We decided it was smarter than having him come out here, in case anyone was watching him."

"Wait." Kenzi held up a hand. "You think the cartel would be following a policeman?"

Slade nodded. "They've done it before, and not just here. Everywhere the cartel locates itself, the first thing they did was study the law enforcement agencies, figure out who they might be able to buy and who's a danger to them. It's how they keep selling the damn drugs in ever greater quantities without anyone but low-level dealers getting caught."

She shook her head. "I knew they were everywhere, but not how intense."

"What did Joe have to say?" Brock prompted.

"He'd had a meeting with his connections at the local DEA office. They had received a tip in their Washington office some time ago that the Lopez Garcia cartel was about to stretch its boundaries to other countries. That they're setting up a structure to be able to funnel money through, launder it and have it come out clean the other end. All in the guise of respectable businesses."

"I thought they already had that," Kari commented. "The Feds always have someone on trial for money laundering. In fact, they just finished a big one and put the three men away for a good long time. The verdict just came down two days ago."

"I'm sure that's why the Lopez Garcia cartel is in a rush. They want to slide in before anyone else does. They were just spreading their wings on an international basis."

"According to the information given to Trainor," Slade told her, "their plan is also going beyond current boundaries. The flow will begin here, in San Antonio, and in Mexico, then move to Europe, the Middle East and even Australia. Someone very respected in the community, with no known ties to the cartel, is making it all happen."

"Alex Reyes." The name popped out before Kenzi could stop herself, and she had a sudden urge to throw up.

Everyone looked at her. She wanted to take the words back and seal her mouth shut.

"I mean…"

"Interesting you should bring up his name," Slade drawled, "because Joe Trainor also talked about him. What is he to you?"

If only she could evaporate and disappear. She was grateful when Trey reached for her hand and gave it a reassuring squeeze.

"Go ahead, Kenzi," he urged. "Tell them what's going on."

"I can't." She wanted to cry in frustration. "He's a client and I can't breach client confidentiality. I could get fired or sued or worse."

"Even if the knowledge you have is critical?"

"She's right," Kari said. "But let's see if we can get around it. Kenzi, from what you aren't saying, I'm assuming something about him is disturbing you?"

Kenzi nodded.

"Okay. I know he's from an old, well-respected, uber-wealthy family. He's quite the well-known figure in both the city and the county. Half his family still manages the holdings in Mexico. How am I doing so far?"

"Good." Kenzi nodded her head. "That stuff is public knowledge, anyway."

"I take it since he's a client of your firm that you're working on a project for him."

"Yes. Again, public knowledge. Everything except the project itself." She nibbled on her bottom lip, a habit she thought she'd been overdoing lately.

"Then let me lay this on the table." Slade leaned forward. "The DEA has had its eye on your firm's client, Alex Reyes, for some time. They got a tip some time ago from a very reliable source and since then they've been watching him carefully. They think he and his cousin in Mexico are connected to Hector Lopez Garcia, and have been for some time. That Alex and his cousin are leading the new expansion of the Lopez Garcia cartel. And that they're giving whatever is in the works the image of respectability."

Kenzi felt sick to her stomach. She had suspected something like this but hearing it as a reality was something else.

"I still can't give you any information," she repeated. "You know that."

Slade nodded. "Let's just consider this giving you advance warning that stuff might come down."

Kenzi shivered as a sudden chill washed over her and the headache began to increase in her left temple. She rubbed at it absently with the tips of her fingers, but she was afraid nothing would ease it. She might have had her suspicions about Alex Reyes, but never in a million years had she suspected anything like this.

"I never even thought about drugs," she blurted. "I thought maybe he was trying to figure out a way to hide money, so he didn't have to pay taxes, but drugs? A cartel connection? Not even on my horizon."

Dana cleared her throat. "I can't be positive, but something makes me think my source works for Reyes in some capacity, and this is what he or she wants to tell me about."

Trey hiked an eyebrow. "You don't know if it's a male or a female?"

She shook her head. "Whoever it is has been smart enough to use something to disguise their voice on the rare phone calls. Usually the contact is by text or email."

Slade rubbed his hand over his head. "Dana, I realize it's not my decision, but I still can't believe you're putting your life in jeopardy for someone when you don't even know the sex. It's no secret Lopez Garcia wants you dead. I think this might just be a trap."

"I'll say it again. They could have killed me already. And with all of you handling my security for it, I'll be well protected." She looked around the table. "Right?"

He nodded. "We'll be doing our damndest."

"But maybe," Kari said, "the cartel knows there's a snitch. But they don't know who, and this is a trap for both of you."

"We've been over that," Slade told her. "The best we can do is make sure we keep her safe."

Kenzi cleared her throat. "Dana, you said you had new arrangements. What are they?"

"I've talked it all out with Slade," her sister told her. "That's one of the things we're going to discuss now."

"What boggles my mind," Kenzi said in a slow voice, "is the fact that a senior partner in one of the city's oldest, most respected law firms has a man involved in drugs big-time as a client. And apparently has for years. I can't believe he's not aware that what we're working on is for that business. If, indeed, it is." She inhaled and let out a slow breath. "And now I'm involved in whatever it is."

"That's something I want to talk to you about," Trey told her. "I think you should figure out a way to call in sick. Starting tomorrow."

"What?" She stared at him. "No. I can't do that. Calhoun specifically told me to be in early tomorrow. Told, not asked. The mood he was in when we met, if I call in sick, he just might fire me."

"The way things look to be coming down," Axel drawled, "that might not be such a bad thing."

"If not tomorrow," Slade told her, "then within the next few days. You can lead up to it. I'm serious, Kenzi. The DEA is getting ready to lower the boom on him. They're just waiting for the paperwork to go in and confiscate all the files."

"You won't want to get caught up in that," Kari added. "Trust me."

Kenzi dropped her head into her hands. The pressure of the headache was increasing.

"You probably all think I am an idiot for not being more suspicious than I was—"

"Stop." Trey cupped her chin and turned her face toward him.

Just the warm touch of his hand began to settle her nerves.

"But—"

He rushed his lips over hers. "Nobody thinks that. There was no reason for you to suspect anything. Kenzi, you've worked at that firm for ten years without anything at all looking honkey. The firm has an impeccable reputation and its clients are the cream of the business world and San Antonio society. Why would the thought of a cartel connection even occur to you? Tax evasion for the mountains of money from cattle and minerals would be more logical."

She shrugged. "Always a possibility with the filthy rich."

Teo stuck his head into the room. "Steaks are ready."

Slade stood up. "Let's get our food and we can continue this over dinner. We got a little sidetracked here, so we should set up the situation with Dana first then see what we can do about your situation, Kenzi. Okay?"

"Sure. Yes. Okay." But she leaned into Trey and whispered, "I don't think I'm very hungry."

"Just eat whatever you can. I don't want you getting sick for real." He put his arm around her and pulled her closer to his body. "We'll figure something out. That's one of my specialties."

Then he leaned down and placed a soft kiss on her lips. And all she wanted to do was crawl into him and pretend none of this was happening.

Chapter Fourteen

Hector Lopez Garcia knew that he should have waited for Diego to get back to him, but there wasn't a big margin for patience here. He took a deep breath, slowly exhaled, and dialed the familiar number.

"*Hola, jefe.*" Diego's voice sounded raspy, as if he'd been talking a lot. "I know you are calling about our thorny problem and be assured, I am still working on this."

"We are running out of time, Diego." He bit down on the cigar clamped between his teeth. "Please tell me you have information for me."

"Some, but I don't think you'll be happy with it."

"Damn it. Well, give me what you've got. Where has everyone disappeared to?"

"The reporter did go off with the sister when she left the hangar, as well as one of the two men involved in this fiasco. And, Hector? You will like this even less. We managed to get someone into the hospital and up to Ignacio's room in scrubs. He managed to talk to him before the guard demanded identification. It seems they have a list of personnel allowed to treat him."

"Fuck." Hector spat the word.

"Indeed. But he did find out something of value. If you recall, Ignacio is one of the few survivors of the massacre in Quintana Roo. You won't like this. He said the two men with the women are part of the team that led that disaster."

Hector ground his teeth. "Go on."

"You won't like this, either. It appears the sister is involved with the man who drove her today, although we were not able to ascertain just how deep that relationship went."

"It doesn't matter," Hector growled.

"But let me tell you who the sister is."

When he finished, Hector was filled with a murderous rage. Who had he offended that brought down such bad luck on his head, and on all the parts of the cartel? He would have to make yet another distasteful telephone call, and who the hell knew what that would bring about?

This fucking reporter had connections that might give her access to information the cartel could not afford her to have. *Mierda!* That created a major quandary. If the order was given to kill her, they would have to bury her where no one would find her. Otherwise her death would raise far too many questions.

"If the work she is doing looks to her like nothing more than what it purports to be," he said slowly, "then we will do nothing. Just watch and wait. Perhaps she will just take it at face value. She has no reason, at this point, to think otherwise."

"But the reporter sister has uncovered information about the plans," Diego reminded him. "What if she shares them?"

"I say again, there is still no visible link between the two situations. We need to clean things up before there is. Getting rid of that reporter is now our top priority. Damn it. How did everything get so fucked up? How are so many coincidences poised to destroy something we've worked a long time for?"

"This is not good news," Diego commented.

As if I don't know that.

"Adding in the soldiers only worsens things," Hector pointed out. "Of all the damn fucking men to get involved with. Someone is raining curses down on us. So. Where did they go when they left the hangar?"

The moment of silence that hummed across the connection did nothing to assuage Hector's rapidly exploding temper.

"We're still working on that." Diego's voice was edged with frustration. "The information on these men is so hidden even their home addresses are difficult to ascertain. But," he added hastily, "we will get the information, I promise you. Have I ever let you down?"

"No, and I don't want this to be the first time. Work harder," Hector demanded. "We are on a time limit here. The organization is poised to move forward with its massive expansion plans, and nothing can interfere with that. You certainly know the DEA is ready to jump on our organization if they sniff anything at all." *Goddamn the DEA, anyway.* "Who knows if the person the reporter is talking to is going to the DEA or even has already done so?"

"They have not made a move on us," Diego pointed out.

"That means nothing. They could even now be investigating, looking for weak links, gathering information to do so. And let's not forget the sister could be a danger in her own way." He thought for a moment. "I don't care what you have to do, but by the end of day I want to know where these women are and who they are with. And any hint at all of who is betraying us. *Comprende?*"

"I will get on it again as soon as we hang up," Diego assured him.

"Do that. I count on you, Diego."

He hung up, fighting to control his anger fuming. He was used to demanding things and having them done at once. Loose threads were snipped. Troublesome people disappeared. Problems were eliminated at the snap of a finger. But now people who didn't know enough to be afraid, or who were clever in their own right, were threatening the empire he had built. And the one he and his family were about to take to new heights. They had to be eliminated, and quickly.

Hector sat for a long moment after he disconnected. Although he did not have proof, long experience and his own senses told him they had one or more leaks in key places. He did not know how that was possible, as the cartel had people they paid too much money to in order give them sufficient warning if that happened. If that was indeed the case, they had serious problems because traitors had slipped by them.

He would have to make another phone call, and he hated that fact. He saw it as a sign of weakness, and he had spent his life doing all manner of things to ensure that no one ever attached that word to him. Worse yet, he was going to again ask for help from a person who it was his responsibility to help. When he had finally identified all the people who had created this situation, he would kill them all himself. Starting with the fucking reporter and maybe her damn sister.

With great reluctance and dreading the conversation that was about to take place, he called the number he had used the day before. In concise sentences, he outlined the situation.

"We must take care of this before things get any more out of hand than they already are."

"I thought that was your responsibility," the refined voice answered.

Hector cleared his throat. "There are places I cannot go, people I cannot reach out to without creating a problem. And while I can take care of the reporter, her sister is your problem. We want to make absolutely sure whether she does or does not suspect anything before we get rid of her."

"Yes. I will take care of that, without raising any eyebrows. But the reporter is your responsibility. If the job hadn't been botched the first time, none of this would even be happening."

"I'm aware of that." Hector's jaw tightened. If he ground his teeth any more, they'd be down to the roots.

"So, then, what is it you want from me, besides verification of the sister's knowledge?"

"I need to know where the reporter had disappeared to and how involved her sister is. You can help on that end."

Silence. Then, "I will find the best way to assess the situation, but if it becomes awkward, you are on your own. I am not going to mess up this move forward by putting anyone on alert. We have worked too hard for it."

Hector drew in a deep breath and reached for his famous control.

"Yes. All of us have." He stared out of the window. "Another unpleasant bit of information. There is also a possibility that whoever this reporter is meeting with has gone to the DEA. I will—"

"*Hijo de puta.* What the hell, Hector? You are the one who is supposed to keep a lid on all of this. Maybe it's time to make an example of someone again."

"And maybe that someone looking to betray us is from your end of the business and not mine." Hector was getting sick of this. "I'll clean my house, but you might do well to take a look in yours. Get that information."

More silence

"All right, *primo*. Let's take a deep breath here and regroup. I will take care of my business, you will take care of yours, and when the mess is cleaned up, we will have taken a giant step forward, ahead of the other cartels."

The connection went dead. Hector stared at the silent phone. *Fuck. Just fuck.* Now this thing had them at each other's throats and that had never happened before. Not to mention the fact that the only way their entire setup worked was when connections were kept to a carefully regulated minimum. They never stepped into each other's worlds. No one objected because it had been that way for decades. The financial rewards to everyone involved were more than worth it.

Anger surged through him and he barely restrained himself from throwing the phone against the wall. Tomorrow he would have to call back and mend his fences.

* * * *

Kenzi leaned back in her seat in the car and closed her eyes. Thoughts about the night before made her feel as if every nerve in her body had been scraped raw. After dinner they had all sat at the dining room table to plan out Dana's rescheduled meet with her source. That had happened after she'd finished a lengthy call with her editor, who'd apparently had a come-to-Jesus meeting with himself and decided no story was worth collecting bodies over, especially if one of those bodies turned out to be hers. But her stubborn sister hadn't budged.

Kenzi had shamelessly eavesdropped while Dana had pleaded with her editor, even going so far as to tell him she was getting the damn story anyway, and if he didn't want it, she knew plenty of places that did. Kenzi had wanted desperately to shake her sister, or smack her, or something. Trey had calmed her down, fed her a glass of wine and she had managed to keep her shit together for the rest of the evening.

Dana's source apparently was not able to get free again for three more days, which made nobody happy, least of all Dana. Yes, she'd agreed, she saw the wisdom of staying at the ranch until then. And yes, how fortunate that Slade had the room, and that everyone on the ranch was armed to the teeth, just in case. But damn, she might just go crazy.

No one had been happy with the source choosing the place for the meet, but there had been no wiggle room there.

'I'm the one in danger here,' the mechanically altered voice had said. *'I will choose the place. It will definitely be worth your while.'*

By the end of the evening, they had decided to scope out the location—even knowing it could be changed at the last minute—and had set up an effective plan to keep Dana as safe as possible. Kenzi still hadn't been convinced. Anything could go wrong. But at that point, she'd realized it wasn't her call.

She had other problems—a headache blooming at the base of her skull and a feeling that somehow she was going to put her foot in her mouth and piss off Reed Calhoun or Reyes himself or both.

"I still wish you had called in sick today," Trey said as they headed away from her apartment complex.

"Truthfully? I wish I could, too. But Calhoun knows I would never do that when we're crunching unless I was at death's door."

His laugh had little humor in it. "That's probably not a good metaphor in this particular situation."

"Yeah." She sighed. "I guess you're right. Don't worry, I'll be okay. Nothing is going to happen at work, and I am going to be careful not to let any of my suspicions show. Anyway, Reed Calhoun knows you deliver me and pick me up and we're together the rest of the time when I'm not working."

"Just watch yourself, okay?"

"I promise." She chuckled. "Did you notice Dana turn green when Axel said he'd take her out riding today? She's never been on a horse in her life."

"Well, he grew up on a ranch, like Slade, so she's in good hands. It will take her mind off the situation."

"Still, I hope someone takes pictures. So Slade's meeting with Detective Trainor again today?"

"He is. He hopes to find out more about what the DEA knows." He pulled into the curb. "Here you go, babe. You be careful, and keep your cell with you all the time, just in case."

She gave him a lopsided grin. "You gonna ride to my rescue if they're mean to me? I'll be okay. I promise. I'll watch what I say. And maybe I'm completely wrong to be suspicious. Everything could be perfectly legit."

"Maybe. But you know the old saying. Hope for the best and prepare for the worst."

She unfastened her seatbelt and reached across the console to pull his head down to hers. Then she pressed her open mouth to his and thrust her tongue inside, sliding it over his and sucking. When she finally pulled back, he looked at her with intense hunger in his eyes.

"You'll pay for that when we get home tonight."

"Oh." She laughed. "I hope so."

Then she opened her door, slid out of the car and took one last look at him to carry her through the day.

She stepped off the elevator and into the firm's reception area at eight on the dot. When she got to her office, Susan was waiting for her.

"Mr. Calhoun has already been here for an hour," she told Kenzi in a low voice. "He's set up in the conference room. He had me order up the special pastry tray from Flour Power and actually asked for brewed coffee instead of using the pods. The fancy stuff he keeps locked up." She dropped her voice. "What's going on, Kenzi? How come his own secretary doesn't take care of what he calls the details? And are you going to get any credit for all the work you did?"

Kenzi drew in a calming breath. "Our client is coming in this morning. He's probably got his secretary printing out the files he needs."

"I've never seen him this uptight." Susan lowered her voice even more. "Is everything okay?"

Kenzi nodded. "Yes, but for whatever reason, Calhoun wants this particular project to be letter perfect." She squeezed Susan's arm. "It's all good. I promise."

"If you say so. Just tell me what you need from me."

"Right now, a cup of coffee would be fabulous."

"Coming right up."

Kenzi dropped into her chair and blew out a breath. Maybe this entire business had nothing to do with Dana's situation. Maybe a lot of things. But whatever the reason, she couldn't get the idea of the connection out of her mind. The bigger question, if it was true, was whether Reed Calhoun had known and was in some way involved. She'd just have to watch how she behaved and be on top of her game today.

She had just opened both her desktop and laptop computers when Susan arrived with her coffee

"He's here." She looked over her shoulder as if someone was standing behind her. "He was whisked right into Mr. Calhoun's office."

"Then we just wait to see if I'm needed. In the meantime, let's get back to work on the Park Place project."

At least a dozen times as she worked on documents, she was tempted to call Trey and see if anything had changed with Dana. Last night Slade and his team had outlined several possible scenarios and how they would handle each. Then, while Trey had taken Kenzi home and Teo had stood guard with Dana, the rest had gone to scope the place out under cover of darkness so they could fine-tune things.

Now all they could do was wait.

At last, shortly before noon, when her nerves were raw and she was about to jump out of her skin, Susan knocked on her door and opened it.

"Mr. Calhoun just buzzed and asked for you to join them in the conference room."

For a moment, panic slid over her like a cold cloth. Then she drew in a breath and exhaled slowly.

"Okay. Here we go. Wish me luck."

Susan squeezed her arm. "Of course."

Kenzi checked to make sure all her files were in order on her laptop, then picked it up along with a notepad and a pen. She was pretty sure Reed had shown *Señor* Reyes the final documents to review today, but there might be some last-minute changes. She knocked once on the conference room door and when she heard, "Come in," opened the door and entered.

The two men were sitting at one end of the table, cattycorner to each other, each with a mug of coffee. A stack of documents sat in front of Reed.

"Good morning." She smiled at both of them. "Nice to see you again, Mr. Reyes."

Kenzi took a moment to study him carefully. Alex Reyes was tall, well over six feet, and his lean body was clothed in a suit she was sure had cost more than her weekly salary. His close-cropped black hair was liberally sprinkled with grey, the kind that gave him a distinguished look, and onyx black eyes looked out from beneath thick black eyebrows. She could practically feel the power emanating from him.

He rose with athletic grace and held out his hand. "Nice to see you again also, Miss Bryant. Reed says the bulk of the work on this is yours, so I wanted to thank you personally. You've done an excellent job."

"Thank you." She spoke in what she hoped was her best professional tone of voice. "It's been a great pleasure and an honor to work on this. I wish you very good luck with the endeavor."

He nodded. "Thank you. In today's global marketplace, more and more people are discovering the value of international business. Setting up the corporate framework for it can be tricky, with all the different regulations in so many countries."

"I agree. But be assured, every regulation was checked and double checked."

"I'm sure it was. I wouldn't expect anything less of this office." He looked at Reed. "*Señor* Calhoun and I go back a long way."

"Yes." Kenzi dipped her head. "He's told me."

"I am sure you know, Miss Bryant, that I have been a client of this firm for many years, a relationship that continues to grow stronger."

"Which we are all excited about," Kenzi assured him. Why was he looking at her as if he was trying to see under her skin? *What does he expect to find?*

"One of the many reasons is the absolute confidence in the respect of confidentiality by every member of the firm." *Including you*, his tone seemed to imply.

"Of course. And every one of us takes this seriously."

"Good. I am glad to hear that."

She cocked an eyebrow. She had to make him believe she did not suspect a single thing.

"Was there a problem with something?"

"No, no, of course not. That's why I wanted you to know how much I appreciated the hours you spent on this. You've created corporate structures like this before? Reed said that's why he asked you to work on this with him."

"Of course. Not many, but the ones I've done have also been complicated." Again, she dug up a smile. "I find it an area of the law that fascinates me."

"What did I tell you?" Reed chimed in. "You have no worries here. Have we failed you in all these years? Trust, Alex. Well-placed trust. That's why you bring everything to us, and it will always be the same."

Kenzi looked from one to the other. "Excuse me, am I missing something here? Is there a problem I'm not aware of?"

"Not at all." Reed shook his head. "But this is a very big project, right? We discussed that at the very beginning."

"And you know it has had my undivided attention and total confidentiality. And that will continue."

"Yes, confidentiality," Reyes repeated. "I'm glad you mention that again. I don't mean to be insulting, but this is not something you discuss at home with your husband, right?"

"I don't have a husband," she told him, "but if I did the answer would be no. The nature of my work never makes it to dinner table conversation. That would be a violation of trust."

Reyes looked at her for a long, silent moment and for a brief second, she wondered if he could see inside her head. Then his lips formed a wintry smile and a sudden chill raced down her spine.

"Thank you. I don't mean to imply that I think you would do this, but with something that has a scope this enormous, I'm sure you can understand my desire to cross every T and dot every I. Thank you for being so diligent with my project."

"Of course." She looked at Reed Calhoun. "Was there anything else?"

"No." He shook his head. "Excellent job, as usual. When this project goes forward and all the pieces are smoothly in place, we'll need to talk about moving you up the ladder."

"Thank you." Under other circumstances she would have been sizzling with excitement. Now she felt as if the ground beneath her was shifting. "If you don't need me anymore, I should get back to my office."

"Of course. Good job."

Both men smiled at her, but as she walked out of the conference room she could feel two sets of eyes boring into her back like hot pokers. Had Reed called her into the conference room just so Alex Reyes could congratulate and thank her, or did he have an ulterior motive? Had she given either of them any reason to suspect her or to sense that she knew about the real Reyes under the public façade? She could hardly wait for today to be over.

Even though she was now deep in another project with a different client, and should have been completely absorbed in it, the afternoon hours dragged. Every time her phone buzzed or there was a knock on the door, she jumped. Telling herself she had to get her act together did nothing at all.

When five o'clock rolled around, she'd had enough. She checked to make sure Reed Calhoun had left for the day, then called Trey to come and fetch her. When she nearly fell into the car, he grabbed her chin and turned her face to him.

"Rough day?"

"You might call it that."

She gave him a snapshot of the little scene with Reed Calhoun and Alex Reyes and the vibe she'd gotten.

"He just kept poking at it." She raked her hair back from her face and tucked it behind her ears. "Asking me again and again. Even wanted to know if I discussed it at the dinner table."

"You think he suspects anything?" Trey asked.

"I don't know why he should," she told him. "I've done the work and been careful not to ask the wrong questions or say the wrong things."

"Do either of them know Dana is your sister? And would they have been following her stories in the media?"

Kenzi shrugged. "Maybe they saw the news clips of her rescue, but I'm not sure if they've paid attention to her story. If we're wrong, if the DEA is wrong, and Reyes is not part of the cartel, it wouldn't amount to a hill of beans to him. But if they're right and he is," she pointed out, "and they put me and Dana together, it means I'll have eyes on me."

"I'm with Slade. I think you need to call in sick until this is over."

She shook her head. "I never get sick. "

"Huh. Not in all the time you've been working there?"

"Not once." She laughed. "I'm disgustingly healthy."

"I don't think there's anything disgusting about it at all." His voice had dropped an octave and one hand squeezed her thigh. "People get sick without warning all the time. Have you taken many sick days?"

She shook her head. "No, but...."

"Let's check with Slade and see what he thinks. I'll call him when we get home."

"How's Dana doing?" Kenzi grinned. "Did Axel get her on a horse for real today?"

Slade laughed. "Only after a great amount of teasing. He just took her down a short trail into the woods and back. Good thing, too, because Slade said she's getting antsy about hiding out at the ranch and being surrounded by so many people."

"Yeah, she's pretty much a loner. She 'll take any chance at all just to get a story because she's so damn sure she's got everything under control."

"She does realize she's got vicious killers after her, right?" Trey asked.

"I'd like to think she does, but she's spent her professional life walking into dangerous situations by herself. She's had to claw her way up to where she is now, fighting a lot of male reporters in what is still a male-dominated profession, so she never gives an inch."

"She'll have to accept protection for her meeting or we may not let her go."

Kenzi burst out laughing. "Stop my sister? That's something I'd pay to see. I'm just glad she focused on riding horses today instead of figuring out how to ditch everyone."

"She did that for sure. And I think she enjoyed it once they got going."

"And hopefully it took her mind off the situation."

Even as she said it, Kenzi thought the words should be capitalized — The Situation.

Seconds later Trey pulled into the parking lot, then they were inside, where she could shut out everything else. The door was barely closed before Trey pulled her into his arms, pressing her against his lean, hard body. She felt every muscle, every inch of him, including the swollen length of his cock that threatened to push its way through his fly.

"Wow." The corners of her mouth ticked up in a grin. "Someone's glad to see me."

"You have no idea."

He thrust his fingers through her hair to cup her head. He held it in place while he drove his tongue deep into her mouth. The flavor that was uniquely Trey flooded her senses, surging through a body relaxing at last after a bitch of a day. She stroked her tongue over his and pressed her body against him, wiggling her hips just a little to create friction.

When Trey lifted his mouth from hers, they were both breathing heavily.

"I needed that," she told him.

"Ditto." He licked just a corner of her lips. "I've half a mind to strip you down and take you on the floor right here," he growled.

God, it was so good to be inside, with Trey teasing all her senses awake. It was just what she needed after the last few hours.

"Well, hang on to the other half," she teased. "You need to call Slade and I need a shower in the worst way, just to wash off the stink of my meeting."

"If you insist. But fair warning." His gaze burned into hers. "I'm hornier than hell."

"Good. That's just what I need."

Chapter Fifteen

Alex Reyes leaned back in his chair and took a sip of the aged bourbon in the crystal rocks glass. He was doing his best to project an outward appearance of calm, because the Alex Reyes the public saw was always calm, even in the most stressful circumstances. Today, however, it was particularly difficult. His well-paid spies had let him know the DEA had been gathering evidence at an alarming rate and could be poised to shut everything down—even the cattle and mineral operation—at any moment.

He had pushed Reed Calhoun to get all the paperwork in order for the shift in operations, his brother had been informed and they were just days away from implementing it and protecting themselves. What had begun as a way to expand beyond the operations of the other Mexican cartels had now turned into a lifesaver for their entire operation, but only if they could get it moving in time.

Now, when he needed it least, he was having to deal with additional unpleasantness, in the form of the man sitting across from him. This man, who he had nurtured and coached and directed and made a crucial and integral part of the organization, had suddenly become a devil who was turning on the very people who had made him what he was.

They sat in a corner of the lounge at the Athletic Club, angled toward each other in deep armchairs upholstered in rich leather. The facility neither catered to athletics nor operated as a real club. It was, however, a very private place for the uber-wealthy whose businesses included drugs, guns, sex trafficking and other enterprises that crossed international borders, operated outside the law and raked in millions.

No expense had been spared to guard against electronic eavesdropping or cell phone location, or any other snooping devices. Here key people could have a drink or a gourmet meal and discuss business away from the public without fear of discovery, which was why Alex had asked Bruno Cerda to meet here. Their presence would be ignored, never acknowledged by others, and all conversations would be private.

Cerda was both an *accionista* — a shareholder — and a *commercializador*, someone who helped run the legitimate enterprises of the cartel. He had been with them since they were all young men, and had performed very well, earning him a permanent seat at the table. Unless, of course, he said something today to fuck it up.

He swallowed a smile as it occurred to him that if he had to kill the man, what better place to do it? By tacit agreement, no one would pay attention.

Cerda took a healthy swallow of the single malt liquor he was drinking and looked at Alex over the rim of his glass.

"I assume this meeting is your attempt to tell me my request has been denied and why."

Alex stared at the man for a moment longer, trying to determine what had prompted the man to do this, and if there was something he'd missed all along.

"Let's take a look at where we are," he began. "Just to set the stage."

"I think the stage is already set," Cerda told him. "In less than a month, your international corporate structure will be in place and you will begin the operation. Correct?"

Alex nodded. "That's the plan."

"You are going to make millions, Alex." He shook his head. "No, billions. Tapping into the three most profitable businesses Lopez Garcia runs—drugs, guns and sex—you will increase your income at least tenfold."

"We will," Alex acknowledged. "And your share will increase exponentially. You will never be able to spend all the money you will be making."

"Aah, so you say." The man took another drink from his glass. "But a pittance compared to what you and the other two will rake in. I deserve a bigger cut and you know it."

Alex studied him again. "So, your point is, you deserve a share equal to ours?"

Cerda shrugged. "Not equal. I would not ask for that. You take all the risks, after all. But certainly I hope for a share larger than what I'm getting now."

Why is there always someone whose greed is so out of control that they'll risk destroying everything for it?

He swallowed a sigh. "We discussed this before. Until everything is in operation and we see what the actual risk and reward is, it isn't wise to change the financial structure. Agreed?"

Cerda sat for a moment, staring into his glass. Alex did not for one moment believe the man was thinking. It was his little trick, his little tell, that he truly believed helped him to get his point across. So, he sat quietly, waiting him out.

"Perhaps I would settle for more upfront compensation," Bruno said at last. "Others have tried this before and failed, chased away by those already in control who destroyed competition. Maybe it would be to my advantage to settle for less but get it up front."

Alex sipped his drink again and took his time answering. It was his way of keeping the other person off balance.

"We've been doing this for more than twenty years," he reminded Cerda. "Something's got you twisted up about this. Enough that you even went to see Reed Calhoun, a stupid mistake that could have created many problems. Everyone knows that the only one who has contact with Calhoun is me."

"Because your ego wants to keep that spot for yourself, so you can always be the one in control."

Alex studied the other man through narrowed eyes. Something was off here. Bruno had never wanted to move out of his position as money manager in all the years he'd been part of the organization. The public tended to think of members of a cartel, even the leaders, as uneducated, bloodthirsty killers who sucked up power like babies sucked up candy. And while that described ninety-eight percent of cartel members worldwide, there was that upper echelon who knew how to manage power and wealth and were accepted and welcomed everywhere.

The Lopez Garcia cartel was different from others in significant ways. For one thing, both he and his brother had bachelor's and master's degrees. While the third leader, the face of the cartel, wielded brutality like a sword to keep people in line, Alex and his brother traveled in the top levels of society as wealthy businessmen, building connections for their traffic in drugs, guns and sex.

Bruno Cerda also boasted a degree in finance from a top university. That was what made him so valuable. He understood more than any of them the fluctuations of international currency and foreign stock exchanges. He was always ready with information on where and how to move money around, clean it, refresh it and reinvest it so their dollars were always making dollars. Many more dollars. But if he persisted in his demand, it might be time to retire him. Permanently.

He lifted the cover of the handcrafted humidor on the table beside him and removed a Cohiba cigar made specially for the members of the club, snipped the end and with slow, deliberate movement, lit it and drew in its essence. Just as slowly, he exhaled a stream of smoke.

"Why don't you just spit out what's really bothering you, Bruno? Don't waste my time beating around the bush."

"All right. Fine," Cerda drained the last of his drink, set the glass down and leaned forward. "It's this damn fucking reporter. She is going to ruin it all. The DEA will identify and target all the key people including you, Antonio and yes, even Hector. We will be dead in the water just like the Medellin cartel. We will lose everything. I want as much as I can get before we all go down the drain."

Alex had to exert maximum control to keep from gripping the cigar so hard that he bit off the end. He didn't know who he was angrier with—Bruno, the fucking reporter or Felix, Hector's nephew, who'd tried to ransom her instead of killing her as he was ordered to. Since then she'd been guarded like Fort Knox, two bodyguards with her at all times. It was a damn fucking miracle they'd been able to make the switch when they did, but that had been an even greater disaster. And now it seemed she was protected by the very lethal soldiers who had executed so many of Hector's men in Quintana Roo. He should have told Hector to have the guards kill her and they'd ferret out the snitch themselves.

Draining the last of his drink, he fixed Bruno with a hard stare.

"The reporter will be dealt with. You can bank on that. And one of the reasons we are setting up this structure in Europe and the Far East is so if it all goes to hell in Mexico, we will have places to relocate and continue our business. The structure and shares will remain the same. Only the amounts will differ. They will increase."

"So you say."

"And it is the truth." He shrugged. "But if you aren't happy, we will be happy to release you from your obligations. No problem."

Beneath his olive skin, Bruno's complexion paled. Alex did not have to explain to him what that meant. He sat there for a long moment, silent, while Alex smoked his cigar. At last he nodded.

"You are right, as always. I have not thought it through and jumped to an unreasonable conclusion. Of course you will take care of the reporter, and anyone else who endangers our operation. Forgive me for being precipitous." He shook his head. "I can't believe I actually let myself be disturbed over it. Please forgive me, *jefe*."

Jefe. All right. He was acknowledging the power structure again.

"No problem." Alex drew on the cigar again. "I will be meeting with Antonio next week, at his *finca*. On Monday, as a matter of fact. All the paperwork is ready, and we need to move forward. It would be good if you joined us. Perhaps he can allay your fears even more."

Alex did not miss the flash of panic in the other man's eyes. He knew Cerda was trying to decide whether he was going to a business meeting or his own execution.

"Yes." He nodded. "It would be good to begin implementing the structure. I will gather all the information on foreign exchange to bring with me, as well as companies that we will want to, shall we say, acquire."

"Excellent. The meeting will be on Monday. I will have a car pick you up and bring you to my place. As you know, I keep my plane on my own property. Much more convenient. Shall we say nine in the morning?"

"Yes. That works." Cerda rose and extended a hand. "I apologize for my moment of panic and look forward to further ventures. We have, after all, been together for many years."

Alex shook the proffered hand. "Of course. I expect this to be a productive meeting as we finalize our plans to move forward."

He remained standing while Cerda walked out of the lounge toward the elevator that would take him to the street level lobby. When he was sure the man was gone, he sat down and took out his cell, selecting one of the numbers he had on speed dial.

"You were right," he said when the call was answered. "He's getting itchy and greedy. It just goes to prove no matter how rich you make someone, they always want more."

"It saddens me to be correct," his brother said. "Is he coming to the meeting?"

"Yes. He is." The answering sigh echoed across the connection.

"All right, then. We will take care of the problem. I will handle it. I take responsibility for bringing him into the organization."

"The responsibility belongs to both of us," his brother told him. "And we will both correct the problem."

He signaled a waiter to bring him a fresh drink and took another draw on his cigar. *Why is it some people just have to find a way to fuck up a good situation?*

Alex continued to sit there, smoking his cigar and taking slow sips of his fresh drink. Betrayal was a greater sin than almost anything else, to Alex's way of thinking. It was the ultimate offense someone could commit. Loyalty was rewarded while traitors never saw the light of day again. He saw Bruno Cerda's request as another form of betrayal, no better than whoever was planning to tell all their secrets.

It frustrated him that no matter how he tried, he could not find out who it was. They certainly paid off enough people in the right places to keep them informed of things. If not for the person on their payroll who worked for Dana Roberts' employer, for example, they might not even have known about her focus on the cartel until it was too late.

And their well-paid informant at the DEA had given them the head's-up that put their project into overdrive. Somehow the DEA had gathered information—or stumbled onto it—about their new plans, and their informant had made them aware of how critical the situation had become. Far from having the weeks they needed to put their plan in place effectively, they had days, and he didn't know how many of those. How had years and months of building and weeks of careful planning gotten so fucked up? *Does that attorney in Reed Calhoun's office play a part in this?* To him she was just a nonentity who did the legal grunt work.

But he didn't think whoever Dana Roberts was talking to was either of those people. So who in the fucking hell was it? It had to be someone high enough up to have information worth all the trouble the woman was going to. Was it Bruno Cerda? It didn't seem logical for him to run his mouth before he found out if he was getting a bigger slice of the pie. Things were falling apart and he had to plug the cracks pronto.

Generations had built the organization—he preferred that word to cartel—with great success. This new intricate expansion with diversification would solidify them along with millions of dollars—no, billions—well into the future. Only three things could rock that boat—the fucking reporter, Cerda and the unknown traitor.

He'd take care of them and things would proceed as planned.

Resting his cigar in the ash tray at his elbow, he punched in a single number.

"The reporter is our top priority. Find her—I don't care how—and follow her to her meeting with the traitor. Eliminate her and dispose of the body. Bring the traitor to me. And do it quickly, *amigo*. We are at a crisis point."

He listened to the response.

"If it was easy, I wouldn't need you to take care of it. Keep me updated."

Disconnecting, he sat back in his chair. Usually he was a patient person. That was how he and his family had amassed their billions. But the time for patience had passed. Now what he needed was action, and quickly.

* * * *

Kenzi closed her eyes and let the water from the rain shower head spray her body. She hoped it would wash away not only the fatigue that had suddenly gripped her but also the tension of the brief encounter with Alex Reyes. Did he suspect that she knew something? Was that why he'd asked to see her? She'd felt his eyes boring right through her, even with that polite smile on his face.

According to Slade's source, the DEA had its eye on the cartel and was watching the whole process. She just wished they'd get busy, sweep up the leaders and shut the damn thing down. Then she could draw a full breath, both for herself and Dana.

She was standing there, eyes closed, enjoying the heat of the water, when she heard the door to the shower open. In a moment she felt Trey's hands on her shoulders and his wonderful, familiar scent drifting across her nostrils.

"You doing okay?"

His husky voice echoed through her, an aphrodisiac to her tense body. The little bite on her earlobe wasn't bad, either. His strong fingers massaged her shoulders as he slid his mouth along the side of her neck and moved his mouth to nibble on the other ear.

"Better now," she murmured, pressing back against him.

She loved the hard, lean feel of him, the flat abs and corded muscles. He moved his hips and the swollen length of his cock prodded at the cleft of her ass. Dark heat coursed through her at the touch and she couldn't stop the hum of pleasure that vibrated in her throat.

"Every time I touch you," he said, his voice a sexy rumble, "I want to suck your nipples and squeeze your breasts, run my hands over every place on your body. Feel you here…" He slid his hands over the curve of her hips and the swell of her abdomen. "And here…" He eased them together so he was cupping her sex, his thumbs and forefingers squeezing the wet lips. "And especially here."

He eased his hand back, away from her pussy, over the curve of her buttocks until he found that cleft again. He drifted his fingers into that hot crevice for a few seconds before easing them back.

"Oh!" She pushed against him, but he'd moved his hands again by that time. Now he wasn't touching her at all, and she moaned in protest.

The rumble of his laugh was low and rough and sexy, and vibrated through every nerve and muscle in her body.

"You want my cock here, sugar?"

She closed her eyes and nodded, trying to clench the cheeks of her ass around him.

"Patience. All good things come to those who wait. Just keep your eyes closed."

That was no problem. It magnified every sensation and allowed her to linger in a state of anticipation and arousal. Of course, she felt that way whenever they were together. More than any man she'd ever met, Trey McIntyre pushed every erotic button in her body and made her want an abundance of everything. Made her want things she'd never desired with anyone else, things so intimate she blushed when she thought of them, and she was far from a sexual novice.

She sensed him moving behind her, and in the next moment he lifted her hands and placed them ahead of her on the shower wall. He trailed the tips of his fingers along her arms and down her sides, reaching around to give her nipples a gentle pinch before taking a step back. In the next moment his hands, coated with the scented body wash she used, spread the lather slowly over her body. Shoulders. Arms. Sides. Then gone, and she wanted to protest the loss of his touch.

But then he was back, this time reaching around to her front to cup her breasts and give them a gentle squeeze. His fingers worked her nipples, lightly pinching them and teasing them with his nails. Every touch sent an arrow of heat straight to her core, setting her inner muscle flexing, seeking something solid to grip and milk.

With the next application of lather, he slid his fingers down her belly, over her mound and between the lips of her pussy, stroking the slippery flesh. With each movement of his fingers he paused long enough to pinch her now throbbing clit. Then he moved his hands away and began the journey again.

By the time he'd covered every inch of her front with the scented liquid, she was a quivering mass. Her nerves felt as if someone had set a match to them and the walls of her sex begged for something to fill the greedy space there. The little nip at the base of her neck didn't help, either, lighting any nerves that might still be sleeping. Then he cast his hand over her again, slowly, from neck to thigh and everything in between, fraying her control.

She waited, biting her lip to maintain some semblance of control and not start begging him to slide his fingers or his tongue or his cock into her. But rather than turning her around, he began massaging the body wash into her shoulders and down her spine. His big hands smoothed it over the curves of her ass, squeezing gently and kneading them. The feel of his hands sliding between her thighs made her even hotter, and she couldn't contain the moan that slid from her mouth.

"Please," she begged. "Oh, please."

That low, rough, sexy laugh vibrated through her again.

"Please what?"

"Anything. Everything. Something."

She was so aroused by this time that she didn't care what he did as long as she could fall into her orgasm. She wanted to cry in frustration when he removed his touch from her body. Then his hands were back, and this time he slipped the fingers of one, slick with body wash, into the cleft of her buttocks. The tip of one pressed against the opening there and her entire body clenched.

"Like that, do you?" He whispered the words into her ear.

"Yesssss." She tried to push back against his touch, but with his other arm banded around her waist, he held her in place.

"Don't. Move." He bit her earlobe. "Do not move."

She drew in a deep breath and forced herself to remain still as he eased one long finger into her body, moving slowly until he had intruded all the way to the knuckle.

Oh!

Sensations chased through her, so intense she found it hard to remain standing. Trey worked his finger slowly in and out, taking his time, getting her used to the feel of him. Then he added a second finger, stretching her inner tissues and scraping back and forth until she was nearly out of her mind with sensation. She wanted to come so badly, but he kept her teetering on the edge. She couldn't even squeeze her thighs together because he was using his leg to keep them apart.

"Please," she begged again. "Please, please, please."

"Please what?" he whispered. "Please let you come?"

"Yes."

He kept moving his fingers and she was sobbing with need.

"Well, why didn't you say so?"

With his other hand he reached around, found her clit and began stroking it in coordinated rhythm. Kenzi rocked as much as she could, scraping herself along his touch in both places. When she was about to lose her mind, he thrust his fingers into her anus and pinched her clit, hard.

And she exploded, her body shivering and shaking and her inner muscles spasming so hard she thought she might shake herself apart. She was still coming when he turned her around and lifted her, thrusting his cock deep into her pussy. She vaguely was aware that his cock was sheathed in a condom and she wondered if he'd had it on all this time.

Then her brain disconnected as he drove into her over and over, so hard the tip of his cock bumped the mouth of her womb. Her muscles clenched his shaft, milking him, and she wound her legs around him, digging her heels into the small of his back to keep them sealed together.

She collapsed against him, held in place by her legs, and her arms around his neck. Her heart still pounded with a furious rhythm and her breathing was ragged and uneven.

Then, at last, it was finished. She leaned into him, weak as a piece of tissue paper, resting her head on his shoulder, and stayed that way for a long time.

"That take the edge off things?" he murmured.

She let out a long sigh. "More than. I don't know how you're still upright," she said with a tiny grin. "I'm not sure I can even stand."

He chuckled. "Then I think we should get you lying down right away."

Somehow, being firm and gentle at the same time, he managed to get them both cleaned up, rinsed off and dried, even helping her blow-dry her hair. Then he carried her into the bedroom, pulled back the covers and slid her into bed. The kiss he placed on her lips was so soft and tender it nearly made her cry.

"Aren't you lying down with me?"

"Not yet. Besides," he teased, "I think after that I need to feed the inner man. Don't tell me you're not hungry. Just a little bit?"

As if in response, a soft rumble sounded in her stomach. The heat crept up her cheeks.

"I guess I am."

"Close your eyes for a few minutes. I'm going to check in with Slade and order some dinner. Cooking isn't on the agenda for tonight. And I picked up a bottle of some really fine bourbon today. I don't think wine will do it after the day you've had. Sound good?"

"Mmm. Sounds wonderful."

"Okay. Take one of your quickie naps and I'll be right back."

Kenzi did as he suggested, lying there, enjoying the feeling of being well and truly fucked and trying to push everything out of her mind. She was halfway between wakefulness and sleep when Trey came back into the room.

"Dinner will be here in thirty. Meanwhile, come on and get up. I'm pouring drinks. After what Slade told me I think we'll both need them."

Chapter Sixteen

Mierda! Hijo di puta! La madre que to pario!
Damn it all to hell, anyway.

Alex Reyes slammed his cell phone down on his desk. Things were unraveling so fast. How the hell had this happened? He'd planned carefully, covered all the details, made sure to cross every T and dot every I. That was his trademark, his and Antonio's. Always had been. And now, because of some stupid bitch of a reporter and an unknown traitor, decades of careful planning were in danger of coming undone.

The plan itself was excellent. They had worked on it for months, making sure all the necessary components would be in place. Doing the research. Working hard to stay ahead of the bubble. And now, suddenly, it was all falling apart.

He was not a man given to pacing or showing agitation in any way. He had built a solid reputation as a self-contained, uber-wealthy rancher and. businessman, the third generation to hold this position.

He took pride in being able to control his environment so that image never shattered. Now, people he didn't even know, people he should have been able to crush like bugs, were tearing down his structure and destroying his respectability.

He had barely pulled himself together after his meeting with Bruno Cerda and returned home where more disaster had loomed. The phone call he'd just received was the latest in a series of catastrophies that never should have taken place. At his meeting with Reed Calhoun today, they had agreed the urgency of the situation called for them to move forward with filing all the paperwork immediately. Although he and Antonio would still meet on Monday, Reed had faxed everything to him to review so the process could begin tomorrow.

On Monday they would deal with Bruno, another unpleasant matter.

But the telephone call he had just received from one of his paid informants had placed an even greater urgency on the situation. He needed to discuss with Reed the best way to prevent the DEA from raiding their offices and confiscating all files related to him and every one of his businesses, especially the new corporate structure he'd just signed off on. For whatever reason, the DEA was upping their timetable.

Reed had told him he'd be at the courthouse himself taking care of what had to be done today and tomorrow. He needed those new entities in place as quickly as possible. Was it possible that once the new structure was legally in place they would be out of reach of the DEA, or did they run the risk of them shutting everything down? How fast could they move in foreign countries? Didn't they have to reach out to other agencies to do that? Reed would know. He knew all of that. He'd be able to tell him how to proceed. Only, at the moment, Reed Calhoun was tied up at dinner with another client and, as was his habit, he had his phone shut off.

Then there was the junior attorney who had worked on this project with Reed. How much did Kenzi Bryant actually know about the projects she worked on? Reed would never have told her the real purpose behind this complicated structure, yet Alex's sixth sense told him there was something going on there. No way could she have discovered anything, but he couldn't take a chance.

He picked up the half-empty glass of bourbon he'd been drinking and took a healthy swallow.

Careful, Alex. This is no time to get drunk.

If someone didn't call back shortly with answers to at least one of his problems, he might actually resort to that.

He started at the sound of a knock on the door to his den.

"Yes? Come in."

The door opened and his wife, Mercedes, entered. He took a moment to enjoy the sight of her. At fifty-five she was as beautiful as the day he'd met her, but richer-looking, more mature. Ebony hair that curled softly around her face showed little grey and her skin was as smooth as the girl he'd married, thanks to the expensive spa she visited regularly. Her work with her personal trainer kept her figure trim and athletic, yet without losing the soft curves he loved so much.

Sometimes he was swept up by the nostalgia of their early days, when he had just moved into his role in all the family businesses, when the sex had been hot, when their life together had been exciting. When the children had come along, she'd stepped into the role of mother as if she'd been born to it. And although she was aware of his cartel activities — her father had been one of his business associates — he was careful to keep everything isolated from *la familia*. No meetings at the house and Hector did all the dirty work. That was the arrangement and had been throughout their families for generations.

Their marriage had continued to be successful as the years passed. He was not like others in his position who disrespected their wives by taking other sexual partners. He remembered all the special occasions and always had unique gifts for her birthday. The children had grown older and gone off to college. Alicia now worked for a marketing firm, her activities as far from the cartel as it was possible to get. And Sebastian was…was where it had all started to come apart.

At last Mercedes had come to fully understand and accept the situation, and for the most part, things had returned to the way they had been. They could have been any happy, well-to-do couple in the world. *Almost.* There was still a fine edge to her, a slight distance, but then he wondered if he was just imagining it. Maybe when they got the new structure off the ground, he would take her on a trip to Europe, or a cruise. Something to smooth out the wrinkles and be sure everything between them had returned to the way it should be.

In the meantime, he had taken steps to reassure himself that she had not quietly gone off the rails. If she ever found out… But no, there was no reason for him to check anything on her phone or her car. She trusted him completely, a fact that gave him a twinge now and then. But then he'd remind himself of everything that was at stake — and hope it didn't blow up in his face along with everything else.

"I am sorry to disturb you," she said in her soft, musical voice. "I just wanted to remind you that we are meeting the Mannions for dinner in an hour." She studied him carefully with her deep violet eyes. "Alex, if you need to take care of business, I can call them and reschedule. That won't be a problem."

He managed to find a smile for her and felt himself relax just a fraction. If only this could be the tenor of their lives all the time. If only —

"No, it will be fine. I may have to excuse myself to take some calls during the meal, but I will make it quick."

"You do what you have to." She studied him for a moment. "Is everything all right? You seem stressed lately."

Was it that noticeable? If he was going to pull this off, he had to appear as if nothing was wrong.

"No. It's all good. Just a glitch with a new contract. I'll be ready to leave on time."

"Very well. I'll go and get changed."

The moment the door closed, his phone rang again. He hoped that this call brought him good news for a change.

"Please tell me you have something positive to tell me," he said, forgoing any salutation.

"The best I can tell you," Hector Lopez Garcia told him, "is that we are getting closer. I want to find these people as much as you do, believe me, but locating them is not easy. They are trained to be invisible."

"I don't care. We are approaching disaster here. Find them. Find the reporter. And find the fucking traitor."

"You know the best way to do the last item is to find the reporter and trail her," Lopez Garcia pointed out.

"That's supposed to be your specialty, so do it. I have too much to lose here."

"As do I," Garcia pointed out. "And Antonio as well."

"Then find them, or all this work will have been for nothing."

He disconnected and barely restrained himself from throwing the phone across the room. Exhaling a settling breath, he punched in the speed dial number for Reed Calhoun. Voicemail again. *Of course.*

"Call me. We are at a crisis point."

He finished his drink and carried the glass into the kitchen. Time to shower and change and put on his game face. Paulo Mannion was a powerful figure in the state cattleman's association, paving the way for certain changes Alex had needed over the years. This was no time to offend anyone or alienate them. Not when he had no idea what the next day would bring.

And that reminded him to call his son later tonight. Another situation he needed to be sure was safely in place.

* * * *

Trey looked around the table at the people assembled—his teammates, plus their women, plus Dana Roberts. Slade had called them the moment he'd hung up from his call with his commanding officer. With Trey's situation in crisis, none of them wanted to pack their gear and head off to the jungle or the desert or wherever they were being sent this time. Ninety-nine percent of the time, he loved Delta Force and its core mission. This was in the one percent that he didn't.

The moment Slade had called, he'd cancelled their dinner order, they'd thrown on their clothes and hauled ass to the ranch. Now they sat around Slade's big dining table eating pizza, absorbing his news and dissecting the situation. Dana sat between Brock and Axel, tension lining her face. No one looked happy. Beside him, Trey could practically feel the tension vibrating from Kenzi's body as Slade relayed the information from his captain that they'd be reporting in the morning, earlier than expected, for a mission that had come up out of the blue.

"I called the others with the news," Slade told everyone, "but I didn't see any need for them to haul ass out here tonight. Better they have one more night with their ladies and be here first thing in the morning. I tried to push things back a couple of days, but the captain said time is of the essence with this one. Orders came down from JSOC, so that's that."

Trey couldn't argue with that, damn it. They all knew no one never argued with JSOC—Joint Special Operations Command, the planning and oversight of certain Special Forces units and their missions.

"They sure couldn't have picked a worse time." Trey raked a hand through his hair.

"I don't think there's ever a good time," Kari Donovan pointed out. "If there was, they wouldn't need you. Right?"

"The thing is," Slade went on, "We've only got a few hours to put the backup plan in place. I called Mike Elliott and he and his agency are on board with this. In fact, he should be here any time now to meet you all and get briefed."

"I know he's good and all," Trey said in a tight voice, "except his guys aren't us."

"But they're the next best thing," Slade reminded him. He looked at Dana. "Your safety is a high priority here. We don't want to see you kidnapped again, or worse, lying dead someplace. You get that, right?"

"I do." Dana nodded. "I'm sorry if I've seemed ungrateful. I'm just not used to having so many people crowding my space. And however you handle this, my source can't know I've got an army hanging out, waiting to drag me away."

"That's not a problem. These guys are way better than good."

"I'm surprised he or she wants to meet in broad daylight." Trey shook his head. "Don't people like this usually want to do this when it's dark out and detection isn't so easy?"

"Apparently whoever it is can only meet during the day." She shrugged. "The original meet we had set for the evening was apparently an anomaly. I can't tell you any more than that."

Slade opened his mouth to say something but stopped when they heard a knock on the front door.

"I'll get it," Teo called from the kitchen.

Two minutes later two men were ushered into the room, one tall and muscular, with dark hair and a scruff beard, the other lean with slightly long blond hair. Trey thought they both looked as if they ate nails for breakfast and could take down a roomful of bad guys without breaking a sweat. If these were the men who would be protecting Kenzi and Dana, the tension in his body eased just a hair.

Slade rose from his chair and shook hands with them.

"Thanks for coming." He turned to everyone at the table. "Meet Mike Elliott, who runs the best damn security agency in twenty-five states."

The tall, dark-haired man laughed. "Just twenty-five? I must be losing my touch. But thanks. This is Jay Cooper, my senior agent."

Mike glanced at Slade. "Have you briefed everyone on our creds or do you want me to do that?"

"You're good. Everyone but Brock and Axel remembers you from the last time you helped us, so we're all set."

"Then how about filling in the details for us so we can put some plans together? And when do you leave?"

"Tomorrow morning. Teo will fly us to the base. We have to be there by oh-eight-hundred."

Trey reached for Kenzi's hand under the table and gave it a gentle squeeze. She linked her fingers through his and squeezed back. The last thing he wanted to do was leave her right now and, for the first time in his life, he wanted to let a woman know he was there for her. Maybe he could get Mike to convince her, where he couldn't, that she should take sick leave from the law firm until this all got resolved. They had no idea how involved Reed Calhoun was in Alex Reyes' cartel business or if he even knew about it. But if the shit was going to hit the fan, he didn't want her to be in the line of fire.

Teo brought two carafes of coffee to the table and set them on hot pads.

"Holler if you need more," he told them before making himself scarce.

"Okay." Mike Elliott hitched his chair forward. "Slade, you gave me a basic outline here, and of course I know all about the fiasco at the hangar and the dead bodyguards in New York. Let's have the rest of the details."

It took the better part of a half hour to get all the details out there and give Mike and Jay a complete picture. Slade also passed along all the information from Joe Trainor.

"The DEA is getting ready to drop the hammer on Reyes," he added. "We need to make sure these two women are protected. Kenzi, I really think you ought to call in sick to your office. Get yourself out of the line of fire. Trust me. you don't want to be there when it happens."

"Amen to that." Trey slid a glance at the woman next to him. "I know you think it might cause some kind of problem, but don't people at that firm ever take sick days?"

Next to him, Kenzi let out a sigh. "Yes, they do, and I know you're right. Slade. Did Detective Trainor tell you when this was going to happen?"

"Not the exact day, but the last word I had with him was sometime this week. Maybe in the next couple of days. And you need to be somewhere safe."

"You need to stay here with your sister." What Trey really wished for was the ability to lock her down until this was all over. Part of Kenzi's appeal was her independence and her insistence on not leaning on anyone, but sometimes that could also be a detriment.

"I'll consider it. But let's talk about how the meeting tomorrow is going to be handled."

Mike Elliot cleared his throat. "Dana, you're meeting this person tomorrow at noon, right?"

Dana nodded. "Yes. I'm surprised it's not a night meeting again, but I have to go with whatever I'm handed."

"Okay. Exactly where is this supposed to take place?"

At that moment Dana's phone buzzed and she looked at the screen.

"Hold on. This is a text from my informant. Well, at least I can be pretty sure now it's a woman."

"Why?" The question came from Slade.

"Because of where the meeting is." Dana nibbled on her bottom lip for a moment. "At a spa in Northwest San Antonio. Tomorrow at two o'clock."

"A spa?" Trey's eyebrows lifted. "So, this person is a woman? And why didn't you say so before? It might have helped narrow down who it is."

"I only knew for sure right now when she texted me the location. Although — and don't ask me why — I've thought so from the beginning. And, of course, a man would not be able to meet me in a spa."

"Then let's make our plan." Mike took out his own cell. "Let me pull up a picture of the place and we'll figure the best way to do this."

"I don't —" She squirmed in her chair. "I'm afraid if I show up with an army, I'll scare this person off. I hated it when my bosses hired them in New York and I'm not too happy with the situation here. I'm just meeting one person. I'll get my interview and get the hell out of there."

"Dana." Kenzi leaned forward. "Even I know you can't do this without protection. Please be smart about this."

"Having bodyguards didn't help before," she pointed out. "Maybe if you and your guys hadn't shown up, the meeting would have happened, and I'd be writing my story. Now."

"Are you nuts?" Trey exploded. "If we hadn't shown up there, they'd have hidden you away until it was time for the meeting, taken you there so they could find out who the snitch is and killed both of you. Have you forgotten your real bodyguards were killed? And, by the way, the cartel replacements had identification that looked so authentic it fooled you and others. Your meeting might have happened, but you'd both be dead."

Beside him, Trey sensed the tension in Kenzi and heard her slightly indrawn breath. He kept his eyes on Dana, knowing that somehow whatever she did was going to involve her sister. Her skin paled and for a moment she said nothing.

"Look." Kenzi sighed. "I know this is your very big deal and I get how important the meeting is to you. But let's go back to what triggered all this security. You were kidnapped. *Kidnapped*, Dana."

"I hear you," Dana told her.

Trey watched the woman, studying her reaction, deciding Kenzi was right. Whatever she said now was probably masked whatever was going on in her mind. How could one person be so foolhardy and gamble like this with her life?

Mike Elliot tapped the screen of his phone to bring up Notes. "Fine. It is what it is. The problem with the spa is, Jay and I will not be able to go inside. Most spas have a hard and fast No Men rule."

Kenzi looked around the table. "She'll be safe inside. I've been there a few times when I wanted to give myself a real treat. No one can sneak in, the way it's laid out, and a man would stick out like a sore thumb."

"We need to be ready and available," Mike insisted. "Jay and I will scope out the place tonight and put some plans together. We'll figure it out." He nodded at Slade. "It's what we do. You know that."

Trey was well aware that none of them were happy with the situation, but short of chaining her to a piece of furniture, there was no stopping Dana from doing what she wanted. Mike and Jay would just have to figure the best way to handle it. And that was something they were very good at.

He was about to refill his coffee mug when Kenzi spoke up and he nearly dropped the crockery.

"Okay, Here's my two cents. I'm going with my sister." *Not a question. A statement.*

Trey nearly choked on his own hot drink. "The fuck you are. I'm not letting you put your life in danger."

"Oh?" Kenzi glared at each of the men. "You're not letting me? Is that what you said?"

Trey swallowed a sigh along with his irritation. "Perhaps I phrased that incorrectly. It would be foolhardy for you to walk into this when there's no need for it."

"The need is for me to be with my sister," she snapped. "Besides, I won't raise any eyebrows. I'll just be a woman arriving for her appointment. The text to Dana said someone at the front desk would give her further instructions. And obviously we'll be well protected."

They all exchanged angry glances, but at last Trey nodded.

"Fine. But you do exactly what Mike and Jay tell you. Understood?"

He could tell she wanted to smack him, but instead she huffed a sigh. "Understood."

"Okay." He looked at Dana then at Mike. "Let's make some plans."

* * * *

It was late by the time they left the ranch. The drive into the city was accomplished for the most part in silence. When they walked into her little foyer, he dropped the keys on the tiny table there, grabbed her and pulled her up to his body.

"I know you're probably pissed at me right now," he ground out, "but my only concern is for your safety. I'm heading out of here in the morning to who the fuck knows what kind of mess, and I need to know you'll be okay. Can you please understand that?"

For a moment she stood there, stiff in his grip, eyes flashing. Then she nodded and the tension in both their bodies eased.

"I don't want you to go off on a mission with your brain tangled up because you think I might do something stupid. I'll call in sick tomorrow, if you think I should. And I guess I don't want to be there when the DEA comes swooping into the office." She frowned. "I wish I knew which day they were planning to move on this."

"All Joe Trainor told Slade was it would be this week. They got a judge to sign the court orders in secret so they could keep it hush-hush."

Kenzi shook her head. "That's going to be a huge shock for Reed Calhoun, not to mention his partners."

"Do you think he knows what Alex is really up to?"

She shrugged. "I have no idea. I'd like to think not, but anything is possible. I know Alex Reyes was the firm's first big client and opened the door to a lot of others. They've accumulated quite a client list in fifteen years."

"I want you to promise you'll call in the morning and tell them you need a few days off. Calhoun shouldn't give you any hassle after all the hours you just put in."

She laughed. "That's the life of an attorney. If you plan on hanging around with me, you'd better get used to it."

He stood there, suddenly frozen in place. "Am I?"

She quirked an eyebrow. "Are you what?"

"Planning on hanging around?"

The grin disappeared and she stared hard into his eyes. "I think that's a question for you to answer, not me. Don't you think?"

"Let's not play games, Kenzi." He pulled her close to him so their bodies were pressed together. "We both know that despite how lightly this started out, how casual, something has changed. Right?"

He didn't ever remember being so uptight waiting for a woman to answer a question. Where had the old love 'em and leave 'em Trey disappeared to? It suddenly hit him with the force of a sledgehammer that for the first time in forever, he'd met a woman who he did not want to walk away from. But did she want more?

She wet her lips as she stared into his eyes. He saw such a mass of emotions whirling there that for a moment, he was afraid she was going to walk away from him.

"I—" She stopped, swallowed, started again. "My rule has always been to keep it casual. Except..."

"Except?" he prompted.

"Except this time something happened, and..." She took a deep breath. "...I don't want it to end."

He blew out a breath. "Thank god. Because I don't want that either." He slid his palms up to cradle her face. "I don't know how good I'll be at this relationship business, Kenzi. It's never been on my to-do list. But I want to make it happen with you."

"Me, too," she whispered.

"Then let's go to bed and seal the deal. Morning's gonna be here way too fast."

Chapter Seventeen

By the time he'd reached Reed Calhoun the night before, Alex Reyes had been ready to jump out of his skin. His source in the DEA's office had called again to let him know the Feds had received signed court orders to raid the offices of Byrnes, Calhoun and Raven within the next forty-eight hours and to confiscate all Reed's files. And not just the ones to do with Reyes' business.

'They want to see if Calhoun does legal work for anyone else in the cartel that's connected to you.'

'How the fuck did they even get onto this?' Reyes had barked. *'We've been well covered for years.'*

'Just like you have a spy, Señor *Reyes, so do they. It's the way the game is played.'*

'This is not a game,' he'd snapped. *'An entire empire could crumble because of this.'*

'Then you'd better cover your ass. And be sure to deposit my latest stipend in the account.'

He'd slept very little, rising finally at five o'clock and spending an hour in his home gym. At fifty-five, he was proud of the condition he kept himself in. He just hoped nothing was going to happen to alter that.

Reed had done his best to explain why it would be impossible to just destroy all the records and files. For one thing, his partners had no idea that the law firm had been funded with drug money or that Alex was one third of the triumvirate that ruled the Lopez Garcia cartel. For another, if indeed this all went down the toilet, he was going to do his best to distance himself from the whole mess and claim he thought he was handling legal work for straight business deals.

He would give his left nut to find out who had sicced the DEA onto him and who was trying to bring him down. It couldn't be Bruno Cerda. The man had made his pitch and would wait at least until after the meeting Monday to do anything. His greed would prevent him from taking revenge until he knew exactly what the score was.

For a moment the image of Kenzi Bryant, the associate in Reed Calhoun's office, popped into his head. No, now he was reaching. But there was something off about her. She had worked on other projects with Reed before, but it seemed there was something about this one that had made her uneasy, and he had no idea why. He'd had her investigated thoroughly, going around Reed so he didn't have to have a confrontation over it, but nothing had turned up.

So who the hell is it?

And damn it all to hell. There was still no sign of the fucking reporter. How did someone like her just disappear off the face of the earth? What was she doing with the members of the Delta Force team that had raided Hector's *finca* and killed so many of his men while rescuing her? And how the hell could he find out their names and where they lived? Even his best sources couldn't get him wat he wanted, telling him definitively the government kept that information secret.

He wasn't hungry for breakfast, but he could use a good cup of coffee. Ana, their live-in housekeeper, should be up by now and hustling around the kitchen.

"*Buenos Dias, Señor* Reyes." She turned and smiled at him when he walked in. "Coffee will be ready in a moment."

"Excellent. Thank you."

He sat at one of the bar stools at the island counter to wait, taking out his phone to check for messages. There was one from a number he did not recognize, so he debated with himself before opening it. He didn't want to infect the cell with a virus, or plant some kind of program that would allow the DEA or anyone else to access his phone. And there was no name attached to it, only a number.

Finally, deciding these days he needed any bit of information he could get, he opened the email. And almost dropped the phone.

Señor *Reyes, my name is Marc Phillips. A friend of yours who met with an accident gave me this number. He said if I ever provided you with any information, you would remember me if I ever needed anything. Now I need protection from the DEA who is investigating everything that took place that day. What I need is a way out of this country and a place to hide. Attached are photos I took at the hangar where two men were shot. I'm sure you know where. One is the reporter I transported. The other is her sister. I am sending them in good faith. Let me know if this helps you and you are willing to reciprocate.*

Jesús, María y José.

Shock gripped his body, followed by a surge of anger. *Of course.* He had sensed something, and he was seldom wrong. One of the women was, indeed, Dana Roberts, the fucking bitch who had dropped off the face of the earth. He was about to call Hector and tell him to offer a bonus to the first man who located her.

The other was the real bombshell, although it reinforced his belief in his internal antenna. Slightly turned away from the camera was Kenzi Bryant, the associate he'd worked with at Reed Calhoun's offices. And she was Roberts' sister? *Goddamn it all to fucking hell anyway.* He'd been right when he'd sensed something off there. He was cursed, that was it.

He closed his eyes for a moment, drew in a deep breath and pulled himself together. It would not do for the man many referred to as the Iceman to turn into a raving maniac.

"Ana, please bring my coffee to my office. I have some work to do."

"*Si, Señor* Reyes."

Once at his desk, he settled himself and took a minute to collect his scattered thoughts again. First, he contacted one of his lieutenants, gave him the pilot's cell number and told him to get the man out of the country. The he called Hector, who was anything but pleased to be roused at this hour of the morning.

"Do you know what fucking time it is?" he griped into the phone.

"Time for us to take care of business," he told him, "or we won't have any to take care of. I am texting you a picture. One of the women is that bitch reporter. The other is an associate from my attorney's office who is either a relative or a very close friend." He explained about the text from the pilot. "I am offering a one-hundred-thousand-dollar bonus to the man who finds them and kills them."

"*Jesucristo!*" Hector whistled. "That much?"

"Hector, we have very little time to find them and get rid of them. The DEA is poised to raid my attorney's office and the last thing I want is for these two women to talk to them. I think Reed Calhoun and I can deal with the DEA, but those women are a stick of dynamite. Someone is snitching on us and we need to clean this up before whoever it is meets with the reporter."

"Are you sure that hasn't already happened?"

"Yes. Because if it had, I'd be in federal custody instead of in my office at home. Now get busy and put the word out. I'm calling my attorney to take care of things on this end. You find that damn fucking reporter and take care of her once and for all."

He barely restrained himself from slamming the phone on his desk. Only the knock on the door stopped him.

"Come in," he called out.

"Your coffee, *Señor* Reyes." Ana stepped into the room and carried a tray with his coffee and two small warm pastries to his desk.

"*Gracias.*"

Without being told, she closed the door on her way out. Alex took a sip of the hot coffee, savoring the smooth bite of it on his tongue and the flow of heat through his veins, blunting the sharp edge of his nerves. Another sip. And after the third had gone down smoothly, he texted the photo to Hector. Then he answered the pilot's email and told him someone would contact him to be sure he was properly rewarded. At the moment, Alex wasn't sure if he was going to pay him or have Hector eliminate him. If the bastard had sent the photo the day it was taken, a lot of things might be different.

That done, he punched a speed dial number on his phone for Reed Calhoun's private cell.

"Jesus Christ, Alex," Calhoun swore. "It's not even seven o'clock."

"I'm calling to make sure you're moving the file to a secure location before the Feds show up, and that you have everything stashed somewhere to pull it up when this dies down."

"It's taken care of. I worked late last night and, no, no one suspected because I often work late hours."

"Excellent."

"I can't believe that's all you called about, so what now?"

"What now is the fact that your charming and diligent associate Kenzi Bryant has some sort of close relationship to our favorite bitch reporter, Dana Roberts."

Dead silence filled the air.

"Reed?" he prompted.

"Where did you get this information?" Reed asked in a tight voice.

Alex explained to him, giving him the circumstances in which the picture was taken.

More silence. Then—

"Fuck. Absolute fuck."

"My sentiments exactly. How likely is it that Dana Roberts, who is on a crusade to destroy the Lopez Garcia cartel, your associate, two of the Delta Force soldiers who rescued the reporter and killed more than a dozen cartel soldiers, are all in a hangar where two more cartel soldiers are taken down and it's all very innocent?"

"Please," Calhoun snorted. "I don't believe in fairy tales."

"It must be in her personnel files. How did you miss it?" Hector demanded.

"Do you think I read everyone's information?" he snapped. "I was only interested in her grades, her degree and her recommendations."

"We have to do something about her," Hector pointed out. "Call me when she gets into the office."

"What do you have in mind?" Calhoun's voice had a wary tone to it. "'Doing something about it' covers an entire spectrum."

"The first thing you have to do is assess whether something has triggered her suspicions." He took another swallow of coffee. "The fact that she knows this reporter and is apparently tight with the Delta Force soldiers makes all my antennae wiggle."

"I can tell you that in all the years she's been here I've never seen any sign of her digging into a client's situation on her own. Plus," he continued, "she's close to being offered a junior partnership. You can believe she's been carefully vetted for that."

"You and I both know," Alex reminded him, "what can be hidden beneath the surface. How would you feel if she managed to dig out the truth about the firm?"

"That won't happen," Reed snapped. "I can assure you of that."

"Be that as it may, today or tomorrow the Feds could descend and if she's there and has any suspicions at all…"

"She doesn't, she won't and if she did, she wouldn't say anything," Calhoun snapped. "I promise you that. And when she arrives, I'm going to have her turn in her office laptop and give her a new one. That way nothing will be hanging out there."

"Really?" Alex tried to hide the skepticism he was feeling. "Fine. I'll take care of things on my end. You'd better do the same."

Still, when he disconnected the call, the edgy feeling of unease still gripped him. One snap of the fingers and everything his family had worked for generations to build could come tumbling down.

On top of that, he had picked up some weird vibes from his wife recently. He could not put his finger on why. Nothing that came back to him showed her going anywhere except her usual places or speaking to anyone out of the ordinary. Maybe all this other business was triggering his receptors. Still…

He picked up his cell again and pressed another number on speed dial.

Ernesto, his head of security, picked up on the first ring. "*Hola*, boss. What's up?"

How to phrase this without giving away his underlying suspicions? No matter how much he trusted his men, he couldn't confide this in them. But fortunately, they knew the real nature of his operations, so he had a logical explanation.

"I am a little nervous about *Señora* Reyes traveling alone today. Some of my business associates have not been too happy lately with the results of our business deals. People get greedy and do unfortunate things. I'd feel better if you kept an eye on her today. You know how she hates to be crowded, though, so be discreet."

"Leave it to us, *Señor* Reyes. We will make sure she is safe, and she'll never know we are around."

"Thank you." He disconnected the call and raked his fingers through his hair. How the hell had all this happened—his carefully constructed façade falling apart, the cartel operation in danger and the niggling suspicions about his wife?

Fuck. Just plain, damn fuck.

Swallowing the last of the coffee, he brought his computer to life. Time to do something he should have done before—research Kenzi Bryant and who she really was.

* * * *

Kenzi rode to the ranch with Trey in the morning, aware of how uptight he was.

"You'd better take a deep breath, soldier," she told him, "or you'll fuck up your mission."

"Never. But I might fuck up this thing between us if I can't figure out how to keep you safe without pissing you off."

She laughed, and it eased the tension.

"You already know me so well." She squeezed his thigh. "Better than any other man, for sure."

"And it's going to stay that way. Count on it."

"I will. I do. You stay safe and everything will be fine. Do not let this distract you from what you have to do."

He lifted her hand and kissed her knuckles. "I'll be coming home to you safe and sound. You stay the same way."

"Promise. I'm going to do my best. Any word on when you'll be back?"

"Slade said the estimate on this mission is five days. We've got good intel. Get in, do our thing and get out." He squeezed her hand. "I'll probably need a lot of special care when I get back," he teased.

"I think that can be arranged."

Fifteen minutes later, she stood with Dana, Kari, Nikki Alvarez—Marc Blanchard's fiancée—and Megan Welles—Beau Williams' fiancée—as they watched the helicopter take off to deliver the men back to base. She did her best to squelch the fear that lodged in her throat—fear for the safety of all of them, but especially for Trey.

Please just let him come back to me safe and sound.

She couldn't lose him just when she realized she'd unexpectedly found the right man for her.

Mike Williams came jogging out of the house. He and Jay had arrived at seven, about the same time as everyone not staying at the ranch.

"Ladies, there's coffee in the kitchen. Teo brewed a fresh pot before they left."

"I'll have another cup before I leave for work," Kari told him. "Then I have to get out of here. I have a court appearance today." She grinned. "High profile. Murder case. The second one I've tried as first chair."

"I bet you knock 'em dead," Nikki said.

"Let's hope."

Jay was on the phone at the kitchen table, with printouts of maps and diagram spread out in front of him.

"Yeah," he was saying, "just like that. Call me back when it's all set."

"When what's all set?" Dana asked.

Mike gestured to the table. "Let's sit down and I'll go over it with you."

She settled into one of the chairs. "You aren't going to fuck this up, are you?"

He grinned at her. "That is definitely not my plan."

"Listen, Dana." Beau pushed back from the table. "If you don't need us, Megan and I are heading out. I have to be at the hospital."

"And I have a deadline," Megan added. "Are you okay with us leaving?"

Dana nodded and reached over for Kenzi's hand. "No, that's fine. You don't need to be in this mess and, besides, I've got my pain-in-the-ass sister with me."

Kenzi actually smiled. "And you're not getting rid of me."

As soon as the two women had left, Mike sat down across from Dana and Kenzi.

"Time to get down to business. Kenzi, the first thing you need to do is call your office and get some sick leave."

She nodded, pulled out her cell and dialed the familiar number. Reed Calhoun was not in, making her wonder exactly where he was this early. She didn't remember him mentioning anything that he had specifically scheduled. She asked for his executive assistant and when the woman answered, did what she thought was a damn good job of impersonating someone with the flu.

"Okay," she told Mike after ending the call. "His exec told me not to come in until I got rid of all my germs, so we're good there. I just hope when the shit hits the fan, he doesn't wonder if my flu has anything to do with it."

"By that time, it won't matter," Mike told her. "And you might think about joining another law firm. We have no idea what all the fallout is going to be here or how high the corruption goes."

She dropped her head into her hands. "You're probably right. Damn."

"I'm sorry if my story is causing any of this," Dana told her.

"No worries." Kenzi looked up at her. "This whole DEA thing is independent of your story. They were already all over it."

Mike refilled his coffee mug. "Now. This spa is located in north San Antonio. We can take the road from the ranch to the Interstate and get off right near where the spa is located."

"Good." Dana nodded. "I was afraid it was in some isolated spot. Those always make me nervous."

Mike grinned. "Don't blame you. I've got some pictures here of the building, the parking lot and the surrounding area. Let's go over everything until it's etched in our brains. Stuff like where we can park to keep an eye on things."

Several times during the morning, Kenzi's phone dinged, first with incoming texts, then with phone calls.

"Don't answer it," Mike told her. "You've got a good excuse. You're sick."

"What if someone comes to check on me and I'm not home?"

"We'll worry about that if it happens. Meanwhile, ignore it."

By lunchtime, Kenzi was sure she had every inch of the area memorized. She'd called the spa and begged for an appointment around two o'clock. Lucky for all of them, they had a spot open. Dana wasn't at all happy with some of Mike Elliot's agents stationing themselves outside, but he'd ridden right over her objections.

"And I have to tell you, Kenzi," Mike said, "Trey would really rather you did not go at all."

"Too bad," she snapped. "I'm a big girl and I'm not a prisoner here. Unless you lock me up—which I really do not recommend—I'm going with my sister. Besides, I think we'll all feel better if she's not in there alone."

Mike threw up his hands. "Fine, but just remember, we'll be right outside and if anything smells weird, we won't wait for you to yell for help."

"This is a spa," Dana bit off. "Filled with women. Don't get your panties in a wad."

"You think women are safer than men?" Jay snorted. "Just look at yourself, Dana."

"Then there should be no worries about us going inside," she snapped.

Kenzi swallowed a laugh and turned away so the men wouldn't see her grin.

At the appointed time, she and Dana drove from the ranch to the spa in her car. Located outside the city in the Hill Country, it was a pretty stone and stucco building surrounded by a parking lot, and beautifully landscaped. It was obvious it catered to a certain class of women. She knew Mike and Jay were close behind her and Mike had managed to get a couple of men working on landscape maintenance around the little building. Kenzi hoped to hell they wouldn't need all that firepower. She wondered if the woman they were meeting was already here or was watching for them and waiting until they arrived. It was hard to tell from outside.

She parked at one end of the lot, as Mike had instructed, in case they needed to make a quick exit. *Does he think this woman has a gun? Or has armed people with her?* Anything was possible.

She pulled open the heavy carved wooden door and they stepped into a beautifully appointed lounge furnished with comfortable chairs and settees. Soft music played through hidden speakers and a credenza held coffee and fruit platters. A receptionist, immaculately dressed in slacks and a silk blouse, gave them a professional smile.

"May I help you?"

"Yes. My name is Dana Roberts. I'm meeting someone here who made this appointment for me. She told me to give you my name and you'd show me to the room where she's waiting."

"Of course. May I see some identification, please?"

"Yes." Dana took out her billfold and displayed her driver's license.

The woman and rose. "One moment, lease."

"Wait." Dana reached out a hand to stop her. "My sister is with me and she made an appointment for the same time. I'd love for her to join us. I was told some of the rooms can accommodate up to four people."

"Let me see your identification, also," she told Kenzi.

"Do you do this with all your clients?" Kenzi asked.

"Those who are here for the first time," the woman told her. "In this particular case, with this special client, extra precautions are always taken. Our client was very specific about the arrangements today. A room for the two of you. That's what she requested."

Dana chewed her bottom lip for a moment. Then she pulled a little notepad from her purse and scribbled something on it, folded it and thrust it at the receptionist.

"Here. Give her this and tell her I would not presume to include anyone who would make her uncomfortable."

The other woman hesitated. Finally, she nodded. "I just hope you aren't getting me in trouble."

They stood at the desk while the woman hurried into the actual salon portion of the spa.

"What did you say in the note?" Kenzi asked, curious, her voice low enough for just the two of them to hear.

"I told her if she needed protection you had the best connection to provide it," Dana whispered. "I said if she trusted me enough to meet me, she could trust my sister."

"We'll see."

When the receptionist reappeared, she seemed slightly disturbed and the smile on her face looked artificial.

"I am to bring you both back to the room," she reported, "but my client has warned me there may be a...dispute. You should know our clientele is comprised of extremely wealthy women who sometime acquire stalkers, so we have security on premises."

Kenzi opened her mouth to comment, but Dana took her hand and squeezed it, signaling her to keep quiet.

"That makes us feel secure also," she said. "Thank you."

From the reception area they were taken into a changing room and handed over to a smiling attendant. They were given lockers to hang their clothes in, and soft, fluffy robes to put on.

"Purses go in the lockers, too," the girl said. "I promise everything will be secure."

When they had stashed everything, they were given wristlets with a key dangling from each one. But Kenzi noticed that Dana, when she was putting things inside the locker, managed to sneak something into her pockets. She'd have bet a month's salary it was a voice-activated recorder.

"This way," the girl told them, her smile still in place.

She led them down a short hallway with doors on either side to a door at the end.

"Enjoy your afternoon," she told them as she opened the door.

The woman waiting for them was dressed in a robe similar to theirs. Although there were three spa chairs in the room, the woman was standing and was obviously nervous. She was of medium height, with thick black hair pulled back into a ponytail. Kenzi had a feeling that style was strictly for the spa. Without makeup to disguise any signs of aging, Kenzi guessed her age to be around fifty-five. But even dressed as she was, there was an ageless grace and beauty about her, and dignity in the way she carried herself, despite the nerves.

Whoever this woman was, she was no low-level snitch.

"I'm Dana." Her sister stepped forward. "I can't tell you how much I appreciate this meeting. You obviously trust me since you requested this meeting. You can put the same trust in my sister. Neither of us will reveal your identity."

"I sincerely hope not." The woman's voice was low and melodious. "Miss Bryant, I'm well aware of the risk I am taking. There's always the chance you could put me in danger if you reveal who I am. I want you to know that."

Kenzi cocked an eyebrow. "And why is that?"

"Because of your business relationship with my husband. I'm Mercedes Reyes."

Chapter Eighteen

Kenzi didn't know who was more stunned, herself or Dana. The last person she'd expected to be their source here was Alex Reyes' wife, and she was sure Dana felt the same. Only long practice and discipline, a byproduct of both their professions, kept them from showing their shock.

Mercedes looked from one to the other.

"I'm sure I'm not the person you were expecting to meet, Miss Roberts. Am I right?"

Dana nodded. "Yes. That's true."

"I trust you, believe it or not, because my husband's cousin had you kidnapped. If you were somehow tied to the cartel, that would never have happened." She turned to Kenzi. "And you, Miss Bryant. I know you have worked on my husband's business projects, but your sister vouches for you. I'll take her word, because if she's wrong, we are all dead. You understand?"

Kenzi nodded. "I do. Is it okay to tell you that for the past few weeks I have had suspicions about his operations myself?"

"Oh?" Mercedes lifted a gracefully arched eyebrow. "And why, may I ask, is that?"

Kenzi shrugged. "Nothing specific I can put my finger on. Just the complicated structure of the new international operations and things my sister has written about the cartels and how they are expanding." She paused. "And forgive me for saying this, but I really don't like your husband."

Mercedes' laugh was anything but humorous. "You're probably part of a very small minority. Alex can charm even the most irritating person."

"I'm sure he can. Just not me."

Mercedes picked up a phone on a table next to one of the chairs and pressed a button. "No coffee is allowed here, but I've ordered some nice herbal tea that I thought would ease the tension a little. Oh, and I paid for your spa service today, even though you won't get to enjoy any. That's so there's a record if anyone looks."

"Thank you," Kenzi said.

"Yes, thank you," Dana added. "But won't your husband wonder at the size of the bill?"

Mercedes shrugged. "Not especially. I am noted for spending a lot of money here."

They waited until a spa attendant brought in a tray, poured their tea and set a cup next to each chair. Once they were seated, Dana looked at Mercedes.

"Before we get started, I have two questions. Do you have any objections to my recording this? I don't want to forget any of the information. And secondly, I'd like to know why you are doing this. Sabotaging your husband this way. It's a very dangerous thing for you to do."

Mercedes nodded. "Understood. I thought long and hard about contacting you, Miss Roberts. But everything I learned about you told me you could be trusted not to betray me."

"I thank you for that. I've worked hard to establish that reputation."

"So yes, you may record this. As for the other, I would say my reasons are my own, but that won't encourage you to believe what I tell you." She sighed. "Alex has been a good husband, and for the most part a good father. Alicia, our daughter, is safely out of his realm, working for a marketing firm in Houston. But Sebastian, our son…"

Kenzi and Dana waited while the woman. gathered her thoughts. They could see that this was a stressor for the woman.

"I'm not a stranger to the cartel," she said at last. "My father was second in command to Hector Lopez Garcia for many years. We lived a rich, charmed life in Mexico, but there was always the danger. I knew Alex was part of the triumvirate that ran everything, but again, we lived a good life and I could ignore the underbelly because it did not intrude on our daily lives. I only asked one thing of my husband."

"And that was?" Dana prompted.

"Not to involve Sebastian in the cartel."

"And he did," Kenzi guessed.

"In a big enough way that there is a price on his head in Mexico, and who knows what will happen here in the States. The only thing I can think of to do is in some way to help destroy the cartel. Then maybe my son can go on to other things, even change his name if he has to. And I can draw a breath again."

Kenzi looked at her sister and saw the same thing in her eyes that she herself felt. Sympathy for the woman, although she had chosen the life for herself. And excitement that this could be the big break in the story.

"All right." Dana pulled the micro recorder from the pocket of her robe and set it on the table between her chair and Mercedes'. "Then let's begin, shall we?"

Kenzi was very impressed listening to her sister lead the other woman through her story. She was stunned at the knowledge Mercedes Reyes had and shocked at some of the things she learned, although she didn't know why. She'd read enough about cartels online to realize the scope of their operations as well as the uncontrolled cruelty.

Kenzi sipped into the locker room twice to check her cell phone, knowing Mike would be antsy not hearing from her. Sure enough, he'd texted her twice asking for an update, so she typed in a quick message.

Going well. Don't know when we'll be finished.

No problem. We've moved the car a few times to avoid attention. Just text when u r done.

They paused at one point when Mercedes called for another tray of the delicious tea, then continued. Kenzi was surprised to see that it was just after five o'clock when at last they finished.

"You must be exhausted," she told the woman. "Telling all this had to be very emotional for you."

"Exhausted, maybe." Her lips curved slightly in a tired smile. "But relieved, also. This wasn't nearly as exhausting as talking to the DEA."

The women stared at her, dumbfounded.

Dana found her voice first. "That was quite a risk. What if your husband was having you followed?"

"Oh." She waved a hand. "I'm sure he does. Since we clashed over Sebastian, I don't think he has quite trusted me. But I'm not as naive as he thinks. I contacted them on a burner phone I managed to buy. Then I drove downtown, parked in the lot for the Rivercenter Mall, spent an hour wandering through stores, watching to see if Alex's men were following me or just waiting by my car. It turned out to be the latter. I shop in the mall a lot, so they had no reason to think that day or the others would be any different. I met up with two agents in a designated spot."

"You have a lot of courage," Kenzi told her.

Mercedes shrugged. "My children are my life. I will do anything to protect them." She looked at her watch, "And now I must go. I am sure Alex had me tracked today, although he knows I come here regularly. That's why it's such a good place to meet. But I wouldn't be surprised if two of his men are in a car outside, hidden someplace, waiting for me to leave."

Kenzi looked at her sister, her nerves suddenly doing a war dance.

Dana nodded at her. "We should let you leave first. I don't know if your husband's men know what we look like, and we do have security out there, but let's not take a chance."

"Oh." Mercedes covered her mouth. "I'm sorry. I didn't think of that. I was so worried about myself I didn't think about putting you in danger."

"It will be fine," Kenzi assured her. "I'll get my phone in a minute and let our team know we'll be out in about fifteen minutes."

Dana thanked Mercedes Reyes profusely, repeated that she would keep the source secret and wished her good luck. Then she and Dana finished a last cup of tea.

"My bosses are going to go nuts over this," Dana said.

"Even though you won't be able to identify your source?"

She nodded. "There's enough factual stuff in here that they can check into it, and I'll do my research, too. Oh, Kenzi, this will really be my big break."

"You really love this, don't you?"

"Beyond anything. And now, I want to get back to the ranch, call my editor and start on the research." She was practically dancing as they headed to the locker room.

When Kenzi pulled her phone from her purse again and turned it back on, she made a noise.

"What?" Dana asked

"This thing is ready to blow up with texts and calls from my office. I can't imagine what on earth is happening. All the documents I gave back to Reed were in top shape. His meeting with Alex Reyes should have been smooth as silk. Except, according to what Mercedes told us, he may have gotten word about the DEA and other things. He'd be in a rush to get the new papers filed and move the money out of this country. I can't imagine what Reed has his shorts in a twist about." She sighed. "Oh, well. I'll deal with it tomorrow."

Next she sent a message to Mike, who texted back at once that they'd be waiting.

Ten minutes later they were out of the building and climbing into Kenzi's car.

"Traffic's a bitch," Dana said. "Sorry you have to drive through this."

"Are you kidding? It's part of my daily menu. And it was worth it for the information you got. Holy shit! Alex Reyes' wife. Who'da thunk it?"

"I know. I'm going to call my editor now and let him know. He's been like a bear on a thistle since the incident at the hangar."

Kenzi laughed. "That's a different way to look at it. An incident."

The Interstate was crowded with the end-of-day traffic, people doing all kinds of crazy things in their hurry to get home, so she concentrated on her driving while Dana made her call.

"He's very excited," her sister said when she hung up, practically bouncing in her seat. "He said to get all my notes down tonight and call him in the morning so we can decide the best way to break this. He said his bosses will practically wet their pants, so he wants to plan for maximum exposure."

"This is your big break, kiddo. The biggest yet."

"Yes." She fist-pumped. "I am so psyched." Then she sobered. "But I do feel bad for Mercedes Reyes. On top of everything, the hammer is going to drop on her husband this week. And while she helped it along, I hope she and her children come out okay."

"No kidding. But she seems like a very strong, smart woman, so my money's on her."

At last they came to the exit for the road to Slade's ranch and were finally out of all the end-of-day Interstate crush. There was usually little to no traffic on the narrow two-lane country road. Besides Slade's place, there were only two other ranches. She checked the rearview mirror to make sure Mike and Jay were behind her, frowning when she saw another car, a large pickup truck, exit the Interstate too.

It probably belongs to one of the other ranches down this way. Practically all the ranch vehicles are pickups.

And this vehicle has to be from one of them, right? Then why did it make her feel uneasy? She couldn't help glancing in the rearview mirror every few seconds. Mike and Jay were still behind them, but now it looked as if the truck was riding their bumper.

"What's wrong?" Dana asked, then turned in her seat enough to see behind her. "Is there a problem?"

"Probably not. I'm just being jittery, I guess. But there's a car behind Mike and Jay that seems to be following them a little too closely."

"They'll take care of it, right? That's part of what they do."

"I hope."

When she looked in the mirror again, she saw the pickup trying to pass Mike and Jay and their car pulling out to block it. But then they swerved around Mike's car and attempt to pass, crowding them toward the shoulder so the truck could pull alongside Kenzi's car. She stepped on the gas, trying to put more distance between herself and the other vehicles. They were coming to a curve up ahead with little passing room, a steep hill and a drop-off on the right, so she tapped her brakes to slow enough for the car to pass.

Mike was driving with its bumper nudging them to the left. But despite Mike's best driving efforts to thwart it, the beast had just enough room to pass and pull alongside Kenzi. The oversized truck hit the car, causing it to skid sideways. Kenzi was startled to see the passenger-side window lower and a hand emerge with a gun. A bullet shattered the window beside her but thankfully missed her.

Holy shit!

"Kenzi?" Fear edged Dana's voice. "What the hell was that?"

But Kenzi was too busy to answer her. A quick glance in the rearview mirror showed her Mike had regained control of his car and was doing his best to catch up to the truck, which she was damn sure was supercharged.

She stepped on the gas, not daring to take time to look in the mirror. She heard the *crack!* of a gunshot again, and when nothing hit her or the car, she figured it came from Mike. She just had to get past the hill and the drop-off. She floored it going up the hill, but despite Mike continuing to shoot at the truck, it stayed beside her. She prayed hard as she reached the crest, the sound of the bullets piercing the air.

Just let me get to the other side. Mike will catch up and shoot the bastard.

She heard a crunch of metal and assumed Mike had rammed the truck, but it didn't appear to stop the beast. Just as she reached the crest, Kenzi felt a huge jolt as the truck banged into her side with all its horsepower. She wrestled with the wheel, the drop-off yawning beside her. Then the truck hit her again, this time the force of its size pushing her to the right no matter what she did. Her tires spun on the gravel of the narrow shoulder as she tried to find purchase, but the truck was relentless. Her tires slid off the edge.

"Kenzi!" Dana screamed. "Oh, my god!"

"Hold on," she yelled as she fought to gain some control of the vehicle, without much success.

The car slid sideways, tumbled off the road and skidded down the hillside, careening as she struggled with the wheel. Then it tipped over on its side and hit something with a loud crash. The airbags deployed, discharging an irritating mist into the car that burned her eyes. The car shifted once more, her head banged the steering wheel and she was dropped into a pit of blackness.

Chapter Nineteen

Alex Reyes stared at the men standing before him in his office.

"This is the truth?" But even as he asked, the sick feeling in his stomach told him it was.

"*Si, jefe.* We followed *Señora* Reyes as usual, but it's a good thing for whatever reason you decided someone should back us up. Just so you know, Hector sent two of his best men here the moment you called him."

"Understood. Now it is to be hoped they can finish the job."

"Yes. Hoped, indeed."

And wipe those women off the face of the earth. It will be well worth the bonus I offered.

Alex fought to get his emotions under control. He had suspected Mercedes had something going on, but he'd prayed he was wrong. The thought that his wife would betray him, not just with the reporter but most assuredly with the DEA, made him physically ill. His insistence on molding Sebastian in his own image, especially with the cartel, had been his undoing, his unshakable belief that he could control everything his downfall.

And now, everything he, Antonio and Hector had worked for since they'd taken over control of the cartel was poised to be destroyed.

Mierda!

"All right," he said at last. "I'll take care of this."

The men nodded and left the room. *Now what?* he asked himself. His life was crumbling before his very eyes. Mercedes had poked her head into the study before to let him know she had returned and that she was giving Ana instructions for dinner. Had her smile been a little strained? Her voice a little tense? Hard to tell, because apparently, she was an excellent actor.

Before he spoke to her — and he still had no idea what he was going to say — he would wait to hear from Javier on the completion of his mission regarding the two women. He would take care of Mercedes, somehow, but if the two women had been eliminated that was one area where he could draw a breath.

His last phone conversation with Reed Calhoun had given him a tiny sliver of hope. The DEA would be descending tomorrow. Reed had managed to bury or disguise all the files relating to his latest endeavor. There was little in the other files going back fifteen years that the Feds could focus on, although he had no doubt they would try. Without either the Bryant woman or the Roberts reporter to question, they had no tangible proof of anything.

It was chancy, but at least if they were dead, it gave him an edge.

The one thing still missing was the Bryant woman's laptop. If she was out of commission, however — or, hopefully, dead—he could have someone break into her apartment and get it. When he'd told Reed Calhoun, who was as stunned as he was, they'd believed that was why she hadn't come to work that day. If his men weren't already taking care of her, he'd kill her himself.

He glanced at his watch. He should be hearing from them any minute now, and it damn well better be with good news. Swallowing a sigh, he poured a glass of bourbon for himself from the bar he kept in his office. He wondered if the entire bottle would be enough to take the edge off his stress.

* * * *

It was the pain that woke Kenzi, pain so sharp and bright it plucked at every nerve in her body. She tried to move and discovered that something heavy was holding her in place. When she tried to shift, she almost passed out from the stab of agony.

"Kenzi?"

Who was that? The voice was familiar.

"Kenzi, can you hear me? Say something."

"Move," she mumbled. "Hurt."

"Lord. Thank god you are still alive." His face was close to hers but at an unusual angle. "Don't move. We'll get you out of here, but we have to wait for some help."

Her head ached as if a sledgehammer had pounded on it.

"Dana?" she asked.

"She's right beside you. We'll get you both out but please don't move until we get some equipment here. Okay? Can you hold still for me?"

"Mmm," as all she said. Then, again, "Hurts."

"I know," the familiar voice said. "Just hang on."

She had no idea how long she lay there, her entire body one large fiery pain, as she fell in and out of consciousness. Then the man was back.

"Only a little longer," he said in a soothing voice. "We've got some equipment here to free you."

She wanted to tell him that was great, except each time she uttered a word, a sharp spear of pain pierced her. She heard some grinding noises, then the door to the car was being pulled off. In the next instant, a pair of male arms reached in to lift her out and place her in some kind of body sling.

"Try not to move," the soothing voice said. "We're getting you up the hill to the ambulance. The emergency techs are waiting to help you."

She gritted her teeth against the pain, so intense that tears rolled down her cheeks.

"Only a couple of minutes. We're going to get Dana out now."

Dana! Thank god.

Then she was placed on a stretched and someone was carefully checking her over.

"Watch it bringing the other woman up," someone shouted. "How is she?"

"Breathing," came the answer. "That's all I can tell at the moment."

"We'd better roll," a female voice said. "Her vitals aren't great, and that leg looks…bad."

Leg? She tried to move one of them and the pain was so intense she almost vomited. She felt tears roll down her cheeks again.

"Don't try to move it, Kenzi. We've got permission to give you something for the pain."

A needle stick and seconds later she fell into blackness again.

Chapter Twenty

Kenzi came awake very slowly, her brain fuzzy. She blinked her eyes to clear her vision and realized at once she was in a hospital room, one leg in a heavy cast. She tried to move and everything hurt.

"Hold on." A male voice that she vaguely recognized pierced the fog in her brain and a hand touched her arm. "Don't try to move or you'll do yourself damage."

She slid her glance sideways to see who it was and saw a very disheveled Mike Elliott sitting there, lines of worry creasing his face.

"What...happened?" she managed to say.

"What didn't." He rubbed a hand over his face. "Long story short, two of Hector Lopez Garcia's goons ran you off the road in one of the biggest pickup trucks I've ever seen. You rolled down that hillside where the big hill is. I'm just damn glad the car didn't catch on fire."

"Dana?"

"Is fine. Broken arm and collarbone, fractured ankle. Two cracked ribs." He gave a rough laugh. "I think she got those when you fell on her."

"Oh, god!" She felt the blood drain from her face.

"No, no." Mike took her hand again. "It could have been a lot worse."

"My injuries?" she persisted.

"Leg with compound fractures, dislocated shoulder, couple of cracked ribs and a sprained wrist. You are both doing pretty much okay, considering."

"Yeah." She twisted her lips in a caricature of a smile. "Lucky."

A nurse bustled into the room, checked Kenzi's vitals and injected medication into her IV. Seconds later, Kenzi was out. When she woke again, Mike was still in the room, but he had obviously showered, shaved and changed and looked only slightly the worse for wear.

"I take it I'll live." She managed to get an entire sentence out.

"You will." Mike nodded and grinned, but his smile bespoke fatigue. "You remember everything I told you before?"

"Yes. What about those two men?"

"In the prison ward of a hospital in San Antonio. Not this one," he was quick to assure her. "With double guards."

"Who are they? Do they work for Alex Reyes?"

Mike shook his head. "Hector Lopez Garcia. No one works for Reyes any more. Let me catch you up to date."

Kenzi listened to him relate how the day after she'd been hurt, the DEA, with ironclad warrants, had raided Alex Reyes' office and pulled every file for every client of his. They had also raided his house, where they found the files he'd tried to hide from the Feds.

"This won't make you too happy, Kenzi. Reed Calhoun has known about Reyes from the beginning. That law firm was funded with cartel money. Calhoun belonged to them from day one. Big scandal in Texas when this story hits the media."

She felt nauseous, and it wasn't from her injuries.

"What about the other two partners?"

"They claimed not to know anything about it, but until everything can be investigated, the law firm is closed." He took her hand. "You and your sister did a foolish but brave thing today. Dana even had me make a copy of her session with Mercedes Reyes to give to the DEA. The cartel is being dismantled one piece at a time."

"But she still gets to write her story, right?"

Mike laughed. "Oh, yeah. Maybe an even better one. The DEA is so grateful for the info she gave them they're giving her an exclusive."

"Good. She deserves it. What about Mercedes Reyes? Did Alex find out she was the snitch? God, I hope she's okay."

"She's fine," Trey assured her. "It seems the DEA also had someone following her, to protect their source. When Reyes' men tried to run her off the road so they could grab her, the agents rescued her and now she's stashed in a safe house until the trial is over and her husband is out of commission for good. I think her daughter's with her. A girl, by the way, who knew nothing of her father's real business, unlike her brother, who was an integral part of it. The DEA grabbed him, also."

"What a mess." Kenzi shook her head. "I guess I'll be looking for a new job as soon as I'm out of here." She started to reach for the water on her nightstand.

"I'll get it." Mike poured some into a cup and handed it to her. "Anyway, first things first. In a few days, they'll start to get you out of bed, with crutches, but right now you're supposed to stay still."

"Can I see Dana?"

He nodded. "I'll arrange to have her brought to your room."

"Listen." She took another sip of water. "You have things to do. A business to run. You don't have to sit here with me."

"Yeah, right," he snorted. "No thanks to me you and your sister were almost killed. I can hardly wait for Trey and Slade to hand me my ass."

She shook her head. "Not your fault. You did everything right. Shit happens."

"I'll be shocked if they see it that way."

"I'll make sure they do," she insisted.

"You just take care of getting well." He stood. "Let me go see what I can do about bringing Dana down here."

* * * *

Trey stood in the doorway to the hospital room, studying the slender figure in the bed, weighted down by the huge cast. His heart ached for what she'd been through.

Two days ago, they had completed their mission, and the moment he had a connection he'd called her number. He'd been shocked when Mike Elliott had answered the phone, and had gone from shocked to furious when he got the details of what happened.

Slade had gotten them back to base as quickly as he could, and Teo had picked them up in the chopper in a neighboring field. As soon as they'd landed, Slade had tossed him the keys to a truck and he'd driven hell bent for leather to the hospital.

Now he stood looking at the woman he had so unexpectedly fallen in love with and wondered what he'd ever do without her. The last thing he'd expected when they'd met at the Huttons' party had been to lose his heart, but as Slade had pointed out to him, fate had a funny way of taking things out of people's hands.

"Are you just going to stand in the doorway, or are you planning to come into the room?"

Her voice was hoarse, but it was the sweetest sound he'd ever heard. In seconds he was beside her, bending over to kiss her. He meant it to be a gentle peck, but she reached up and wove her fingers into his hair, holding his head in place, sliding her small tongue out to touch his lips. That did it for him. He thrust his tongue into her mouth, tasting every inch of her, his heart pounding as he realized how close he'd come to losing her. When he lifted his head, they were both breathless.

"If I wasn't in this state," she whispered, "I'd show you just how glad I am to see you."

"If you weren't in this state, I'd be showing you."

He sat on the edge of the bed, holding her hand, unwilling to break the contact.

"Please don't be made at Mike," she begged. "They actually saved our lives."

"Shit happens," he agreed. "But that's the end of situations that put you in jeopardy. Dana can do whatever the hell she wants, but no more run-ins with thugs for you."

"You won't hear me arguing. Anyway, I've got a ways to go before I hit the playing field again. And I have to look for a new job."

"I have some ideas there," he told her in a tentative voice that completely belied his Delta Force personality. "That is, if you'd like to listen."

"I'm all ears."

He cleared his throat. "My folks have a ranch very much like Slade's, only theirs is in Montana. And I've told them about you."

Her eyes widened. "You did? I thought you were Mister Footloose and Fancy Free."

"So did I. So did everyone, including my family, to their despair." He brushed the hair off her forehead. "But when I wasn't looking, a feisty lawyer stole my heart. I've talked about you enough, told them about what happened when I was on my way here to see you."

"And?"

"And they'd love it if I'd bring you to the ranch to heal. Now wait a minute," he said, when she opened her mouth to protest. "Hear me out. My mother's a registered nurse and my sister's an attorney, so you'd have someone to talk shop with. Please."

He watched the play of emotions across her face while she digested everything he'd said. God, he loved this woman. He'd never expected this, but now he wanted it more than he wanted to breathe.

"And where would you go, anyway?" he persisted. "Your dad's an engineer on the other side of the world, your mother passed away years ago, and your sister is going to be busy healing herself and writing the biggest story of her life." He brushed his mouth over hers. "I love you, Kenzi, and I want to marry you. Let me take you home to my family."

"M-Marry?" she stuttered.

"Mm-hmm. That's what people do when they're in love, or so I'm told. And I do love you, more than I ever thought possible."

She nibbled on her lower lip and Trey could see her thoughts chasing themselves across her face. When she smiled, he relaxed for the first time since he'd entered the room.

"Okay, soldier." She grinned. "I'm convinced."

And the last bit of tension left his body.

"You just wait," he told her. "My family will love you and spoil you to death." He bent his head lower. "And as soon as you're able-bodied again, I'm going to take you to bed and fuck you senseless."

She burst out laughing. "Now there's the Trey McIntyre I know and love. Welcome home, soldier."

And as he laid his head on her breast, he knew that was the truth—he was home. *Finally*.

Want to see more from this author? Here's a taster for you to enjoy!

Corporate Heat: Masquerade
Desiree Holt

Excerpt

Lindsey turned over in bed and checked the time on her little clock. Five a.m. *Holy hell.* She was sure she hadn't gotten more than an hour's worth of sleep combined all night. Most of the time had been spent tossing and turning, trying to get the picture of Craig Wainwright's dead body out of her mind. Seeing the man she'd worked with for the past four years lying in the morgue, battered and bruised, with all the life drained out of him, was painful and gut-wrenching. A sick feeling lodged inside her even as questions kept rattling around in her brain, bumping into one another.

She didn't know which shocked her more — Craig's death and the circumstances, or the fact that his ice-queen of a wife, Natalia, had chosen to contact her as opposed to one of her friends. Or intimate acquaintances, as she called them. After all, their relationship was distantly cordial at best. According to what the police had told them, he'd been killed in a one-car accident on a stretch of road that was not even close to the route to his house. What had he been doing there, anyway? And at that hour of the night?

She looked at the clock again. Five-fifteen. With a sigh, she gave up any attempt to get some sleep and pulled at the covers, which were now all twisted around her body. Disentangling her legs, she pushed herself to a sitting position and dragged herself out of bed.

Today it was important that she be alert and to have all the parts of her brain in maximum working order. As vice-president of Elite Marketing, she was expected to have her shit together all the time. No matter what. Taylor and Noah Cantrell were due at Elite at seven sharp, and that meant being alert and in charge.

When Taylor had brought Elite into the mega-structure of Arroyo Conglomerate four years ago, one condition of the arrangement had been to add another executive-level position to manage the fast-expanding business. Lindsey had been recommended by a business friend of Taylor's. She was well-respected in the industry and had a great understanding when it came to marketing. Plus she had a well-honed business sense. A high-priced education at the University of Pennsylvania and Wharton School of Finance had seen to that.

She recalled worrying that Craig would think his toes were being stepped on, but he'd told her again and again how glad he was to have her there. He was smart enough to see he needed someone who could shoulder the load with him.

"Some of my clients are taking up more and more time," he'd told her. "This will really help a lot, especially managing the staff."

It was important that the Cantrells knew their faith was not misplaced. Besides, she owed it to Craig. Keeping the agency running and increasing revenue was the best tribute she could give him. She was sure the staff, when she told them, would be in upheaval, so she needed to be the steadying hand on the wheel.

She'd hated disturbing the Cantrells last night, and the late hour hadn't helped. However, it was a standing rule with all executives in every Arroyo division that Taylor Cantrell was to be notified at once of anything out of the ordinary relating to her top people. This more than met that qualification.

Although she and Taylor had only had sporadic contact in person since Lindsey had joined Elite, they had a relationship so strong that video and phone calls handled any business without a problem. But the woman had a way of letting people know if they'd disappointed her, even while she was smiling and being polite. Lindsey wanted to make sure she was ready for anything today.

They'd have some decisions to make, and fast, the most important being about who would step into Craig's position. Would Taylor look outside the agency again, and bring in someone new the way she had with Lindsey?

She wasn't looking forward to gathering the staff when they arrived at the office. Giving them the sad news would be extra tough since she had no answers for them. She could visualize organized chaos while everyone absorbed the news and Taylor dug into Elite to make sure nothing was wrong. It wasn't, after all, as if this was a normal auto accident, which in itself would have been bad enough. No, there'd be questions, the same ones she kept asking herself.

Lord, please don't let me lose my shit today.

A hot shower washed away most of the cobwebs, and by the time she had dressed and applied makeup, she felt halfway to being human. By seven o'clock, she had the single serving brewers set up in both the break room and her office, the carousels stocked with a variety of flavors and trays of her favorite pastries set out beside them. The answering service was on notice to continue taking calls for an additional hour. That was all she could do to prepare for what was coming.

She had just taken a deep breath when she heard knocking on the glass doors to the suite of offices.

Here goes.

Stepping into the reception area, she saw the Cantrells standing in the hallway. They were a striking couple, the tall man whose Native American heritage gave him dark, exotic good looks and the woman, with her wavy auburn hair, ocean blue eyes and milky skin a direct contrast to him. They were the quintessential power couple, looking for all the world as if they'd had eight hours' sleep and had nothing more to worry about than where to go for lunch.

How do they do it?

"Good morning." She swung the door wide for them. "I'm sorry, I thought for sure you had keys to the office."

Taylor smiled at her. "Only to be used in case of emergency. I don't want people to think they have no privacy."

And who else would consider that important?

"Please come into my office. I have coffee and pastries. I didn't know if you'd have had a chance for anything on the plane or not."

Taylor smiled. "Very thoughtful of you. Thanks."

Lindsey made sure everyone was served before indicating they should sit in the arranged conversation grouping. She waited for them to take the lead.

Taylor took a swallow of her beverage and set her cup on the little table in front of the couch.

"Okay, Lindsey. Tell me everything you know about last night, starting with when you left the office. I'm assuming Craig was still here?"

Lindsey nodded. "I worked until a little past seven before packing it in. He was in his office, working on a project. Maybe more than one, considering the amount of material spread over his desk. I'm sorry I have no idea what it was, but it might have been photos for a couple of magazine layouts. Or he could have been deciding which models to use, since we had three scheduled for different clients."

"Did he supervise all of them himself?" Taylor asked.

Lindsey wrinkled her forehead. "I don't think so, but we operated independently so it was hard to tell. Jerry Ortiz worked on a lot with him and we met once a week to catch up. Last night I asked Craig if he needed any help and he said no, he was good. He just wanted to wrap up some details before he went home to spend the evening with his wife. I have no idea how he ended up where he was or why. Obviously, something changed."

Why didn't I press him harder? Ask more about what he was doing?

But she'd been tired and more than ready to get out of there. She'd remember that for a long time.

Taylor took another swallow of coffee. "Noah called the police station and had them fax a copy of the report to the house before we left."

"And they did it just like that? I thought the police were cranky about doing things like that, especially for someone they don't know." Then she stopped and heat skimmed her cheeks. "Sorry. I forgot who I was talking to."

Taylor laughed. "Sometimes being who we are has its advantages."

Lindsey nibbled on her lips. "Did it show anything?"

"Not much, but it's just the preliminary report. But at that location, he wasn't even close to being on the way home when he had the accident. I haven't spoken to Natalia, but did she have any idea where he might have been headed? Or why he ended up staying so late at the office?"

Lindsey shook her head. "None at all."

"Had you noticed anything different about him lately?" Taylor asked. "Any change in habits or behavior?"

What could she really say? All she had were vague suspicions. Still…

"Anything you can share," Taylor prompted, "no matter how small, could be helpful. You know I have a lot of confidence in your opinion."

"I just want to make sure I'm not mistaking pressure nerves for something else." She got up to brew another cup of coffee. She'd have to be careful not to drink herself into caffeine overload today. "Craig was smart and savvy, and knew what he was doing. But lately I got the feeling he was dealing with a lot of pressure. Maybe because of some of the large accounts he'd taken on. People who wanted more campaigns and bigger ones."

Taylor frowned. "Do you think they were too much for him to manage?"

"No." Lindsey shook her head. The last thing she wanted was to damage Craig's reputation as a top marketing person in his field. "And you know yourself how good the money was." She paused, choosing her words with care. "But if I'm truthful, the last couple of years he seemed, oh, antsy, I guess, is the best way to put it. Like he was walking some kind of fine line. I have no idea what it could have been, though. Elite is doing extremely well. We almost have more clients than we can handle, especially as we're expanding our international market. In fact, we even discussed bringing another person on board to handle some of the smaller accounts."

Taylor smiled. "An abundance of business is always good to hear. But…"

"Yes." Lindsey nodded. "But. I kept getting the distinct feeling something was off. I was hoping to have something more concrete than just a feeling before I approached him about it."

Noah leaned forward and placed his coffee mug on the table.

"Was it financial, Lindsey? If he was keeping things from you, that could be a problem."

A tiny knot tightened in her stomach and she did her best to keep her voice even. "Truthfully, Mr. Cantrell —"

"Noah," he interrupted. "I think it's time we dispense with formalities."

"Noah." *Can I express my reservations to him without being sure?* The last thing she wanted was to create trouble where there was none.

"Lindsey." Taylor's voice was friendly but firm. This was, after all, business. "The president of a viable marketing company that is a component of Arroyo Enterprises has died both unexpectedly and in odd circumstances. It may turn out to be a sudden heart attack and he may have just been taking a drive to clear his head after a long workday. But I trust your instincts. If there is even a hint of something bothering you, then you need to share it with us. I have to know how we're going to handle things going forward."

The knot in her belly got a little tighter. "Going forward? Do you think you might close the agency?"

"No." The other woman shook her head. "Not at all. Not even a consideration, unless we find something really dire. But we can't have a vacuum here. You know yourself this agency is a moneymaker, and that looks good on the Arroyo balance sheet and to the board of directors. If we need to get in front of something, now is the time to do it."

"And there may be nothing at all to worry about." Lindsey cleared her throat. "Please keep in mind that this is just my impression."

Taylor nodded. "Understood."

"Okay. Like I said before, for the past two years or so, Craig has seemed edgy. Jumpy even, at times. As if he was wrestling with some kind of problem. He was traveling a lot for these photo shoots, much of it out of the country. That wasn't a bad thing. We've expanded at a rapid rate in the global marketplace, which means customers with a wide variety of tastes. Plus, a lot of our clients like the tropical settings for layouts. I offered several times to help ease his load, but he was very proprietary about his clients and insisted on managing everything himself. I had little to do with the foreign trips. Now and then, Natalia went with him on the trips—I think to help corral the models."

Noah lifted an eyebrow. "He didn't ask you to go with him? Or one of the account managers?"

"Sometimes Jerry Ortiz, who worked closely with him, but he usually made it plain he preferred doing it himself." Lindsey shook her head. "I was busy overseeing everything else when he was tied up with one of these projects, and the models were, well, a handful for one of the account managers to handle. They were strictly Craig's baby."

The Cantrells exchanged a glance.

"Would you say there was anything improper going on between Craig and any of the models?" Taylor asked.

"No, nothing like that." Again, Lindsey shook her head. "Not at all. But something was on his mind."

"All right." Taylor leaned back in her chair and again something passed unspoken between her and her husband. "Here's what I'd like to do. Noah's heading to the police station to see if they've learned anything else. They'll have gone over the car by now, to see if there were any mechanical problems."

Maybe that was what it was. But… "Craig kept that car in tiptop condition."

"Mechanical problems can still happen," Noah pointed out. "I want to make sure they've checked every single thing."

Taylor turned to Lindsey. "You and I need to decide what we're going to tell clients and share that with the staff. Additionally, because Elite has a high public profile, as soon as word gets out, the media will be like starving wolves at your door. How about if you draft something and run it by me?"

Lindsey nodded. "I can do that. Are you thinking about a press conference?"

Taylor shook her head. "No. I want to low-key this. In fact, I don't want to make a general announcement. We'll need to call his list of clients, something I think is best you handle. If they ask, we'll send them a brief statement electronically. And we should get ready for calls from others as word trickles out. Maybe even the media, although I hope not. He had a pretty high profile in the Miami–Fort Lauderdale area, right?"

Lindsey nodded. "Okay. I'll get something put together for you to take a look at. Before we do anything, however, I'd like us to meet with the staff. We have to tell them right away. When Craig's in town, he's always in his office early. His absence will raise questions. How about I get them in the conference room as soon as they arrive at work?"

Taylor nodded. "Yes. Let's do that."

Lindsey wet her lips then asked the question she'd been battling with. But it was important that she knew. "I should probably wait until we get past this immediate crisis, so I hope you'll forgive me for asking." She put on her best professional face. "Are you planning to bring someone in from the outside to take over in Craig's place?"

The Cantrells exchanged a look and Noah gestured to his wife.

Your deal, he told her in unspoken acknowledgment.

"We discussed this on the way over here from Texas," Taylor answered. "We'd like you to step in as head of the agency. Think about it. You know the operation and the clients. And we know you. It would be one less thing to worry about. Elite would be in very good hands and both the clients and the staff know you." She paused. "Unless you'd rather not do it. But, Lindsey, you're the logical person."

For a moment Lindsey wasn't sure she'd heard right. "Take charge of Elite?"

"That's not a problem, is it?" Noah asked, his face expressionless.

"Of course not." She was stunned. "But what about Natalia? Won't she inherit Craig's share of Elite? She might not like having me around."

Taylor shook her head. "We prepared for that. In all the Arroyo subsidiaries, if the partner passes away, Arroyo does a buyout with the surviving spouse. If there's no spouse, then with the estate. We can't have unqualified people suddenly in charge of our subsidiaries just because they inherited."

"Makes sense. That means you're buying the other fifty-one percent of whatever business it is, right?"

"That's correct. It then becomes a wholly owned subsidiary of Arroyo, so you don't have to worry about some idiot coming in and making a mess of things. It's your baby, at least for now."

Lindsey didn't know whether to be thrilled or terrified. "Thank you both for having such faith in me."

"Your reputation and history speak for themselves. That's why we sought you out to begin with." Noah rose from his chair and held out his hand. "We know you'll do a great job, Lindsey. And now I'm going to leave you and Taylor to dig into what's going on here and keep things running smoothly while I get on with my business. How about dinner at eight to recap the day and see where we are?"

Lindsey's head was spinning, but she managed to nod. "Whatever you need, I'm there."

"Good. I'm glad we got that settled." Taylor grinned at her husband. "I knew we'd made the right decision."

"Okay, then. I'm out of here."

It said a lot that Noah Cantrell did not leave without kissing his wife goodbye. It was a good indication of the strength of their relationship and how comfortable they felt in their own skins.

As soon as Noah was gone, Taylor refilled her cup. "Okay, Lindsey. Let's get to work."

Home of Erotic Romance

Sign up for our newsletter and find out about all our romance book releases, eBook sales and promotions, sneak peeks and FREE romance books!

About the Author

Today best-selling author, Desiree Holt has produced more than 200 titles and won many awards. She has received an EPIC E-Book Award, the Holt Medallion and many others including Author After Dark's Author of the Year. She has been featured on CBS Sunday Morning and in The Village Voice, The Daily Beast, USA Today, The Wall Street Journal, The London Daily Mail. She lives in Florida with her cats who insist they help her write her books, and is addicted to football.

Desiree loves to hear from readers. You can find her contact information, website details and author profile page at https://www.totallybound.com